ILLICIT PROMISES

STOLEN MOMENTS BOOK II

CATHARINA MAURA

For my beloved readers, especially the ones that have contacted me to let me know how much you loved Stolen Moments. This one is for you.

CONTENTS

CHAPTER 1

milia

I'm trembling as Kate and I walk up to the apartment that Carter and Asher share. My hands are clammy and my heart is hammering in my chest.

Carter and I haven't had a genuine conversation in the last year and a half. Every time he came home, he went out of his way to avoid me. If he was ever forced to speak to me, he'd treat me with such indifference I'd barely recognize him. Ever since the first time he came home, he and I have slowly but surely become strangers. Carter now treats me with the same cold politeness that he used to reserve for Kate's other friends. It's like *he and I* were never friends. Like we weren't so much more than that. I'm terrified of seeing him again. I'm terrified of him pushing me away even further.

I've been in a weird state of denial, telling myself that we're only distant because he's been so far away, but soon I'll be out of excuses. I'm not sure I'm ready to deal with the guy he's become. Carter and I used to be so close, but now I barely know him. All I know is whatever I hear from Kate and Helen, combined with what I see on social media and on the news. He's a rising football star and based on the photos I've seen online, well-loved by the girls at USC. While I know he isn't the guy he used to be, my heart refuses to accept it. In the few interviews he's done on his private life, he made it clear that he doesn't believe in love at all and that he enjoys his bachelor lifestyle. The Carter I used to know wasn't like that. He might never have said it, but I'm pretty sure he used to love me as much as I loved him.

The door opens, and Asher appears, his eyes lingering on Kate. I know the two of them have been seeing each other on and off again — neither of them able to stay away, though they both keep trying. All the while they've done their best to keep it from Carter until they finally decide to make things official, which has yet to happen. For Kate, Carter's graduation party was the start of something new. It was the night she and Asher finally gave in and acted on their feelings, setting in motion the months of push and pull they've gone through. For me, it was the end of the best thing I ever had. The night I spent with Carter was the last night we had together.

Asher pulls Kate toward him and hugs her tightly, his face buried in her hair. When they're still wrapped up in each other minutes later, I clear my throat awkwardly. Asher blinks and looks at me, confused. Yep. He didn't even see me standing here. He blushes and steps back to let us in.

"Hey, Emilia," he murmurs. I roll my eyes and push past him. If they're going to be this obvious about their affection for each other, they might as well not even try to keep it from Carter. They're hardly subtle. For a split second, I wonder what things might have been like if Carter and I started dating two years ago. Would we have made it? Would Helen and Kate have gotten over it? Would he be welcoming me the way Asher is welcoming Kate? My heart aches at the mere thought of all the would-haves and could-haves.

"Make yourself at home," Asher tells us. Kate and I follow him in curiously. The apartment looks so normal. It doesn't look like the bachelor pad I was expecting. It's just a regular two-bedroom apartment with neutral colored furniture. It isn't even messy. The boys can do with a bit of color, but they certainly haven't done a bad job.

We pause in front of Carter's bedroom and Kate sighs. "Is he still asleep?" she asks, her mood souring. I check my watch and bite down on my lip. It's nine am on a Sunday, but he knew we'd get here today. I might not have spoken to him much, but I know Kate has.

Kate rolls her eyes and opens his bedroom door. I hesitate before following her in. Will he be happy to see me at all? Will he be upset if we wake him up? Things haven't been the same between us in months now, but I'm hoping we can at least become friends again now that we'll be seeing a lot of each other.

It's pitch dark when we walk in, and Kate slams her hand against the light switch. Carter's room is bathed in light and he groans. My eyes roam over his room in surprise. His floor is scattered with clothes and other mess. Carter was never super tidy, but he was never this messy either.

He sits up and runs a hand through his hair, an annoyed expression on his face. The sheets fall to his waist and my eyes roam over his body. It looks like he's naked and the sheets barely cover him. He looks mad as hell to have been woken up, but his anger drains away once his eyes land on us. He looks at Asher first, and then at Kate.

"Kate," he says, his voice rough and sleepy. His eyes linger on me for just a few seconds, his expression unreadable. I can't figure out if he's even remotely happy to see me. He dismisses me and looks back at Kate. "When did you get here?" he asks. He grabs his jeans from the floor and pulls them on underneath the covers before standing up.

My heart aches at how easily he ignores me. He's focused entirely on Kate, and it's like I'm not even here. He hasn't so much as smiled at me.

"A few minutes ago," Kate says. She crosses her arms and glares at him. "I told you Milly and I would get here today. Why are you still in bed?"

I look up at him as discreetly as I can. He looks bigger. More muscular and rugged. I'm hit with a familiar sense of longing. My eyes roam over his body and freeze on his lower abdomen. He's got more than a few kiss marks on his skin and I suddenly feel sick. I bite down on my lip to keep my emotions in check. It feels like someone has stabbed me in the heart and then twisted the knife. It's been over a year since Carter and I ended things, so why do I still feel this way? I look away, frozen in place.

I breathe in as deeply as I can, my breath hitching. It hurts. He warned me he'd move on, but I guess I was in denial. Carter has done his best to hide his sex life from Kate and me. I always *knew*, but knowing isn't the same as seeing. I take a step back and rub my chest as though that'll soothe my aching heart.

"I thought Asher told you that our orientation is tomorrow. I literally called you last night to make sure you'd be up in time. I can't believe you're still in bed," she says, snapping at him.

Asher clears his throat and puts his hand on Kate's shoulder. "Come on," he says. "I'll show you my room and the rest of the place while Carter gets ready. It won't take him long."

Kate glares at Carter one more time and then follows Asher. I trail behind them, not wanting to be left alone with Carter.

"I... uh... I'll make some coffee," I say, tipping my head toward the kitchen. I need a moment to pull myself together. Just seeing Carter is so much harder than I thought it would be. It's like feelings I thought were long gone came rushing back at once. I guess part of me hoped there'd still be *something* between us. I never got over him, but it seems like he's defi-

4

nitely moved on. I can't help but blame myself. I should've chosen to be with him while I could.

Kate looks at me worriedly and I smile at her. "Just tired," I tell her, lying through my teeth. She hesitates, but eventually nods and follows Asher.

I walk around the kitchen numbly, working on autopilot. I don't snap out of it until Carter walks in. Looks like he didn't bother getting ready — he's still in nothing but his jeans, his chest exposed. He leans against one of the counters and studies me curiously.

I push a cup of coffee toward him, a small insincere smile on my face. I've been standing here completely spaced out for so long that the coffee is now lukewarm at best. Usually I'd have offered to make him a new cup, but I just don't have it in me today. My heart feels shattered. Is this what Carter and I have become? Strangers that don't even say hi anymore?

My eyes drop to the kiss marks on his skin and I'm hit with another flash of pain. He looks down and traces the marks with his fingers, a small frown on his face. I look away and stare at my cup instead.

"Hmm, looks like my friends and I had a bit too much fun last night," he says, grinning.

I feel sick to my stomach and grit my teeth. "You fuck all your friends?" I ask, my voice harsh and angry. I can't help it. I promised myself I'd be better than this, but I can't help myself.

Carter looks startled and then chuckles. "Emilia, I'm single and I'm a football player. I'm not gonna stand here and pretend I've been a saint. We're at college, for God's sake. It's not like you've been a saint back home. How's Landon these days?"

I frown. "Landon?" I ask, confused. I haven't even thought about him in a year. "We broke up like a year and a half ago," I tell him.

Carter straightens and stares at me with wide eyes. "You *what?*"

I look away and wrap my arms around myself. I broke up with Landon the first time Carter came home from college. I still remember the exact moment I knew Landon and I would never work out. I tried pulling a prank on Carter and he caught me. He had me pressed up against his window, his fingers buried deep inside me. I knew right there and then I'd never want Landon the same way and that it would be unfair to keep dating him, when I knew I was just using him to get over Carter. I broke up with Landon the next day.

"I only dated him because I was wondering what dating might be like. It wasn't really as good as I thought it would be, so I ended things."

Carter blinks in disbelief. "Why didn't you tell me?" he asks, his eyes flashing with anger.

I frown. "When was I supposed to tell you, Carter? Whenever you came home, you ignored me. Besides, why would you even care?"

Carter runs a hand through his hair and looks at me through narrowed eyes. "You said it wasn't that good. *What* wasn't that good? Did you sleep with him?"

I shake my head instinctively and immediately regret it. Carter's lips tug up at the edges and his entire demeanor relaxes. I grit my teeth and glare at him.

"It's none of your business who I have or haven't slept with, you manwhore."

Carter chuckles. "Hmm okay, Minx," he murmurs. My heart skips a beat and I hide my face in my coffee cup. He hasn't called me *Minx* in so long. It's always Emilia these days. To hear him call me the way he used to oddly revives the butterflies I try so hard to keep buried.

"So those two times with me are the only times you've had sex, huh? You're practically still a virgin, Minx. At this rate you might as well keep it up until marriage."

I almost choke on my coffee and cough violently. Carter

6

grins as though my unease is amusing him. I prod his chest angrily. "Whose fault is that, Carter? You kept everyone away from me. Even after you left, most guys didn't dare come near me."

I'm shaking with anger. Even though we always denied it, everyone always saw me as Carter's girl. As the girl that's out of reach unless you want to deal with Carter himself. Long after he left, people would ask me how he's doing. Other than Landon, there weren't many guys that could even look at me without immediately associating me with Carter. Not that it would've mattered. No one captured my interest anyway. In the last two years, I couldn't even imagine sleeping with anyone other than Carter. I still can't.

"Seems like you don't have that issue, huh? You're far from virginal, aren't you?" I say, my voice breaking. I'm consumed with pain and rage that I know I have no right to feel. I glance at my cup, longing to give into my temper and dump the coffee on his head. It won't mend my broken heart, but still.

Carter laughs and tips his head toward me. "Do it. I dare you," he murmurs.

I grit my teeth and glare at him. I can't believe he still reads me so well. I hate it. I hate that he still owns every piece of me. "Don't think I won't," I snap.

Carter crosses his arms and grins at me provocatively. I glare at him and rise to my tiptoes, my coffee cup in hand. I bring it to his head slowly. Carter watches me in amusement, as though he's waiting to see whether I'll actually do it. I hold my cup over his head and empty it slowly, looking him in the eye as the coffee streams down his face. He could've evaded me easily, but instead he leans back against the counter, allowing it to run down his body.

My eyes follow the trail down his abdomen and a moment that should've felt victorious and vindictive instantly turns into *more*. I lick my lips and try to keep my mind off licking the coffee from his body. I swallow hard and Carter's eyes darken as though he knows exactly what I'm thinking.

The moment shatters when my eyes zero in on the kiss marks on his skin. Just looking at them makes me feel like I've been sucker punched. How many girls know exactly what Carter's abs taste like? Hell... some girl probably still has the taste of him on her lips. I look away, equal parts disgusted and heartbroken. It's obvious he's been spending his days fucking around.

He's clearly moved on, just like he said he would. So why am I still stuck in the past? Why am I unable to even want anyone else? Seems like Carter is having great sex and I'm just missing out. I'm missing out because I keep comparing every man I meet to the one I can no longer have. No more. I'm going to live it up at college as much as Carter has. Maybe that's exactly what I need to finally get over him. Seems to have worked just fine for him. I'll find someone to sleep with before the week is over. How hard can it be?

I grit my teeth and Carter grabs my jaw. He turns my face toward his and shakes his head. "It's not happening, Minx. Whatever you have in mind right now, forget about it. It isn't happening."

I glare at him, hating that he can still read me so well. "We'll see about that, Carter."

CHAPTER 2

arter

I feel like a dick even though I haven't done anything wrong. Emilia and I aren't together — we've never actually been together. Yet the way she looked at me when she saw those hickeys on my skin made me feel *guilty*. I've had plenty of wild nights since I went to college, and last night was no exception. Never once have I felt ashamed of my sex life, though. Not until today.

I thought I was over Emilia, but I still can't stand to see her hurting. I didn't expect it to happen, but my heart still races when she smiles at me and I still crave her with every fiber of my being. It doesn't help that she's even hotter now than she used to be. It's not just her body I want, though. I still feel that need to mess with her and to rile her up. Seeing her again brings back so many memories. I still remember all the childish hopes and dreams I had for us and all the things I thought I'd show her when she finally joined me in LA.

My mind drifts back to the day I saw her standing in her bedroom with Landon. I'll always remember that as the day every hope and dream I had for Emilia and me shattered. I'd been so infatuated with her, and so heartbroken to see her with someone else. Things seemed pretty serious with them back then, so it seems odd that she broke up with him so quickly. I can't believe Kate didn't tell me about it either. Not that it would've mattered. She and I never would've worked out. My mother was right. We were too young and my sister never would've gotten over it. Part of me wishes she and I never even got together. If we hadn't, we might've still been close now. We might not have grown apart the way we did. I might not have pushed her away.

I hate to admit it, but I've actually missed her. I've missed the pranks we used to pull and the friendship we shared. I sigh and set up Emilia's little Nespresso machine in the dorm room she'll be sharing with Kate. I glance at her and grin to myself. The way she looked at me with all that coffee streaming down my body... she looked like she was thirsty as fuck. Thirsty for *me*. The chemistry between us is still there, and it's still hot as fuck. I doubt that'll ever change. Emilia's eyes meet mine and I can't help but want to mess with her a little.

"Want some coffee, Minx? You did *spill* the cup you made this morning."

She blushes and tries to look stern but fails. She nods and turns back around. She's been awkward around me all day, and I guess it's weird for her too. It'll take us time to get back to being friends, but I think I know how to make it happen. Pranks have always been the foundation of our friendship.

I smile to myself and make her a cup of coffee. I stir a good spoonful of salt in, a wicked grin on my face. I can't wait to see the look on her face when she takes a sip. I hand it to her with a serene expression. I might not have messed with her in years, but my game face is still on point. Or so I thought. Emilia glances at me suspiciously and I purse my lips. She reads me far too easily. It's been years since I've been able to trick her in person. I always have to do it behind her back.

She takes a sip and spits it right back out, coughing. She glares at me and slams the cup down. "You disgusting devil!" she shouts, her cheeks reddening. Her eyes flash and I burst out laughing. She looks cute as hell.

Emilia grabs my t-shirt and shakes me. Or she tries to, at least. She's unable to move me with her tiny hands. She places her palms against my chest and her brows rise just a little. I watch her intently and see the anger drain away, replaced by a flash of lust. Her hands glide down my chest before she catches herself and pulls away.

"You! Do you want another cup of coffee thrown on you? You're unbelievable, Carter. So childish! I thought you said we were done playing pranks? What the hell!"

She glares at me fiercely, and I instantly remember why I've always loved messing with her. She looks fucking hot when she's all riled up like this. I love getting a rise out of her. Her cheeks are flushed and her eyes are blazing. I wrap my hands around her waist and she melts into me. Her body still fits against mine perfectly. She presses her tits against my chest and I'm instantly hard. I see that hasn't changed either. I always thought I was just easily aroused, but it's only Emilia that makes me feel this way. Her eyes widen when she feels my dick pressed up against her stomach and she looks up at me. She tries to look stern but I know that look all too well. The lust in her eyes is unmistakable, no matter how hard she tries to hide it. Rather than pull away and admonish me, she moves even closer.

"I'm going to get you for this," she whispers. I can't help but grin. I've missed messing with her. I've missed interacting with her. Hell, I've just missed *her*.

"Oh yeah, Emilia? I'm trembling in my boots."

She clenches her jaw and pulls away from me. Her eyes

drop to my jeans and she bites down on her lip when she sees how hard I am. I grin at her as I imagine what those sexy lips are going to feel like wrapped around my cock. I close my eyes and look away. I'm sure things will get more and more interesting from now on.

CHAPTER 3

milia

I'm anxious. It's only been a few weeks and I already feel like I'm falling behind in my classes. I'm more overwhelmed than I thought I'd be. I can't afford to fail anything. If I don't keep my GPA up, I'll lose my scholarship. If I'm already struggling now, then how much more difficult is everything going to get?

I carry my heavy bag to the library, my shoulder aching. I miss having a locker. I wish I could've done what Kate did and just buy all the e-books instead, but my scholarship provided me with the physical books, so I have to suck it up and lug this heavy bag around campus.

I glance up when I hear a familiar voice and find Carter standing by the library entrance. He's standing next to a girl, and the way she's touching his arm and pushing her breasts in his face tells me they're either intimately acquainted, or she'd like them to be. I take in her long blonde hair and the sweet smile on her face. I know this girl. It's *Lisa*. The girl Carter keeps being tagged in photos with. The one I've seen photos of for years now. I may or may not have done some Facebook stalking, and I may or may not know more about her than I should. I know she's a cheerleader — a very good one. On top of that, she's an engineering major, just like Carter. They look good together and they must have so much more in common than he and I ever did.

My heart twists painfully. Just seeing him with someone else still makes me jealous. I can't help but wonder if she's the one that put those kiss marks on him, and if by now she knows his body better than I do. It's been two years since he and I were together, so why do I still feel this way? I can't go down this road with him. I still can't be around him without wanting him.

It doesn't help that he seems to be everywhere. And each time I run into him, he's got another girl on his arm. It's painful and it's weird. He never used to be like that in high school. But then again, he never slept with anyone before me. I guess it's different now.

Carter spots me before I can walk past him and immediately approaches, leaving Lisa staring after him in surprise. She follows with a confused expression on her face, and I'm already done with this shit. I don't ever want to have to compete for a guy's attention.

"Emilia," he says, smiling. My heart skips a beat at the way he looks at me. He looks like he's actually happy to see me. How can my heart feel so full, yet ache at the same time? Lisa catches up to us and smiles at me — it's one of those genuine smiles that make you want to smile back and I hate her all the more for it. I nod at the two of them politely and move to walk past, but Carter throws his arm around my shoulder, stopping me in my tracks.

"You're going to the library to study? We were just headed that way," he murmurs. He grabs my bag and throws it over his shoulder. "Fucking hell, Emilia. What are you carrying in here? Bricks?"

The edges of my lips turn up and I shake my head. "I can

carry it, Carter. You don't need to do that. I also really need to study. I don't have time to mess around with you."

Lisa chuckles and holds her hand out for me. "I'm Lisa," she says. "You have no idea how excited I am to finally meet the infamous Emilia. Carter told me about some of the pranks you two have pulled on each other and that shit is lit."

I shake her hand awkwardly and smile. What am I supposed to say to that? *Yeah, I know all about you too, but that's because I stalked you on Facebook?*

"Lisa and I need to study too. Let's go together," he says. Lisa nods as though she genuinely doesn't mind, and I suddenly feel conflicted. I'm hesitant and tug on my bag, but Carter is holding it hostage. Eventually I give up and walk to the small secluded study corner that I've been using. Carter and Lisa follow and sit down opposite me. Much to my surprise, both of them actually grab their bags and take out their laptops and books. They're so in sync that it's obvious this is their usual routine, and I'm oddly jealous. I've never felt like an outsider in Carter's presence. Even long before he and I were anything but friends, we were each other's *person*. Now it seems like my role in his life belongs to someone else.

"What?" Carter says, smiling. "I have a partial academic scholarship, remember? I have no choice but to keep my GPA up."

I nod and stare at him in disbelief as he pulls out his tablet and starts drawing up complicated equations. Lisa glances at him with such a sweet smile that I'm hit with an instant possessiveness that I'm not entitled to. "No choice, huh? Keeping his GPA up is effortless for him. I swear he's the smartest guy I know."

Her eyes are sparkling with admiration and affection, and I feel like the third wheel here. This is exactly why I've been trying to avoid Carter. I've been clinging to the memory of what we used to be to each other, and every time I see him, I'm hit with the realization that everything has changed. I'm no longer the person who knows him best. I'm not the girl he reaches out to. And I'm definitely not the girl he holds in his arms — not anymore.

Carter smiles at her and drops his arm to the back of her chair. "Says the girl that keeps beating my test scores."

The familiarity and mutual respect between them is obvious, and it's painful. I don't know why I expected her to be mean or... I don't know. I guess it would've been easier. It would've fit the image I built of her in my head so much better.

Lisa smiles at me and then puts in her earphones, tuning us out and focusing on her textbook completely. She and Carter work in tandem, the two of them exchanging notes.

I tear my eyes away from them and blink at my own textbook. I don't understand what's happening in my statistics assignment at all. I glare at it and drop my forehead to the table, beyond frustrated. I'm going to have to get a tutor and my scholarship won't cover that. I feel so stupid and so out of my depth.

Carter chuckles and rises from his seat. He drags his chair to mine and sits down next to me. He leans back and grabs my assignment brief, reading through it patiently. Then he laughs again and shakes his head.

"Minx, this is basic stats," he says. My heart skips a beat. I'm no longer used to him calling me Minx, and what used to be a regular nickname now feels like something intimate. I blush and shake my head.

"It's not," I argue petulantly. "Basic stats is about marbles and shit. This is torture. I don't understand why I need to know this."

Carter grins and puts his arm around my shoulder. I peek at Lisa, but she hasn't so much as looked up at us. I want to know what's going on between them. They're acting like they're just friends, but some of the photos I've seen of the two of them made it look like they were definitely more than that. At least he hasn't introduced her as his girlfriend. What would I have done if he did?

"Come on. I'll explain it to you," he murmurs, and I snap out of my thoughts.

Carter leans in and proceeds to break down every single step of the calculations. He's far more patient than I ever would've expected. He's serious and he doesn't joke around at all. He's explained things to me before back in high school, but it's different this time. I always knew he was ridiculously smart, but I'm impressed nonetheless.

Carter makes up a few examples and hands me his tablet. "Now you try," he tells me. I nod and get to work. Carter returns to his own stuff and occasionally checks in with me to point me in the right direction.

"Shit. I think I get it," I whisper.

Carter chuckles. "If you're struggling with this, then you should probably know it's only going to get harder, Emilia."

I nod and bite down on my lip. I really am going to need a tutor to get through this. There's no way I'll be able to do it otherwise.

"I'll do it," Carter says. I frown at him and tilt my head in question. "I'll be your tutor."

I blink at him in disbelief. "I *do* need a tutor, but I think I'll try learning by myself first. I don't think I can afford one anyway," I murmur. I'll never get over all these feelings that have resurfaced if he tutors me. We'll be too close too often.

Carter grins and grabs my chin. He turns my face toward his and I scowl at him. His eyes drop to my lips, where they linger, until he pulls away.

"Hmm, Minx. You don't have to pay me in cash. You can pay me with your body."

I look at him with wide eyes, and he bursts out laughing. "You can cook for me, Emilia. Cook for me in return for tutoring. I'm happy to get you the ingredients too. Asher and I built some apps that are bringing in a decent amount of cash, but you know I can't cook for shit. I miss the food Mom and you used to make. It'd be nice to have that as a treat every once in a while."

I'm not used to this flirty version of Carter. When we were younger, he was often sweet rather than flirty, and I'm a little thrown off. I hesitate and end up nodding against my better judgement. I know he and I shouldn't spend more time together. The more I find myself alone with him, the harder it gets to resist him. We've finally found ourselves at a stage where we can actually be friends again. I can't mess that up by falling for him all over again.

"Okay," I whisper, unable to resist. "Yeah, I guess that might work."

CHAPTER 4

 arter

The doorbell rings and I walk up to it nervously. I've been antsy waiting for Emilia today. I don't know what I was thinking offering to tutor her. It's obvious there's still something between us. If I want to be friends with her, I shouldn't be finding opportunities to be alone with her. Why the hell do I keep thinking with my dick instead of my head?

"Hey," she says, her voice soft. Emilia looks cute as fuck today. She's got her hair in a messy bun and she's wearing leggings with an oversized tee. She looks comfy and stunning. My heart warms when she starts to fidget with the hem of her tee and bites down on her lip — classic giveaways of her nerves. I grin, relieved that she's just as affected as I am.

"Hey," I murmur. Emilia follows me into the apartment, and I lead her to the living room. "I usually study at the coffee table. We can move to the dining table if you want, though."

She shakes her head and drops to the floor. She's quiet as she unpacks her books. She's been avoiding me lately, and she hasn't responded to any of the little pranks I pulled whenever we ran into each other. I've stuck random dumb stickers on her back, and one time I stuck a fake spider on her backpack, but she hasn't retaliated at all.

I'm low key glad that I've finally found a way to get her to spend time with me. I told myself I'd stay away from her, but now that she's here, I find that I've missed her too much. I miss the bond we used to have. We were good friends before we fucked it all up.

I grab a pillow and sit down next to her, my thigh grazing hers. I'm no longer a teenager, but being near Emilia is still enough to make me hard. I grab another pillow and place it over my lap. Emilia glances at me and stares at the pillow in confusion before it finally clicks. She looks at me in disbelief and blushes. She seems flustered where she used to look smug, and I suddenly feel awkward. It irritates me that I can't control my body's response around her. I *want* to be friends with her, but my body has other ideas.

"So how do you wanna do this?" she asks. I grab her book and start flicking through it.

"How about we both just study, and once you run into a problem, I'll break it down for you."

Emilia nods and starts working. I try to concentrate on my own assignments, but all I can focus on is Emilia. She's still using the same perfume I gave her. Did the bottle last that long or did she buy herself another one? I didn't go home for her birthdays. The last two years were the first birthdays we didn't spend together ever since she walked into my life. Every year I stupidly bought her a new bottle of perfume, though. Just in case I decided to go. I'm pretty sure I have two bottles stuffed somewhere in my sock drawer.

Emilia sighs and I glance over at her. She's got her brows scrunched up in such a cutesy way that I'm instantly filled with tenderness. "What's wrong?" I murmur. She points at a math problem and I glance at it over her shoulder.

"That one is actually quite complicated," I admit. I grab her pen and write out every step to take as I walk her through it. Instead of paying attention, she just looks at me in awe.

"How do you know all this?" she asks.

I chuckle. "I had to take these classes too, Minx. Besides, I'm doing an engineering degree. Almost my entire curriculum is math."

She sighs and rests her head against my shoulder. I can't resist and throw my arm around her before handing her pen back. "You try," I whisper. I drop my chin on top of her shoulder and watch as she successfully solves the equation. "Very good," I murmur. I didn't mean for it to happen, but my angle gives me the perfect view down her t-shirt. It's loose and it's oversized, so I can see her boobs clearly. They look bigger than they used to, and she isn't wearing a bra. I didn't think it'd be possible, but I'm actually even harder now.

I pull away from her. I don't want to be a weird pervert, and I definitely don't want to make Emilia uncomfortable. I don't know why I can't act like a normal person around her. It doesn't help that she seems to be even more beautiful than she used to be.

"Carter?" she says. I look up at her and she looks at me funny. "What are you thinking about?"

I blink. "*Your boobs*," I blurt out. I'm mortified. I can't believe I actually said that. Emilia looks at me with wide eyes and then looks down at her breasts. She blushes and clears her throat.

"Um, well..." she says.

I bury my face in my hands and groan. "Shit, Minx. I'm sorry. I just... *fuck*."

I run a hand through my hair and Emilia nods. She looks down at her breasts again and shrugs. "Well, they *are* great boobs," she says, and I burst out laughing.

"Emilia," I murmur, drawing out her name.

Her eyes roam over my body and she jumps up. "I'm getting hungry. Let me see what you have to make dinner with," she says. I nod and follow her into the kitchen, relieved with the change of subject. She makes herself at home and rummages through all my cupboards. I usually hate it when women so much as wander through my apartment, but I love having her in my space.

She orders me to chop up some vegetables for her while she preps the base of what looks like a healthy and filling dinner. I think she'll make a mushroom and chicken oven dish. Whatever it is already smells amazing. I'm glad she isn't making anything that doesn't fit in with my coach's diet. I guess by now Emilia is as used to my dietary needs as my mom is.

She scoops some sauce off the spoon with her finger, but before she can taste it, I grab her hand and close my lips around her finger. Emilia gulps and stares at me with wide eyes, her lips falling open. She looks at me with desire swirling through those gorgeous eyes of hers. I'm taken back to our childhood instantly. The way she used to look at me and the way she used to make me feel... being around her is dangerous. I can't resist her. I can barely function. My cheeks are just as flushed as hers and I take a step back. It's like I have no self-control when it comes to her.

I take a step back and excuse myself, practically running to the bathroom. I need some distance. My heart still races when Emilia is around. It's been years since we last got together, and even then, we never dated. I guess we were sort of seeing each other, but we were just kids.

I close the bathroom door behind me and sink down to the floor. Emilia and I shouldn't go down this path again. We can't. I still remember the way my heart ached when she refused to try long distance. The way my heart straight up broke when I came home to find her in someone else's arms. Emilia has never felt for me what I feel for her, and I'm not sure I even want her to. I don't want to feel that vulnerable again. I don't have time for complications and I doubt she's up for casual sex. I need to put an end to this somehow.

CHAPTER 5

milia

I exhale in relief when Carter walks out of the kitchen and place my hand over my chest, as though that will calm my racing heart. My heart still skips a beat when he's close to me. I inhale deeply and shake my head. I'm losing it.

I grab my bag to fish out the packet of googly eye stickers I bought on the way over. It's a tame prank for Carter and me, but it'll be funny. I glance behind me and smile. I can't wait to see his reaction when he finally discovers them. He's been trying to revive our feud, and until now I haven't given in. That'll change today, though. Pranks are our way of communicating, and I've missed the bond we had thanks to that. Besides, I've let him get away with sticking weird things on my back whenever we ran into each other and that gross salty coffee. Payback was inevitable.

I work as quickly as I can and put googly eyes on as many things in Carter's fridge as possible, including every single one of his eggs. It looks weird and hilarious as hell. I hear the bathroom door open behind me and try my best to stick just a couple more on the jars in his cupboards before he makes it back to the kitchen. As soon as I hear his footsteps approach, I put the stickers in my t-shirt. I should've thought to wear something with pockets. Rookie mistake.

Carter pauses in front of me and looks at me suspiciously before leaning back against the counter. His eyes roam over my body and he cocks a brow. "What did you do, Minx?" he asks. He peers into the oven and then back at me. "You're eating that too, right?" he asks, his voice tense.

I giggle. I can't help it. It's been years since I've messed with him like this. I forgot how much fun it is. "Yeah, Carter," I reply. "I'm eating it too."

He looks at me with raised brows. "So you didn't mess with the food?"

I shake my head, barely able to suppress my smile. I can't believe he saw through me with a single look. I thought I looked innocent, so how does he know that I've done something? Looks like my poker face needs work.

Carter continues to look around and eventually opens the fridge. He freezes and stares at it in horror. "What the fuck is this?" he whispers, pointing at the eggs with the googly eyes on. "This is fucking horrifying, Emilia. What the fuck are *those*?"

His eyes are wide, and he genuinely looks shocked. His reaction is even better than I expected, and I burst out laughing. Carter's lips tip up at the edges and he smiles at me. "They look like little demons, Minx." He steps away and points at the fridge. "Oh my god, their eyes are following me," he whisper-shouts. He closes the fridge door and turns around to face me. I know he's exaggerating to indulge me, but it's still funny as hell.

"I've thrown fake insects in your bed before yet *this* freaks you out?" I ask. Carter shudders and shakes his head as he walks toward me. I take a step back and my hips bang against the kitchen counter. My heart starts to race and I swallow hard.

Carter places his arms on either side of me and cages me in.

He leans into me and nods. "Yeah. It's the eyes, man. So creepy."

He's standing far too close to me, and I'm so tempted to slide my arms over his chest and around his neck. His body looks broader and stronger, and I want to find out if it feels that way too.

I can't help but wonder if he still feels something for me. Am I crazy for hoping that he does? I know it's better for both of us if we don't go there, but my heart is foolish. Carter takes a step closer until our clothes brush against each other. All I'd need to do to feel him against me is lean in just a little... How would he respond if I press my body against his?

Carter's eyes drop to my lips and my heart beats harder. He closes the distance between us and I almost sigh in relief when my body presses flush against his. I bite down on my lip, and his eyes follow my every move.

The front door slams closed and we both jump apart as Kate's giggles fill the house. Asher and Kate walk in and freeze when they see us standing in the kitchen.

"Hey, what're you doing here?" Kate asks. I'm suddenly flustered, even though I know I have a perfectly good reason to be here.

Carter straightens and looks at Kate sternly. "What are *you* doing here?" he asks. "Why are you coming in with Asher?"

Kate freezes. The way she and Asher look at each other is far too obvious for Carter to miss, yet he doesn't say anything.

"Oh, I was coming to see you," Kate tells him, blatantly lying. "I ran into Asher at the front door," she says. I look away and cringe. Kate isn't a good liar, and Carter is remarkably observant, so I don't understand why they both keep dancing around the obvious. Is he waiting for her to tell him herself? Or maybe he's waiting for Asher to tell him... Either way, it's obvious that he knows about them. Kate seems nervous as she walks into the kitchen.

"You cooked?" she asks, her brows furrowed. I nod and smile tightly. I know I haven't done anything wrong, but I feel like I've wronged her somehow.

"Yeah. It's your mom's recipe for stuffed mushrooms and chicken," I say awkwardly, an immense feeling of guilt sweeping over me. Nothing is happening between Carter and me at all, but I'm on edge around Kate. She grabs my hands and pulls me toward the living room.

"So how come you're here?" she asks, her tone clipped.

I inhale deeply and try to smile at her. "I was falling behind on both stats and calculus, so Carter offered to tutor me in return for me cooking for him every once in a while," I explain. I tip my head toward the books on the table and Kate nods, her shoulders relaxing. I guess she still isn't comfortable with the idea of Carter and me. Part of me kind of hoped that would've changed by now, especially considering her relationship with Asher. I've never really considered Kate to be hypocritical, but I'm starting to. I'm starting to blame her for losing out on what I could've had, even though I made that choice all by myself.

"Why didn't you tell me?" she says, sounding worried.

I shake my head and shrug. Kate and I don't share any classes. She chose to do the easiest ones first, while I just wanted to get the most difficult ones out of the way. "You've been kind of busy. I haven't actually spoken to you much at all since we got here. Our class schedules mostly clash and when we're both free, you tend to hang out with Asher or those girls from your art class. I totally get it, but you know... I just haven't really had a chance to speak to you."

Kate sighs and wraps her arm around me. She drops her head to mine and I'm instantly placated.

"How about we go to a party tomorrow?" she says. "There's one I'm dying to go to, and you haven't done much other than studying. We should both live it up just a little. Besides, we'll have a chance to catch up."

I nod and smile, relieved. I've missed her. Ever since we started college, we've barely spent any time together. We don't share any classes, and she's mostly been concerned with enjoying the college experience. I don't blame her for it, but I *have* felt pretty lonely. She's been staying out late recently, so I'm usually asleep by the time she gets in, and in the mornings we're both in too much of a rush. I'm looking forward to spending some time with her and finally catching up.

CHAPTER 6

milia

"God, this reminds me of Carter's graduation party. Do you remember that?" I ask Kate. She blushes and looks at me with wide eyes. I chuckle. "Of course you remember. You abandoned me and spent all night locked up in your room with Asher. I was so sure Carter was going to catch on."

Kate sticks her hand into my bra, just like she did that night, and helps me create more cleavage. Though these days I don't really need it. I didn't think my body would change much more, but it has. I'm far more curvy than I was two years ago, and I'm certainly not complaining.

"Perfect," Kate says. She forced me into a skintight bodycon dress that puts the phrase *little black dress* to shame. My shoulder-length blonde hair is straightened perfectly, and Kate has worked her magic with my makeup. I look far more seductive than usual. I wish I had her mad makeup skills.

She's outdone herself with her own hair and makeup too. She's wearing a dress not too different from mine, and her long brown hair is perfectly straight too. She's given me a cat eye look, but she's totally rocking her smokey-eye. It really emphasizes her hazel eyes. I don't think I could've pulled it off.

She runs her hands down my shoulders excitedly and smiles. "I'm so excited about tonight's party. It'll be different from the handful of mixers we attended in the first week. This'll be the first *real* party we're attending together."

Her excitement rubs off on me and I giggle as I take another sip of my vodka soda. Kate and I started pre-drinking a couple of hours ago as we got ready, and I'm pleasantly buzzing now.

"Hey," Kate murmurs. "Did you really think I abandoned you at Carter's party? I know back then I was pretty absorbed in Asher, and I know I am now too. I didn't really think I neglected you, but maybe I did. Have I?"

I purse my lips, unsure what to say. I don't want her to feel obligated to spend time with me. I don't want to be needy. "I guess maybe a little?" I end up saying. "I kind of thought that we'd really enjoy college together. We've both worked so hard to get here, and it's all just been a bit... disappointing. My classes are insanely hard and I'm already falling behind, and you're always with Asher or your new friends. It just feels like so much has changed. I thought college would be a lot more fun than it actually is."

Kate looks down in guilt and nods. "I'm sorry, Milly. This was meant to be our time, and I'm just totally neglecting you."

I feel bad because *she* feels bad. It wasn't my intention to make her feel that way at all. I wrap my arm around Kate's shoulder and shake my head. "Well, whatever. Let's just have a good time tonight."

Kate grabs her glass and clinks it to mine. "Yep," she says, her eyes twinkling. We both finish our drinks and make our way to the house party Kate has gotten us an invite too. I'm nervous as we walk into the house while Kate smiles at everyone relaxedly.

She empties her glass, and I bite down on my lip. She already drank far more than I did while we were getting ready. The party has only just started and she's already swaying in her heels. I know she feels more confident when she's had a few drinks, but I can't help but worry about her.

She offers me a shot and I take it reluctantly, my eyes flitting through the room. I freeze when I find Carter standing in the corner, his hand on Lisa's waist. His head is bowed toward her and he seems to be listening to her raptly. The two of them seem close and I just can't help but be filled with intense regret and jealousy. Might Carter and I have been like that if I had agreed to be his? Would he and I have lasted? Would we still be together or would life have torn us away from each other?

I take the second shot Kate hands me, the liquor burning its way through my throat. I barely resist the urge to gag and Kate laughs as she rubs her hand over my back. She flits through the room, chatting to almost everyone, and I can't help but wonder when she even got to know all these people. It seemed like she didn't spend any time with me because she was either in class or with Asher, but now I'm wondering if she spent some of the nights she came back late partying instead. I shake the idea off. Why would she go anywhere without even asking me to join? That doesn't seem likely. I trail behind Kate quietly and nod as she introduces me to one person after the other.

"Girl, we should find you someone to sleep with," she murmurs, giggling. I look at her with wide eyes and shake my head. Kate bursts out laughing. I'm starting to feel pleasantly buzzed and relaxed, so when she hands me another drink, I take it eagerly.

"Thank god," Kate murmurs. "I was so worried you were gonna feel uncomfortable tonight. I'm so glad to see you live it up a little."

I start to reply to her when a girl I don't know grabs Kate's hand and pulls her along toward a game of beer pong. She shrugs at me apologetically and winks. "I'll come find you in a bit! Socialize, girl!"

I nod and sigh. Would it be okay if I just leave already?

CHAPTER 7

arter

I spot Emilia the second she walks in. She's wearing a skintight black mini dress that showcases her body perfectly. Her long legs look fantastic with those heels on, and for a second I imagine myself spreading them, my hands on her thighs. I wonder if her body will still feel the same underneath mine. Will she still moan my name the way she used to?

"Carter!"

I blink and drag my eyes back to Lisa. I bow my head toward hers apologetically and try my best to give her all of my attention, but for the life of me, I can't remember what we were talking about.

"Emilia, huh? You're still so in love with her, it's unreal. It's been two years, dude," she says. There's a slight edge to her tone. but it's fleeting. She's mostly annoyed that I missed half of what she said and she'll have to repeat herself. Lisa knows better than anyone how I feel. She and I have always been clear on what we are and what we *aren't*. We might've started out as fuck buddies just using each other to get over the people we love, but over the years we've become friends. She's one of the few people I actually confide in. One of the few women I enjoy spending time with outside of bed.

"I'm over her," I murmur.

Lisa rolls her eyes. "Is that why you keep looking at her like a lovesick teenager?" she says, an amused expression on her face.

I sigh and wrap my hand around her waist. "What is it, Lisa? You have my undivided attention, okay?"

She looks at me through narrowed eyes and shakes her head. "It's fine. He left just now," she murmurs, her eyes filled with heartbreak. I don't have to glance around the room to know that it's Mason Dalton she's referring to.

"I can't believe you fell for that moron," I chide her gently.

She sighs and drops her forehead to my chest. "He wasn't always like that. When we were younger, he was just the sweetest. He still is when we're alone."

I guess this is exactly why Lisa and I get on so well. We're compatible, but our hearts don't beat for each other. She's been in love with her jackass childhood friend all her life, and when we first met, I was still hopelessly in love with Emilia. Hell, I might still have some feelings for her, if I'm truly honest with myself.

"Fuck, Lisa. You really deserve better. You need to get over that idiot already. How long are you going to watch him fuck one girl after the other?"

She bites down on her lip and shakes her head in denial. "He's not like that. You just don't know him," she says.

I pull a hand through my hair and inhale deeply. No matter what I say, she won't listen. I don't want to see her hurting the way she is, over someone that doesn't deserve her.

I try to give Lisa my undivided attention, but I can't help but notice some guy walk up to Emilia. I watch her from the corner of my eye and tense when she smiles at him. I'm filled with annoyance when he wraps his arm around her. Emilia turns toward me and our eyes meet from across the room. She glances at Lisa and then back at me before she turns away. I watch as she grins and nods at something the jerk that's hitting on her says.

"Go," Lisa whispers. "I know you want to. Emilia has been looking over at us, getting more and more agitated, and you're not doing much better. Go on. I'm fine."

I glance back at Emilia to find her taking yet another shot. Did no one remind her *not* to take drinks from strangers? Why the hell is she having drinks with this asshole? She's swaying in her heels and she looks drunk as fuck. Lisa pushes against my arm and I smile at her gratefully before making my way to Emilia.

"Hey, Minx," I murmur, suppressing my annoyance. Emilia looks up at me and her eyes roam over my body before turning back to the guy she's with. He stares at me wide-eyed and then looks back at Emilia.

"Carter Clarke," he says, before clearing his throat and repeating my name loudly. Emilia glances at me through narrowed eyes when douchebag's attention shifts from her to me. "You're amazing on the field, man," he says, rambling on and on about my own damn stats as if I don't know them myself.

I smile at him and tip my head toward the door. "Thanks. I need a moment with Emilia here," I say, barely able to contain my irritation. I'm not sure *why* I'm so annoyed. Douchebag takes the hint and walks off, but not before smiling at Emilia. She turns to watch him walk away before glancing at me.

"Carter," she murmurs, her eyes narrowed. "Didn't think you'd be able to pull yourself away from *Lisa*."

Her voice drips with venom and I try my best not to smile. I shouldn't feel so pleased to find her acting jealous — Emilia and I were over years ago.

"You're drunk."

She shakes her head and sways a little. I grab her by her waist, my hands closing around her almost entirely. I've always loved holding her like this.

"Where's Kate?"

She shakes her head again and looks around the room in search for her. She deflates when neither of us spots her, and I wrap my arm around her. "Come on, let me take you home."

Emilia shakes her head. "I didn't bring my access card. I can't get into the dorm," she says, pouting. "I'd have left ages ago if I could have."

She looks angry and jealous, and I love it way too fucking much. "Come on, baby. Let's go."

As soon as we're outside, I sweep her into my arms and carry her to my apartment a few blocks down. She rests her head against my chest and closes her eyes.

"Are you sure you can just leave *Lisa*?"

I chuckle. "Why do you say her name like that?"

Emilia pouts, and I bite back a smile. "She's *nice*. And pretty."

"She is, but you don't sound very pleased about it."

Emilia glares at me. "I'm not. I wish she was a bitch."

I burst out laughing. "Why would you want that?"

Emilia leans back a little and looks into my eyes. "Because I don't want to like her. I don't want to like the girl that took my place in your life. I don't want to be happy for you. I don't want to acknowledge that she's better for you than I ever could be."

I pause with her in my arms right in front of my door and put her down carefully to grab my keys. She stares at the ground, looking lost as fuck. I inhale deeply and unlock my door before carrying her into my apartment. I set her down on my bed and she kicks off her heels. She's quiet and I have no idea what to say to her either.

"Emilia, you know Lisa didn't replace you, right?" I say eventually, my voice soft. "She's *her* and you are *you.*"

I don't know how to explain it any better than that, and I'm not sure why I even want to. Emilia and I aren't what we used to be. I owe her nothing.

"Are you dating her?"

I knit my brows and shake my head. "No. It's not like that between us. She's just a friend."

Emilia frowns and looks up at me with her big blue eyes, the hopelessness in them hitting me right in the chest.

"Just a friend, huh? Is she the *friend* that left all those kiss marks on your body?"

I freeze and swallow hard, unable to answer her. I suddenly feel like I've wronged her somehow, when I know I haven't.

"I wish it were me," she says, her voice so soft I almost missed her words.

"You don't," I say, my tone harsh. "Don't say shit like that so thoughtlessly, Emilia. I'm trying my best to be friends with you again, to salvage the friendship you and I both wrecked. Don't complicate things now."

She looks up at me with heartbreak in her eyes and I immediately want to take my words back.

"I know, and I'm sorry, Carter. But I just need to know... do you love her?"

She looks at me like I'm holding her life in my hands. For a second I consider lying to her just to make sure she and I don't end up in the same situation we're only just recovering from, but I can't do that to her.

"No, Emilia. I don't love her. I stopped believing in love years ago."

She looks up at me with a small smile on her lips, a tiny spark of hope lighting up her eyes. Part of me wants to crush it as soon as I see it, but I can't. I can't, because it's Emilia, and she might have broken my heart, but she still owns my soul.

CHAPTER 8

$\mathcal{E}$milia

I wake up feeling groggy and exhausted. My head is pounding and I feel like I haven't had a sip of water in years. I blink, completely disoriented, and then freeze when I see Carter lying beside me. He's got his arm underneath his head, his long lashes fluttering slightly. My heart starts to pound right along with my head and I inhale sharply as I look around, trying to catch my bearings.

Why am I in Carter's bedroom? I run my hands over my body and exhale in relief when I find myself still in the dress I wore last night. Last night's events slowly run through my mind. Carter with Lisa, Kate disappearing on me, me forgetting to bring my access card and Carter taking me home with him. I vaguely remember saying something that I feel I shouldn't have, but I can't for the life of me remember what it was. Just how much did I drink? More than I ever have before, that's for sure.

Carter moves slightly and sighs, still half asleep. He whispers my name so softly that I barely even hear it. His lashes tremble, as though he's about to wake up. He reaches for me and pulls me close, his arms wrapping around me. Carter pushes his face into my hair and then shifts to get more comfortable, settling his lips against the most sensitive part of my neck. His free hand moves over my body, until he's got my ass in his palm. He squeezes and I jump, surprised. Carter freezes and pulls away from me suddenly.

"Shit," he says, breathing hard. He blinks, disoriented, and then closes his eyes and groans as he runs a hand through his hair. "I'm sorry, Emilia," he murmurs, his voice groggy.

I bite back a smile and nod at him. Did he think me being here with him was a dream? That's kinda cute.

Carter covers his face with his arm, and I turn onto my side to look at him. He seems so flustered now that I almost want to tease him even more. Before I have a chance, he clears his throat and looks at me, a serious expression on his face.

"How are you feeling? You got pretty damn drunk last night. You're not used to drinking, so even a few drinks will hit you real quick all of a sudden."

He's got his serious face on, and I pout. "I know, Carter. I just..." I don't even know how to explain. I don't want to admit that I drank more than I planned to because I was upset to see him with Lisa. I have no right to be upset and I don't want him to find out I still have feelings for him.

My conversation with him slowly comes back to me and my cheeks heat up. I close my eyes and groan. I can't believe I asked him if he's dating Lisa or if he loves her. That's none of my damn business. What the hell was I thinking?

Carter sits up and crosses his arms. "I'm serious, Emilia. What would you have done if I hadn't been there last night? You could barely stand straight."

I sit up too and comb through my hair with my hands. The way he's looking at me, as though I'm some sort of fuck up he needs to lecture, pisses me off. "I would've just found someone to spend the night with," I say, my voice dripping with venom.

Carter's eyes flash and for a second I'm sure I saw hurt in them. "Fine," he says, his tone harsh. "I'll just leave you alone next time, then. Seems like you'd have had no trouble finding someone to sleep with anyway."

I sigh and close my eyes. Why did I have to say that? He and I both know I'd never go home with just anybody.

"I'm sorry," I whisper. "Thank you for taking care of me last night."

Carter shakes his head and falls back on his pillow. He puts his arms behind his head and stares up at the ceiling. I've never felt this awkward around Carter before. What am I supposed to do here? Do I just leave now?

I grab my phone and frown when I see dozens of texts from Kate. She wasn't replying when I called and texted her last night. I check the time stamp and they're all from the last hour or so.

Kate: *Did you get home okay?*

Kate: *I'm at Asher's, and I think Carter is home.*

Kate: *How am I supposed to sneak out of here without him noticing?*

Kate: *Asher is still asleep so he can't even distract Carter*

Kate: *Pretty please, Milly, will you come save me?*

Kate: *I just need you to distract Carter for a bit.*

Kate: *Please, Milly!*

I glance at Carter and sigh before texting her back.

Emilia: *I can try, but no guarantees.*

I put my phone back on his nightstand before finally taking in his bedroom. Most of his furniture is dark and masculine. His room looks far less messy than it did the first day I walked in here, so many weeks ago. It actually looks kind of stylish.

"I'm sorry, Carter," I murmur.

He looks at me and smiles tightly. "I'm sorry too," he says.

"You're old enough to make your own choices. I made plenty of dumb choices in my freshman year, so I can't really expect you and Kate not to make any."

I freeze. Somehow I don't like being grouped with Kate. It makes me feel like he sees me like a sister.

"Um, yeah," I murmur. "Can I take you for breakfast to thank you for last night? I *was* just a little irresponsible and you took great care of me. Besides, outside of tutoring we haven't really hung out or anything. It might be nice to catch up," I say carefully.

I'm hungover like crazy, and even though I want to have some food, I'd much rather go back to sleep. I can't just leave Kate to her own devices, though.

I'm holding my breath as Carter looks at me. I'm terrified he might reject me. Until the question left my lips I didn't realize I've been longing to spend time with him.

Carter smiles and I breathe a sigh of relief. "Sure, Emilia. That sounds like fun."

CHAPTER 9

milia

Carter drives us to a cute little restaurant away from campus. I couldn't relax at all as we both got ready just now. I nearly had a mental breakdown thinking Kate would come storming into the bathroom just as I was rummaging through Carter's cupboard for a spare toothbrush. It's not until we left the house that I could breathe easy.

"This place is cute," I tell Carter. He smiles at me and points out his favorite dishes. We both end up ordering eggs, toast and bacon. Can't go wrong with the basics.

I almost moan out loud when I take my first bite and Carter laughs at me. "The options here are simple, but everything is so good."

Part of me wants to know how he discovered this place and how it came to be his favorite breakfast place, but a larger part of me fears I wouldn't like the answer.

I sip my coffee silently, feeling oddly out of it. Every once in a while I catch a glimpse of the guy he used to be. Sometimes I catch him looking at me a certain way that makes me think he must still have some feelings for me. But other times it's like it's only fleeting lust and nothing more. Like I'm just another girl he finds hot.

"How has college been, Milly? It's been, what, three months?"

I freeze and stare at him with wide eyes. "Don't call me that," I snap. He looks up at me in surprise and smiles before looking away. I clear my throat awkwardly. Carter has never once called me *Milly*, not even when we were kids. It's always been a name that only family has ever used, and I've never seen Carter as family. He's always been so much more than that. Even when we were younger, I never saw him like my brother, even though I've always thought of Kate as my sister.

"I'm sorry, Carter. I mean, of course you can call me that. That was unwarranted."

He chuckles and takes another sip of coffee. "It's fine, Emilia. I guess we aren't close enough for me to call you Milly, huh?"

My heart clenches and I'm not sure how to explain, how to talk myself out of this one. "You've never called me Milly before so I was just a little startled, that's all."

Carter looks at me and smiles. "I see. But my parents and Kate call you that, so isn't it only natural that I'd call you that too?"

My heart twists even more and I nod, my head moving only slightly, as though I can only just make myself do it. "I...yeah, of course. Of course, Carter."

It's weird that something as simple as this makes me feel so damn heartbroken. He's drawing a line between us. Is he saying he's going to start seeing and treating me as family now, or am I overthinking it?

"Never mind," he murmurs. "You'll always be Emilia to me. You'll always be my Minx."

I look into his eyes, startled. I bite down on my lip and look away, clearing my throat.

"College has been fine. Not as fun as I thought it'd be. I'm mostly just studying, actually. I'm more homesick than I ever thought I'd be. It's crazy, but it's actually *your* mom I miss most."

Carter nods in understanding. "That's not crazy at all. You two are so close. I'm sure she misses you too. You two been calling or texting?"

I nod. "We text every morning and every night, and I try to call her every other day or so too."

Carter smiles at me adoringly. "That's why you're Mom's favorite. She texts Kate and me too, but I bet you're the only one that never fails to text her back."

I shake my head. "I'm not her favorite," I say. Carter looks at me in disbelief and I smile at him.

"College is more than just studying though, Emilia. You should have some fun too. I'm sorry for not checking in with you more. I know things between us... have been different. But if we can, I'd like for us to be friends again. Let's try, okay?"

I nod, my heart beating wildly. I'll take whatever Carter will give me. "Yeah, let's try," I murmur. I'd want nothing more than to have Carter back in my life, fully.

We're both quiet as Carter drives me back to my dorm. It's like we both want to get back to where we were, but neither one of us can pretend that we're truly just friends.

He hugs me as we reach the building, and I smile up at him. He brushes my hair out of my face tenderly. "Tutoring session next week?" he asks. "We need to get you back on track so you can actually start to enjoy college."

I nod gratefully and wave as he walks away. I feel all out of sorts, my stomach is fluttering excitedly and my heart feels lighter than it's been in weeks. God, I hope I'm still drunk.

I walk to my dorm room lost in thought and jump in

44

surprise when Kate walks up to me before I reach the door. She hugs me tightly.

"Thank you, Milly. God, I'd be so dead if Carter caught me."

She grabs my hand and drags me into our dorm room, her eyes roaming over my body. "Wait a minute. Why are you still in last night's clothes?"

I roll my eyes and cross my arms. "I couldn't get in because I didn't bring my key card, and you freaking left me. What the hell, Kate?"

She groans and runs a hand through her hair. "Shit, I didn't know you didn't have your card. I wouldn't have left with Asher if I'd known."

"I don't get why you left without telling me at all."

Kate's eyes flash with mild annoyance. "We really need to find you a boyfriend, or like, a hook-up or something. You'll get it then."

I walk to my bed and sit down, ignoring her comment. Kate's expression turns dreamy and she smiles as she sits down next to me. "Ugh, Asher is amazing. We decided we wouldn't be together officially. We're both just having fun, that's all."

I bite down on my lip, unsure what to say to her. "He lives with Carter, though. It's not like you can keep it from him forever."

Kate purses her lips and looks away. "Yeah, well, we aren't dating. And to be honest, I don't think it'd really matter if we did. Carter and Asher's friendship isn't really like ours. Asher is never at our house, and our families aren't friends and all that stuff. Even if we dated, I don't think it'd be so bad."

I have no idea what to say to any of this. I don't understand their relationship at all. I can't tell who is stringing who along, and for once, I don't have it in me to care. Even if I warn her, she won't listen, anyway.

CHAPTER 10

 arter

I stare at my watch for the thousandth time. Just ten more minutes until Emilia gets here. I look over my living room, pleased with how tidy it is. I've felt bad about the way I snapped at her for getting drunk when I was much worse at her age. It's like I lose all my rationality when it comes to her.

It's not just my rationality I lose... it's my willpower too. Most of the time I manage to keep her at a distance, but fuck, I didn't think it'd be this difficult.

The doorbell rings and I jump up. I open the door far too quickly and Emilia looks up, startled. My heart skips a beat when she looks into my eyes.

She smiles and steps forward, pushing herself against my body and wrapping her arms around me. I hug her back and rest my chin on top of her head. She fits into me so perfectly. I inhale deeply and my heart skips another beat when I catch a whiff of her perfume — the one I bought for her.

"Hey," she says, pulling away.

"Hey." I walk into my house, feeling somewhat flustered. No one has ever made me feel the way Emilia does.

She takes a seat on the floor in what has become her usual spot, and I drop down beside her. She takes out her books and gets to work, but I can't for the life of me focus on my own work.

I sigh and work on autopilot as best as I can, occasionally running a hand through my hair. Coding has always come easy to me. I love the binary part of it.

"Hey, what're you up to?" Emilia asks, her voice soft. I shake my head and turn to look at her. I'm startled to find her so close and my heart starts to race.

"Wow, this looks so cool. What is this?"

She leans into me as she peers at my laptop, her back against my arm. I move without thinking and wrap my arm around her the way I used to. I rest my chin on her shoulder, and if I wasn't so close to her, I'd have missed her sharp intake of breath.

"It's a platform that Asher and I are building. It's based on blockchain, and if all goes well, we should be able to build an exchange of sorts. Almost like a stock exchange. We're trying to build a platform that'll rival banks as we currently know it."

Emilia turns her head to look at me in awe, and she's so close that my nose almost brushes against hers. Her eyes widen, and for a second, her gaze drops to my lips.

"Wow, that's seriously so cool. I have no idea what blockchain is, though."

She leans her head against my shoulder, and I rest my head against hers. "Blockchain is basically data that's extremely secure and as far as we're aware, impossible to hack. If implemented well, it will transform the current banking industry. Can you imagine being at the forefront of that?"

Emilia shakes her head and looks at me, her eyes filled with wonder. "No, I can't. But I can imagine *you* being at the forefront of that. I always knew you'd go on to do something amazing. You have so much freaking potential, Carter. I always thought you'd either get drafted into the NFL or you'd do something else really cool."

My cheeks heat up, and I look away. Emilia has always believed in me. Even when she and I acted like each other's worst enemies, she always had my back when it came down to it.

"Yeah, well... coach thinks I still have a chance at getting drafted if I work hard enough, but I'm not sure about that. Football training is so fucking rough, Minx. It's such hard work that I barely even enjoy it anymore. I'm still thrilled when I'm on the field, but it's not the same as it was in school. I don't know. I guess we'll see which direction life will end up taking me."

Emilia nods. "Whatever you do, just make sure you're happy. Don't get so caught up making a living—"

"—that you forget to build a life," I finish, quoting the words my mother drummed into us. Emilia laughs and nods.

"What about you, Minx? You still want to be a lawyer like your dad?"

She nods absentmindedly, as though she isn't quite sure. "Yeah, I do. I'm not sure what I want to specialize in, though. I don't think I want to get into criminal law. I'm thinking corporate? I don't know. Plenty of time to decide, I guess."

"How about I build a huge company and you become my in-house council? We'd make a killer team."

She smiles at me, her eyes filled with hope for the future, and my heart skips a beat. Emilia and I working together... the thought hadn't occurred to me before, but now I'd love to see it happen.

My doorbell rings and we both frown. Asher is meant to be at work for the rest of the day — I specifically scheduled my tutoring session with Emilia so we'd have some alone time. I'm annoyed as I walk to the front door and yank it open.

Lisa stands in front of me, black tear marks on her face. She's crying and starts to sob as she throws herself in my arms.

"Carter," she murmurs. I wrap my arms around her and hug her back as I gently steer her into the house. She's clinging onto me as though the world fell from underneath her feet. I sigh as I stroke her hair.

"What happened?" I whisper. She shakes her head and continues to cry her heart out. I rest my head on top of hers and let her be. If she's crying like this, then that can only mean one thing. Fucking Mason found a way to hurt her again. I'm tempted to rough that asshole up a little, but Lisa would never forgive me, and coach would fucking bench me.

I steer her to the living room as best as I can, but she won't budge. I groan and lift her into my arms instead. Her entire body is shaking from the force of her tears.

I carry her into the living room and come eye to eye with Emilia, who's looking at me with eyes filled with heartache. She swallows hard and looks away as she takes a step back, nearly stumbling over my coffee table. *Fuck*.

I try to put Lisa down on the sofa, but she won't let go of me. I glance at Emilia apologetically, but she isn't even looking at me. Instead, she's packing up her bag. I know how she feels about Lisa, and even though Emilia and I aren't together, I still don't want to hurt her.

"I... he — Carter... I can't," Lisa says in between sobs. I sit down on the sofa with her still in my lap and what should've felt like consoling a good friend suddenly makes me feel like I'm the worst person alive.

"I should go," Emilia says, her voice shaky.

Lisa pulls away from me and turns to find Emilia standing in the middle of my living room. She scrambles off my lap and looks up at her. "Emilia," she says. "No, please don't go."

Emilia looks at Lisa and tries her best to smile, but she fails. "I, uh... I won't interrupt you guys," she says. She picks up her bag with trembling hands and Lisa shakes her head. She grabs Emilia's arm and pulls her toward her with so much force that they almost collide.

"I'm sorry," Lisa says. She throws herself at Emilia and starts crying all over again. Emilia looks at me with wide eyes, but I shake my head. I have no idea what's going on, or what could've happened. I breathe a sigh of relief when she hugs Lisa back and moves her hand over her back soothingly.

I lean back against the sofa and look at the two girls. "Was it Mason?" I ask. Lisa nods against Emilia's shoulder and tries her best to stop crying, but every few seconds a sob tears through her throat.

"I... I was supposed to... I was going over. We were g-gonna have lunch together. H-he was still asleep, but there was a girl. He was in bed with a girl."

I don't doubt for a second that Mason orchestrated it so Lisa would see that. I don't get that guy at all. Something has gotta be wrong with him for him to treat her the way he does.

"He's an asshole, Lisa. Fuck him. You could have any guy you wanted the moment you set your eyes on them. Why the fuck does it need to be him? He doesn't fucking deserve you."

Emilia looks at me over Lisa's shoulder and I can see the gears in her mind whirling. I just know she's going to overthink and overanalyze what I said, and part of me wishes I could take it back. She looks down and avoids my gaze, doing her best to console Lisa instead.

Lisa pulls away and turns to face me. "But I only want him," she says. I sigh and nod. I know the feeling — that's exactly how I used to feel about Emilia. Hell, part of me still does.

CHAPTER 11

arter

I stare at the text from my sister in annoyance and glance up at Asher who is pacing in the living room.

"So, Kate just texted me, saying she wants to come over to study. Says she needs some help?"

Asher's eyes widen, and he nods nervously. "Oh, yeah? Yeah, that's fine. I mean, we don't have any plans tonight, right? She can come over. I mean, if you're busy, I can tutor her?"

I roll my eyes and walk to the sofa. This has gone on too long now. "So, is there anything you want to tell me?" I say, throwing the most cliché line I can think of at Asher. He deflates and joins me on the sofa, his eyes moving from me to the TV. I grab the remote and turn it off.

"I — I guess... I mean, yeah."

I pinch the bridge of my nose. This is going to be painful as fuck. I've been ignoring whatever is going on with them because I was avoiding *this*. Asher's awkward behavior.

"I mean, we aren't seeing each other. I, no, that's not it. I mean, Kate and I, we..."

I run a hand through my hair and frown at my best friend. He's the guy I'm starting a company with and he may well be the smartest guy I know, but when he gets nervous, he gets awkward as fuck. It wasn't so bad when he was still playing ball, but since he tore his Achilles tendon, his confidence has been more shot than usual.

"Are you dating my sister?"

Asher blinks and stares at his hands. "Um, sort of. She and I... Kate and I, we aren't dating. She isn't looking for commitment, and I guess she's scared about letting you down? I don't really know."

I inhale deeply and rest my head against the sofa. I was hoping for better than that. To think the two of them are just seeing each other but aren't actually dating makes me uncomfortable.

"I see."

"I'm so sorry, man. I didn't mean for it to happen. I don't know how to even explain. I'm sorry."

I shake my head and clap him on the back. "It's fine, Asher. I just wish you'd told me. You'll always be my best friend, you know? Can't say I'm particularly happy about what's going on with Kate and you, but my sister isn't a child. I won't interfere with the choices you guys are making."

How *could I* interfere? I'd just be a hypocrite. After all, for the longest time I was chasing Emilia. How can I condemn my sister for doing the same thing I was doing?

Asher runs a hand through his hair and looks up at me. "Will you tell her you know?"

I shake my head. "Nah, since you two aren't dating officially, it'll just be awkward. What am I supposed to say? If it gets serious, she'll tell me herself."

Asher exhales in relief and smiles. "Fuck, I've been wanting to tell you for so long. I've felt so guilty for ages."

"You do realize I knew all along, right? I saw you disappear into her bedroom at my graduation party."

Asher looks at me with wide eyes, and I shake my head.

"So, are we good?"

I nod. "We're good."

Asher jumps up when the doorbell rings, as though he can't get away from this conversation quick enough. I bite back a smile and wonder if I should've made it a bit harder on him. He's seeing my *sister*, for God's sake. I should've made him suffer just a little more.

I'm surprised when Emilia follows Kate in. Kate didn't mention that she was coming with her. Not that it matters, but still. I look down at my clothes. I'm in sleeping bottoms my Mom got me and a tee. If I'd known she was coming, I'd at least have put on a bit of body spray or something, damn it.

Emilia has been avoiding me since the last time I saw her. She consoled Lisa as best as she could and then quietly left. I've been wanting to reach out but stopped myself from doing so. After all, the misunderstandings work in my favor. They keep Emilia at a distance, which is exactly where I need her to be.

"Hey," she says, her voice soft and unsure.

"Hi," I murmur. I extend my hand and point toward the coffee table where we've studied before. Emilia takes her usual seat while Kate and Asher sit down opposite us.

Much to my surprise, we all manage to get some work done without too many interruptions. It doesn't take Kate too long to drop her pen in annoyance, though.

"I'm bored," she says. She gets up and walks to the kitchen to rummage through the cupboards. She returns with a bottle of tequila and four shot glasses.

I groan when she hands each of us one and then proceeds to fill us all up. "Let's play a game," she says. "How about *never have I ever*?"

I shrug and close my textbooks. It's a Friday night. I didn't think we were gonna get that much studying done, anyway.

"Okay, I'll start," Kate says. "Never have I ever cheated on an exam."

Everyone but Emilia drinks and Kate rolls her eyes at her. "Seriously, Milly? Never?"

Trust my sister to tweak this game so we all get drunk. She isn't supposed to be mentioning things she's guilty of herself, but fuck it. Emilia shakes her head, a small smile on her lips. I guess she wouldn't ever have cheated on an exam. She just doesn't have it in her.

Asher raises his glass. "Never have I ever trespassed."

This time all of us drink, and Asher frowns at Emilia. "Technically, I was trespassing the day I met Kate and Carter," she tells him, making him laugh.

I hold up my glass and try my best not to look directly at Emilia. "Never have I ever skinny dipped."

I take my shot while Emilia's cheeks redden and smile to myself. Her hand is trembling, as though she wants to drink but doesn't dare to. Eventually she raises her glass to her lips and takes a sip. She smiles at Kate and shrugs. "Technically we have, remember those inflatable pools your mom used to fill up for us?"

Kate laughs and nods, taking a sip of her drink.

Emilia looks at me and grins before raising her glass. "Never have I ever put fake weed in someone's locker."

I groan and take another shot. She's got me there.

Asher raises his glass and shrugs. "Never have I ever dumped someone over text."

Emilia blanches and takes her shot, coughing as it goes down wrong. I look at her with wide eyes and Kate bursts out laughing. "Shit, I forgot you did that to Landon. Poor guy."

I smile to myself, even though I know I shouldn't. She dumped him over text? What the fuck?

Kate lifts her glass and grins at Emilia, and I know that whatever she's going to say is guaranteed to make Emilia drink. "Never have I ever snuck into someone's room."

She groans and glances at me before taking a shot. I can't even count the amount of times she's snuck into my room. I raise my glass and grin to myself. "Never have I ever watched someone masturbate."

Kate and Asher both blanch and take a shot, both of them avoiding looking at each other. Ugh, disgusting.

Emilia looks at me with wide eyes and coughs. She rubs her chest and gets up. "I need some water," she says between coughs. I stand up and follow her into the kitchen, my shot glass in hand.

Her cheeks are bright red and she's leaning against the sink, looking all hot and bothered. Is she thinking of when I gave her that little show through our windows?

She looks up when I walk toward her, and her cheeks get even redder. Her blush spreads to her chest and my eyes drop to her breasts, where they linger.

"You owe me a shot, Minx," I murmur, my voice gravely. I hold it out for her and she looks at me with heated eyes. She's breathing hard and I barely manage to resist. I want her so fucking bad. I want Emilia pushed up against my kitchen counter, her lips on mine.

"I don't know what you're talking about."

I smile and bring my shot glass to her lips. Emilia looks down and then smiles before emptying my glass, her head tipped back.

"I thought you said you didn't know what I was talking about?"

Emilia grins at me as her eyes run over my body, showing me some of the bravado I'm used to from her. One thing I've always found really fucking hot about Emilia is how fucking brazen she is. None of that modest bullshit.

"I don't."

I chuckle and grab a bottle of vodka, refilling the glass. "Fine. Never have I ever fucked someone in a treehouse."

She takes the glass and drinks half, offering me the other half. Fair enough. I raise it to my lips and empty it. Emilia takes it from me and refills it.

"Never have I ever made out with someone in open waters," she says, her voice husky.

My mind flashes back to that very first kiss she and I ever shared. Things have always been intense between us, and that night was no exception. I still want her as much as I did then. I want her wrapped around my body, my hands roaming over her skin. I take a step closer to her and place my hand around her waist, giving into temptation. Emilia melts into me, her chest rising and falling rapidly. She's breathing as hard as I am, and the way she pushes her hips against mine makes me want more.

I take the glass she hands me and empty half of it, offering her the rest. She places her palm flat against my chest and grins as she tips the glass up. Her fingers trace over my pecs and she looks up at me with a clear challenge in her eyes.

I'm about to tempt her into more reminiscing when Asher walks into the kitchen. I step away from Emilia and thankfully Asher pretends like he didn't just walk in on us having a moment.

"Kate is a bit drunk, how're you feeling, Emilia?" he asks.

Emilia shrugs. She's definitely tipsy, but she seems fine otherwise.

"I thought maybe we could let the girls crash here?" Asher says.

I nod. "They can have my room. I'll take the sofa."

Asher nods and walks back into the living room. "You're fine staying, right? I can take you home if you want to. I can't drive right now, but we can take a cab if you want."

Emilia shakes her head, a sweet smile on her lips. "No, that's okay. We can stay over. It's getting late anyway, and I do feel a little tipsy."

I nod and escort her to my bedroom, wishing it could be me sharing that bed with her tonight, and not my sister.

CHAPTER 12

arter

I struggle to sleep on the sofa and keep twisting and turning. Our sofa is huge, but so am I. I sigh and stare up at the ceiling, willing myself to go to sleep already.

I tense when my bedroom door opens and strain my ears. I can hear soft footsteps followed by the sound of Asher's bedroom door opening. Kate? She sure has some guts going into Asher's room knowing I'm right here. I can barely stomach the mental image, let alone the real thing, or I'd have just walked in on them like I know Mom would've done.

I close my eyes and try my best to fall asleep, but all I can think about is how Emilia is in my bed right now, all by herself. Kate won't return to until early in the morning. I toss and turn for the next thirty minutes and just give up.

I purse my lips and grin. This is the perfect chance for me to play a trick on Emilia — I can't sleep, anyway. I get up and rummage through my bag until I find one of my markers, and then I walk up to my bedroom as quietly as I can.

I pause in front of the door and twist the door handle as

silently as I can. If there's anything I've honed during my seasoned prank career, it's stealth. I sneak into the room in dead silence and leave the door ajar, so Emilia won't hear it click.

I tense when I hear soft sounds coming from my bed. It's barely above a whisper, but in the silence of my room I can hear it clearly. My heart starts to race and I quietly make my way toward my bed.

Another soft moan escapes Emilia's lips and the sound of it goes straight to my dick. I'm instantly so fucking hard. I stand a few steps away and look at her. Her eyes are closed and her hands are hidden underneath my sheets, but the way she's moving her body tells me she's riding her hand *hard*. She moans louder and it sounds like she's close.

"Carter," she whispers, and I bite down on my lip to keep my own groans in. She's fucking thinking about me while touching herself like that?

I inhale a shaky breath and make up my mind. I walk to my bed and lean on it with one knee; the bed dipping under my weight. Emilia's eyes open wide and she looks at me in shock.

I pull the sheets away from her, my eyes running over her body. She's wearing one of my favorite t-shirts and her hand is buried in her black underwear. She lies there, frozen and embarrassed as hell, and I chuckle.

It's like the sound of my laughter snaps her out of it, because she pulls her hand back and hides it underneath her t-shirt.

"Did I interrupt something?"

Emilia gulps and looks up at me, her cheeks bright crimson. I get into bed next to her and cover us both up.

"You... w-what are you doing here?"

I hold the marker I have in my hand up for her. "Was planning on drawing some cat ears on your face or something.

Maybe some dicks. Seems like you might prefer the dicks, Minx..."

Emilia looks up at me, her chest rising and falling rapidly. Her eyes roam over my face and down to my chest. The way she's staring takes me back to how she used to look at me, so many years ago. The way she moaned my name and the way she messed with me... Emilia's eyes fall to my lips and she inches closer.

I trace my hand over the side of her face, brushing her hair out of the way. Her eyes flutter closed and she sighs happily before looking into my eyes. I lean in just slightly. She's so close. Closer than she's been in years. How many times have I dreamt of having her this close to me? Of having her lips on mine again.

Emilia raises her hand and brushes her fingers over my neck before cupping the side. Her thumb grazes my throat, back and forth. My heart is racing and I'm breathing as hard as she is.

It's been so fucking long. I've done so well resisting her since she walked back in my life. I keep trying to convince myself that I don't want her, but I do. I fucking do.

I tilt my head toward her and let my eyes fall closed. Just one kiss. Just one taste of her.

My lips brush over hers, and a soft sigh escapes her lips. Emilia's hand moves to my hair and she pulls me closer, her tongue brushing over mine. I moan and roll on top of her, our lips colliding hungrily. I push her legs apart and settle between them, my dick pressing up against her. Emilia's hands roam over my back and she tugs on my t-shirt.

"Emilia," I whisper. I can taste the tequila on her tongue. I can't help but wonder if it's liquid courage that's fueling her bravado. "Baby, how much did you drink?" I'm worried she isn't thinking clearly. I want her, but I never want to take advantage of her.

"Please, Carter," she whispers. She tugs my t-shirt and I sit up long enough to take it off entirely. Emilia pulls me back and kisses me with the same passion I'm feeling. Her tongue tangles with mine while my hands roam over her body. My fingers trail downwards, over her underwear, until the tips of my fingers graze her pussy. She inhales sharply and grabs my hair. She pushes her hips up in a silent bid for more, and I push her panties aside. My fingers slip into her easily — she's fucking soaking wet.

Emilia moans and I grin before biting down on her lower lip. "Shh, baby," I whisper. I tease her clit and keep her right on the edge, riling her up. I can't help but mess with her.

"Carter, *please*."

I give her what she wants and feel her body fall apart against mine, my lips swallowing every single one of her moans. She's so fucking sexy. She collapses against my pillow and the way she smiles up at me makes me feel things I haven't felt in years.

She pulls me closer and kisses me so sweetly that I'm suddenly filled with emotions I thought I buried long ago. I kiss her back slowly and gently before dropping my forehead against hers.

The lust is fading, and rationality is taking its place. I told myself I wouldn't do this with her again, yet I didn't last more than three months before I found myself in bed with her again.

I don't want to put my heart on the line again. I don't want to go through the roller coaster ride that any relationship with Emilia would be. I don't want to risk upsetting my family. Mom might not have said anything, but it broke her heart when I wouldn't come home for Emilia's birthday or other family occasions. We finally got over that, we're finally in a place where we can be friends again... I can't fuck that up again — but I want to.

CHAPTER 13

*E*milia

I've been nervous and giddy all morning. Carter and I spent most of last night together, kissing and touching in ways I've been craving. Just having his hands on me makes everything in the world feel right. I have no idea what time he snuck out. All I remember is falling asleep in his arms and waking up next to Kate.

"I must've been crazy. Shit, I'd be so dead if Carter caught me. Oh my god, the next time I so much as attempt to kiss Asher when Carter is nearby just smack me. Like, right across the face."

I glance at Kate and shake my head. "Like that would actually stop you once you have your mind set on something."

She purses her lips and nods. "Yeah, okay, good point."

I chuckle and get dressed as quickly as I can. I'm eager to see Carter again. I'm glad he remembered to sneak out, but at the same time I was pretty disappointed when I didn't wake up in his arms.

The entire house smells like bacon and my stomach growls

loudly as I make my way to the kitchen. Carter and Asher are already sipping their coffee, both of them on their laptops at the kitchen counter.

"Morning," I murmur, my voice betraying my giddiness. Asher barely looks up from his work, but Carter raises his head to look at me. I expected to find the same excitement in his eyes that I'm feeling, but instead he looks at me warily and smiles tightly. He looks back down without so much as bidding me a good morning, and all my excitement leaves me at once. I'm left feeling deflated, and I guess part of me is a bit humiliated. To think I was so excited when Carter seems to think I'm an inconvenience.

I grab a cup of coffee with shaking hands and stare out the kitchen window as I take a sip. Carter has always been the only one that's capable of doing this to me. He makes me feel high highs and lower lows. A single look from him can drive me insane and his dismissal still hurts as much as it used to — perhaps even more. I promised myself I wouldn't go down this road with him. We've been here before and we know where it leads. Yet, last night I just couldn't resist. I thought Carter felt the same intense need that I was feeling... that inability to stay away for even a second longer. Was I wrong? It's so easy to forget that he isn't the guy I used to know. It's been two years since he and I were even friends, let alone more than that.

Asher groans and gets up to walk to his room, his expression stormy. I glance at Carter to find him already looking at me, his expression carefully blank. Now that we're alone in the kitchen, I'm suddenly nervous. This has gotta be the first time I'd rather have Kate interrupt us.

"Emilia," he says, his voice calm and even. How can he possibly be this calm after the way he touched me last night? He gets up and approaches me. He leans back against the kitchen counter, leaving more than enough space between us.

"We should talk."

I nod and bury my face in my coffee cup. Why does my heart already feel like it's breaking?

"Look, Emilia, we both had a bit too much tequila. I mean, I did find you in my bed touching yourself and whispering my name... How could I not have been turned on? That doesn't mean I should've acted on it, though. We shouldn't have done what we did. I'm all for casual hook-ups, but you and I both know that we're awful together. I'm not up for that mess again, and I'm sure you're not either."

My stomach twists uncomfortably, a dull ache spreading through my body. He regrets last night. Of course he does.

I look up at Carter and try my best to smile at him, but I'm sure I failed. "Yeah, no, of course," I murmur, unsure what else to say. Part of me wants to question him, to ask him whether last night meant anything to him at all, but my pride won't let me. I don't want him to think I'm hurt or that I'm hung up on him or something. I don't want to do anything that might endanger the delicate friendship we've rebuilt. I can't risk losing Carter entirely, not again.

He exhales in relief and smiles at me — a real smile this time. "I knew you'd understand, but *fuck*, I was so worried. I think by now we know that we're better off as friends, but I was worried I might've given you the wrong idea last night. I'm glad we're on the same page, Minx."

"Yeah, of course. So last night... was just a hook-up?"

Carter's cheeks redden and he nods. "Yeah, well, I guess. Not much of a hook-up, though. All we did was make out."

I instantly start to overthink his words. If this isn't much of a hook-up, then what is? The idea of him with anyone else breaks my heart. I can't help but think back to how he held Lisa in his arms and how he told her she could have anyone she wanted as soon as she decides on it. Did *anyone* include *him*? It's obvious they've hooked up before, and it's becoming a lot clearer what that actually entails. I've been seeing photos of them for two years now. Does that mean he's been sleeping with her for years? Has he been falling for her, bit by bit, throughout that time? I've never seen him be as delicate with anyone as he was that night. I thought I was the only one that ever saw that side of him, but I was obviously wrong. While I was pining after him, he's been moving on — with a girl that's far more suitable for him. If she'd given him an honest chance, last night probably never would've happened.

"We're good, right?"

Carter sounds anxious, as though the idea of me thinking last night meant anything at all terrifies him. My messed-up mind can't help but wonder if it's because of Lisa. Is he worried I might ruin things for him?

"Yeah, of course. We're good."

I breathe a sigh of relief when Kate walks into the kitchen, a bright smile on her face. "Morning," she hums. She's obviously in a great mood, undoubtedly because she got laid last night. Too bad I never got that far. I'm such a freaking fool. Who pines after their high school crush? Carter was never even my boyfriend, and it's been two whole years since we last had sex. Why am I even remotely surprised he's moved on? I need to work harder to make sure I move on too, or I'll end up ruining our friendship all over again.

CHAPTER 14

$\mathcal{E}$milia

I can barely focus on what the professor is saying and yawn again.

"You're Emilia, right?" the girl on my right says. I turn to look at her and smile.

"Yeah. Dawn, right?" I remember her from my first week here. She was super nice at that first mixer Kate and I attended.

She nods excitedly. "I've seen you in class a few times before, but you're always so focused during lectures I'm scared to talk to you, even though we sit near each other all the time. This is my twin brother, Lucas."

I glance over her shoulder at the tall blonde guy next to her, the resemblance between them is striking. He leans over his sister and offers me his hand.

"Hey," he says, a friendly smile on his face.

"Hi," I murmur awkwardly as I shake his hand. He grins at me and leans back in his seat.

"Looks like you're struggling to pay attention. Can't blame ya, this lecture is boring as hell," Dawn says. I laugh and nod in silent agreement. She scrolls through her social media and holds her phone up for me. "Are you going to this? I don't think I've actually seen you out since the first week."

I glance at the Facebook post with raised brows. "Looks like a house party at some jock's place?"

She looks at me open-mouthed and shakes her head slowly. "You're kidding, right? Please tell me you know who Noah Johnson is?"

I shrug. "Never heard of the guy."

Dawn fans herself and shakes her head. "No way. He's a football *God*. You're coming tonight. I cannot believe you don't know who he is. Impossible."

My first instinct is to say no, but then I think about Carter. I promised myself I'd try harder to move on. "Yeah, sure, why not?"

Dawn squeals and grabs my hands. "Oh my god, I'm so excited!" I chuckle and squeeze her hand slightly. She reminds me a little bit of Kate. Not the estranged Kate that she's become, but Kate before Gabby. I grab my phone and decide to text her. Lately she's been really into parties, so she might want to come tonight. Unless we're with Carter and Asher, we don't really spend much time together lately.

Emilia: *Hey, do you want to come to some Noah guy's party tonight? One of the girls in my lecture invited me.*

Kate: *Oh my god, Noah Johnson?*

Hmm, seems like I really am the only one that hasn't heard of this guy. But then again, I've purposely been avoiding all mention of the football team... of *Carter*.

Emilia: *Yep, that's the one*

Kate: *Shit, I would've loved to, but Asher told me he booked a hotel for us tonight*

I sigh, discouraged. It would've been so much more fun with Kate there. I want to try to step outside of my comfort zone, but I selfishly wanted her with me to give me that final push.

For the rest of the day, I'm anxious just thinking about this party. By the time evening comes around I've changed outfits eleven times, and I've straightened my hair so many times that I'm not sure it's ever going to have any texture again. I ended up deciding on a little black dress that doesn't make me look over-dressed but still makes me feel sexy. I paired it with red lipstick and the eye makeup Kate taught me to put on. It's not quite the metamorphosis I undergo when Kate dresses me up, but I'm happy and I feel confident.

That confidence doesn't last long, though. By the time I reach Noah Johnson's front door, I've already had to convince myself to go in a handful of times. I agreed to meet Dawn inside, yet I can't quite make myself go in. I make it as far as the porch and just give up. I end up walking around the corner of the huge house and lean back against the wall.

What am I doing here? If it's this hard just to show up at a house party, how will I ever find someone to hook up with?

"You look like you're deep in thought."

I jump when I hear a voice; I thought I was alone. I look around and lay eyes on a tall, muscular guy that looks vaguely familiar. He's leaning back in a dark corner, as though he's hiding.

"I'm sorry, I thought I was alone here," I murmur. "I didn't mean to interrupt. I can go."

He shakes his head. "That's okay. We can share this solitude."

He walks over, and the small amount of porch light illuminates his face. His eyes are the brightest green I've ever seen and his half-long brown hair looks roguish instead of douchy. I have to admit he's sort of handsome.

The green-eyed stranger sinks down to the floor next to me

and extends his legs, crossing his ankles as he leans back against the wall. I follow his lead and sit down beside him.

I stare at the sky. I came here with such grand ambitions. I was going to take the first step toward getting over Carter... yet here I am.

"You look so sullen. What's wrong?"

I shake my head and smile. "You don't want to know."

"I've had a spectacularly shitty day. Humor me."

I turn to look at him and inhale deeply. "I'm still in love with a guy that got over me years ago. We sort of got together a few days ago, but to him it was nothing more than a drunken hook-up. I can see him falling for someone that's far better for him than I could ever be, but I can't let go. I actually came here tonight determined to hook up with someone and finally start getting over him, but I can't even make myself walk through the door."

I draw in a shaky breath and swallow hard.

"I'm not much better," the guy says. "I'm in love with my brother's girlfriend, and the worst thing is... I think she feels something for me too. No matter how hard I try to push her away, she won't go. I'm tired of hurting her. I'm tired of wanting her."

I drop my head back against the wall. "We're both fucked."

He starts laughing and turns to look at me, a cute smile on his face. "I'm Mason," he says.

His name rings a bell, but I can't quite place him. "Are you in one of my lectures? Your name sounds familiar."

Mason shakes his head and grins. "Nah, there's no way I'd forget a girl as beautiful as you. I'd have introduced myself long ago."

I giggle and look away shyly. When is the last time someone called me beautiful? Someone other than Helen or Kate.

"Will you tell me your name?"

I smile. "It's Emilia."

Mason rises and grabs my hand. "Come on, Emilia. Let's try to make the most of tonight. You made it this far, might as well go in."

I nod and clench Mason's hand as we walk into the house, my heart beating wildly. It's clear that he's popular because almost everyone nods at him and some of the guys fist bump him, but he doesn't stop walking, and he doesn't let go of my hand.

"First, drinks. There's no way either of us is getting through tonight without them."

I laugh and nod in agreement. Mason hands me a shot of tequila and I'm instantly reminded of Carter. I have a feeling tequila is always going to remind me of him, and what likely was the last night I ever spent with him.

"What's wrong?" Mason asks. He brushes the hair out of my face and I shake my head before I take my shot of tequila.

"You've got it bad, huh, Emilia?"

Mason grabs my hand, and I cling to him happily. "I warned you. I'm a freaking mess. Even the tequila reminds me of him. How dumb is that?"

Mason raises our joint hands to his lips and kisses my knuckles gently. "Not dumb at all. Just for tonight, though, I'll make you forget all about him."

I blink, caught off guard, and Mason chuckles. "No expectations, Emilia. I meant we can just hang out and have a good time. If it leads to more, then it does. If it doesn't, then that's fine too."

I nod and take the vodka mixer Mason is handing me. He tenses suddenly, and when I follow his line of sight, I follow suit.

Lisa and Carter just walked into the kitchen, their hands entwined the way Mason and mine are. Lisa is dragging Carter along and walks up to us. She glares at me before looking at Mason.

"*Mason*," she says, and it finally clicks. Mason is the guy she was crying about? Shit. I glance over at Carter and he looks furious, probably on Lisa's behalf.

Lisa looks at me and frowns. "Why are you with Mason, Emilia?"

Mason stiffens and looks at me with raised brows. "You two know each other?"

I bite down on my lip and nod. Carter lets go of her hand and wraps it around her waist instead. He might as well have stabbed me in the heart. I can't stand seeing him with her.

Mason follows my line of sight and then looks at my face. I must not be hiding my feelings well because his eyes light up with understanding. He turns toward me and gently brushes my hair behind my ear before leaning in.

"Come on, let's get out of here."

I hesitate. I've never done this before, and even though I like Mason, I don't like him *like that*. I barely even know him. I want to be one of those girls that can do one-night stands, but try as I might, I don't think I can.

"Over my dead body," Carter says through gritted teeth. He grabs my wrist and pulls me toward him. I stumble and crash into his chest, and he wraps his arms around me. I push against him and glare up at him.

"Why do you seem to think you have a say in this?"

Hurt flashes through Carter's eyes briefly and hope surges through me. My stupid heart just won't give up.

"You want to go home with Mason?" he asks, his voice harsh.

I shrug. "Yeah, why not?"

Mason chuckles and hands me another shot of tequila. I down it and look up at Carter with a wicked smile on my face.

"Tequila makes me feel... like I don't want to spend tonight alone."

Mason barks out a laugh and wraps an arm around my

waist, earning me another glare from Lisa. He leans in and whispers into my ear. "Do you think Carter Clarke might actually kill me?"

I laugh and turn to face him, my nose brushing against his. I'm startled — somehow I didn't expect him to be this close. Guess those shots are hitting me quicker than expected. "No," I whisper. "Not because of me, anyway."

Carter pulls on my hand and yanks me back again. This time he bends down and lifts me into his arms before I have a chance to pull away. I gasp and hit his arm, but he ignores me and walks straight to the front door, leaving a throng of shocked people in his wake. My eyes meet Dawn's as we walk past the entrance, and she looks at me with raised brows. Carter walks so quickly I don't even have a chance to explain to her what's going on.

Carter is trembling with anger by the time he puts me in his car. I was planning on arguing with him further, but I know that riling him up further isn't going to do me any good.

He gets behind the wheel and I buckle myself in. "Carter, did you drink?" I ask, my voice soft. He looks at me and clenches his jaw before shaking his head.

"Didn't have a chance to grab a fucking drink. When I walked into the kitchen, you were all tangled up with Mason. Do you really think I'd get behind the wheel drunk, Emilia? Do you think that little of me?"

Carter is clenching the steering wheel so tightly that his knuckles are white. I shake my head and he drives us to his apartment in silence. I thought he was going to drop me off at my dorm, so why are we here?

CHAPTER 15

arter

Emilia is silent as she follows me into my apartment. Everything is quiet and dark, and I don't bother to turn the lights on. I turn to face her as soon as the door closes, barely in control of my anger. Just seeing her with Mason, his arm wrapped around her waist, their faces so close together...

"Why did you bring me here?" Emilia asks. She crosses her arms, inadvertently pushing her tits out. She looks so damn beautiful in the small amount of light streaming through the windows. The idea of her going home with Mason tonight fucking tears me apart. What if Lisa hadn't dragged me to that party? Would Emilia have gone home with him?

"Why were you with Mason?"

Emilia rolls her eyes and looks away. "That's none of your business, Carter."

"Do you even know him? He's not a good guy, Emilia. He wouldn't treat you well. What were you thinking?"

She barks out a humorless laugh and looks up at me in

disbelief. "I wasn't expecting him to treat me well. Hell, I was *counting* on it. I wasn't planning on dating the guy."

I clench my jaw and do my best to ignore the mental image. "So what *were* you planning on? Would you have fucked him?"

She shrugs. "I was leaning toward it, yeah. I don't get the problem here. Didn't you say you're all for casual hook-ups? Or are you just upset that I got with your little girlfriend's man?"

"Is this the tequila talking?" I say through clenched teeth. Granted, Lisa would be really fucking upset if Emilia and Mason got together, but nowhere near as upset as *I* would be. I wasn't thinking of Lisa at all when I carried Emilia out of there.

She laughs and bites down on her lip. "Hmm, tequila... I guess the tequila does make me want more of what we did a couple of nights ago. You said that was barely a hook-up, though, didn't you? I think it's about time I find out what a *real* hook-up entails."

I walk up to her and bury my hand in her hair. Her body still responds to me the way it used to. She pushes her chest out a little more and her eyes darken with interest. "If it's me you want, then why the fuck were you with Mason?"

Emilia grins up at me. "But you said you and I would be awful together, right? That we're better off as friends?"

I did say that, and I fucking lied. Fuck. I know she and I shouldn't do this, but I can't stand here and watch her walk into someone else's arms either. I just can't. I tighten my grip on her and tilt her head toward mine. Emilia's arms find their way around my neck and I pull her flush against me.

"Fuck what I said. If it's me you're trying to get out of your system, then the only one you should be fucking is *me*, Emilia."

She looks into my eyes heatedly and I groan as my lips come crashing down on hers. She moans as soon as we touch. I lift her up and she wraps her legs around my hips as I push her against the wall. Her hands roam over my body impatiently while our tongues tangle together. I need her so fucking badly.

Her hands find their way underneath my t-shirt and she lifts it up. I let go of her long enough to let her take it off, and then my hands are back on her.

"Baby, I need you," I murmur against her lips. Emilia nods and her lips move toward my neck. She kisses and bites me in all the right places, driving me insane. I grab her ass and tug her dress up. She leans back a little; just enough to let me take it off her. I drop it on the floor and walk us toward my bedroom. "I need to be inside you, Emilia."

She groans in agreement and sucks down on my neck, sending a delicious thrill through my body. I lay her down on my bed and lean over her. She half sits up and yanks on the button on my jeans, eager to get it off. I chuckle and shrug out of it before joining her in bed. She looks so fucking hot, lying here in her underwear. I've been dreaming about having her in my bed like this. Ever since she stayed over a few nights ago, I keep wanting her back in bed with me.

Emilia bites on my lip and drops her forehead against mine, pulling her lips away. "I thought you said you didn't want me?"

I grab her hand and wrap it around my erection. She giggles and presses her lips against mine. I kiss her deeply, wanting to lose myself in her. I reach behind her and undo her bra easily. Emilia frowns and looks at me in annoyance. "I see you've gotten better at that," she snaps. I smirk and kiss her before she can overthink it. My fingers trail over her breasts and every time I touch her just right, a small shiver runs through her body. I fucking love it.

She squirms underneath me impatiently and I smile against her lips. Within seconds we're both finally naked. I reach over to grab a condom and she looks at me through lowered lashes as I put it on. I don't think I've ever wanted anyone more than her.

Emilia parts her legs for me and pulls me on top of her eagerly. "Now, Carter," she whispers. I lean over her, my forearms on either side. I hover over her like that, my eyes on hers and my dick aligned with her perfectly. She squirms underneath me and I push into her slowly, inch by inch, my heart beating wildly. I don't remember the last time I was this nervous.

"Yes," Emilia whispers, and I bite down on my lip to keep myself in check. She's so fucking tight, and all I want is to push into her fully. I sink into her all the way and drop my forehead against hers. I'm panting and my heart is going fucking wild.

Emilia buries her hand in my hair and rakes my scalp with her nails. "Oh God, yes," she whispers. I pull back slightly and then sink back into her, keeping the pace slow and steady. My lips find hers and she kisses me like her life depends on it — like she's feeling the connection the way I am.

Emilia hooks her leg around mine and I pull back to thrust into her harder. The way she moans drives me insane. "Carter," she whispers. Sex with her is unlike anything I've ever experienced before. Being with her is still so fucking incredible.

I thrust into her at an angle and the way she squeezes my dick tells me she fucking loves it. I grin when she kisses me more frantically and fuck her even harder. Her legs start to shake and I struggle to hold on, but I'm intent on making her come all over my dick. "Carter, I can't—"

I feel her muscles spasm around me and she drops her lips to my neck. She sucks down on my skin, right below my ear, where I'm most sensitive. The way her body erupts around me pushes me over the edge and I come harder than I have in a long time.

I collapse on top of her and bury my face in her neck. She wraps her arms around me and I kiss as much of her skin as I can reach, down her neck and the side of her face. Both of us are a sweaty mess, but it couldn't have been more perfect.

I move away from her to take care of the condom and then join her in bed again as quickly as I can. She's always been the only girl I ever want to hold after sex, and I can't imagine not having Emilia in my arms right now. I can't imagine asking her to leave.

She fits in my arms perfectly and sighs. "I thought you said you and I were better off as friends," she says carefully. I kiss her cheek and inhale deeply.

"You and I clearly have some unresolved issues... this thing between us, I don't think it's going away anytime soon. We might as well just get it out of our systems, together."

Emilia tenses in my arms and all of a sudden I feel nervous. I hate all these things she makes me feel. "What does that mean?" she asks.

"I don't know, Minx. I was serious when I said I think we're better off as friends. But maybe you and I... I don't know. Maybe we can be friends with benefits or something?"

Emilia rolls on top of me and holds herself up above me, giving me the perfect view of her boobs. I tease her nipple with my fingers and watch her face as she tries to fight the arousal.

"You and I? Friends with benefits?"

I shrug. "Why not? We clearly still want each other. I don't do feelings, Emilia. We aren't going to date — I don't want any of the mess we got ourselves into years ago. We've already established that we don't want to hurt my family, and that it isn't worth the risk. So let's just get together, no strings attached, just sex. Outside of bed we remain friends, nothing more and nothing less."

Emilia lowers her body on top of mine, her breasts crushed against my chest. "Hmm, I guess. That might work. Fine, but on one condition: while you're sleeping with me, you can't be with anyone else."

I blink in surprise. "You want exclusivity?"

Emilia nods, and I can tell she isn't going to budge on this. Oddly enough, I'm not at all opposed to it. Exclusivity means she can't get with anyone else either. She'll be mine alone.

"Deal."

I grab her and turn us over so I'm on top of her. She giggles when she realizes I'm hard again. I shut her up by trailing my fingers over her inner thigh. I wonder how long it'll take me to make her come again, on my fingers this time.

Emilia jumps at the sound of the front door slamming closed and I glance over my shoulder. "It's fine, babe. It's just Asher. He won't come in."

She frowns as though she's surprised he's here and I grin at her. "He went to the library to study. Says he can't study at home. He's in full-on cram mode."

Emilia looks puzzled and I lower my lips to hers, intent on making her forget everything but me.

CHAPTER 16

milia

I wake up in Carter's arms, our legs tangled together. Last night flashes through my mind, frame by frame. Friends with benefits, huh? If it means I get to have more of what Carter gave me last night, then I'm all for it. I'm glad he agreed to exclusivity. I don't think I could've dealt with the thought of him being with someone else. I'd just wonder if I'm the only one he's sleeping with or if he might've been with someone else shortly before getting into bed with me. I'd be so anxious all the time.

It's petty, but part of me also wants to keep him away from Lisa. It's horrible, and I wish I were a better person. I wish I had it in me to wish the best for him. I know he and I are going to be temporary, but she and him might not be. I'm knowingly standing in the way of that — I'm knowingly keeping him away from her, out of pure selfishness.

My phone buzzes and I reach for it absentmindedly. I pick up without thinking, still sleepy.

"Hello?" I murmur.

"Milly? You didn't text or call last night. Where are you? Is everything okay?"

I sit up, panicked, and Carter groans at my sudden absence. "Baby, come back," he murmurs, his voice gravelly.

Helen clears her throat awkwardly. "Emilia, are you with a boy?"

I feel my cheeks heat and my heart beats a thousand miles an hour. I know she can't see me and she's so far away, but somehow I feel like she just walked in on us.

"I — no... I'm sorry I forgot to call, Helen. I went out last night and I just... I missed your call and then it got so late."

Carter sits up at the mention of his mother's name and he looks at me with wide eyes. I raise a finger to my lips and wrap his bed covers around me.

Carter grins and pulls them away again. He grabs my hand and kisses the inside of my wrist, sending a small shiver of delight through my body.

"I see. That's okay, Milly. You don't need to apologize. It's okay. I was just worried. I know what Carter and Kate are like, so I'm not surprised when they don't call or text, but when it's you... I was just worried. I'm happy to hear you went out last night. Are you finally having some fun, sweetie?"

I pull my hand away from Carter and he grins as he leans in. He kisses my shoulder and I try to swat him away as quietly as I can, but he's having too much fun riling me up.

"Yeah, it was fun. I had a good time," I say, and Carter raises his brow.

Helen chuckles. "I'm glad to hear it, sweetie. You've always worked so hard, so please make sure you enjoy college too. Did Kate go to the party with you?"

Carter pushes me flat on the bed and lowers his lips to my stomach. He kisses me gently and works his way up to the underside of my breast. I glare at him and thread my hand through his hair. I want to pull him away, but I'm enjoying his feather soft kisses too much.

"Hmm, what? Oh, no, she didn't come with me. I did invite her, but she already had plans."

Helen sighs. "I'm worried about her. I barely get to speak to her. She doesn't pick up my calls and doesn't call back. I don't want to be an overbearing mother, but I just want to know that she's doing okay. How has she been?"

I inhale deeply and think of what I should say. I don't want Helen to worry, but I don't want to lie to her either. Carter looks up at me and grins wickedly before kissing my breast. I drop my phone when his tongue swirls around my nipple and I grab it frantically while glaring at Carter yet again. He smiles and I look at him through narrowed eyes as I bring my phone back to my ear.

"She's made a lot of friends here, and she seems much happier than she was at home. I think it's been kind of liberating for her to be here? I'm not sure. Either way, she doesn't seem unhappy or homesick."

Helen is silent for a couple of beats and I worry that she'll see through me. The truth is I barely speak to Kate these days. She seems to be going out a lot and we keep missing each other. We don't share any classes either, and I think she's quite glad about it. I've tried not to take it personally, but I've felt like she's been trying to break away from the person she used to be — and that includes me. I guess college has given her an opportunity to rediscover herself. I know she felt quite lost after the whole Gabby thing, so this might actually be what she needs.

Carter rests his head on my chest and I stroke his hair while he draws circles on my stomach.

"Okay, well, that's good to hear. You girls look after each other, okay? I know you and Carter aren't as close as you used to be, but please reach out to him if you need anything. He'll be there for you, Milly."

I bite down on my lip in guilt and nod. "Uh, yeah, I know. Carter actually offered to tutor me in statistics. He's been very nice."

He looks up at the mention of his name and mouths *nice?* right before taking my nipple between his teeth. I suppress a moan and close my eyes, trying my best to maintain my composure.

"Oh, Milly, I'm so happy to hear that! It'd be great if you two became friends again. I can't wait to have all you kids home for Christmas. How great will that be? Not much longer to go. I'll get to see you again soon."

I smile against my phone, my heart warming. "Yeah, I can't wait to see you either. I miss you."

Helen inhales deeply and I know us being away has been hard on her. "I miss you too, honey. Well, you go and enjoy your day, okay? I'll speak to you tonight."

I sigh and bid her farewell, wishing I could be there to console her. What she needs right now is a tight hug, yet I can't even give her that.

Carter grabs my phone and puts it away before pulling me back in his arms. "Mom will be fine, Minx."

"You little shit," I say. "How can you touch me like that when I'm on the phone with your mom? Are you crazy?"

I sigh and snuggle in closer. It's so surreal that I'm actually lying here with Carter. How long have I been dreaming of this? I know it's just sex, but I'll take whatever I can get.

"You know you loved it," he murmurs. I can't even deny it, because I did. I'm still sore from last night but I already want more.

"Hey, Emilia? I might not have said this before, but I really appreciate the way you speak to Mom every day. I'll try to be better too. I'll try to call her more often."

I lean in and kiss his neck. "Yeah, that'd be nice."

I speak to Helen a lot more than I speak to my dad. I call

82

him once a week or so, but if I don't get in touch with him, he won't bother calling me. It's always me reaching out. I want to believe he loves me and just isn't good at communicating, but it's starting to become draining to always be the person reaching out.

Carter's alarm goes off and he silences it. "Weight training," he murmurs. He kisses me on the cheek and gets up while I lie back in his bed and watch him. His body is magnificent and for the foreseeable future he's going to be all mine. Will I be able to walk away unscathed when the time comes?

CHAPTER 17

*E*milia

I walk into my dorm room quietly. The curtains are drawn and it's pitch dark. I can just about see Kate's head sticking out above the covers, the sharp smell of liquor and *hangover* in the air. I walk to the window and open the curtains, just enough to let some daylight into the room. Kate groans and throws her arm over her face.

"Hey," I murmur. "Thought you'd still be at the hotel with Asher?"

She blinks and looks at me in confusion, but then she nods. "Oh, yeah, I ended up wanting to go home," she says, looking away. I can't help but feel like she's lying.

"Did you two argue or something?"

She groans and turns around, ignoring me.

"What happened?" I ask. "Did you end up going out?"

She turns to face me again, annoyance flashing through her eyes. "God damn it, Milly. Let me sleep. It's like ten in the morning."

I'm surprised by her outburst and step back in alarm. I'm

not sure what to say to that and merely nod as I grab the books I came here to get. I'm flustered all the way to the library. I feel like Kate is being suspicious, but I can't figure out what's going on. Is she seeing someone else, maybe? It hurts that we've grown so far apart that she won't let me in anymore. She's been going out almost every night lately, and every time I ask her where she's going, she's vague in her response. It's obvious she doesn't want to invite me along, and it hurts a little. I don't even like partying, but it'd be nice to get an invite.

I'm absentminded as I walk into the library and don't snap out of it until I hear someone call my name. I turn back to find Mason waving at me and freeze. Now that I know who he is, I'm not sure how to act around him. The way Lisa cried her eyes out was heartbreaking, and I can't believe he managed to hurt her that much. He waves me over and I walk toward him reluctantly.

"Hey," he murmurs, patting the seat next to him. I sit down and edge away a little. "So, what ended up happening last night?"

I blush as memories of last night assail me and Mason chuckles. "Carter seemed really pissed off to find us together," he says, grinning. "I've known the guy for years, but I've never seen him carry a girl off in anger. What happened? Probably safe to assume he's the guy you're in love with?"

I look away awkwardly. "I didn't realize you knew each other," I whisper, scared of being too loud.

Mason chuckles and throws his arm over the back of my chair. "Don't worry, your secret is safe with me. Doesn't seem like Carter moved on, though. The way he pulled you away from me was no joke."

I bite down on my lip and nod. "It's complicated. It's just... unresolved feelings." I turn to face him and raise my brows. "You and Lisa?"

85

His smile drops, and he looks at me cautiously. "That's also complicated."

"Lisa isn't dating anyone. She can't be your brother's girlfriend."

Pure heartbreak flashes through Mason's eyes and he swallows hard. "My brother is dead. He was a soldier. Like I said, it's complicated."

I blink in disbelief. "I'm really sorry for your loss," I whisper, my voice breaking. I can't imagine what it's like to lose your sibling, and to deal with the guilt of falling for the person they loved. Mason smiles tightly and looks back at his textbook. It's as though he's stuck in memories he can't shake himself out of, and I grab his hand. He squeezes back and smiles at me as best as he can.

Our luck must be rotten, because as we're sitting here with our hands entwined and our faces close to each other, Lisa walks up to us. She looks at me with such blazing fury that I shrink back. Mason's grip on my hand tightens and I try to pull it away, but he won't let me. He sends me a pleading look and I look back at him through narrowed eyes.

"Mason, you're early," Lisa says. Her eyes drop to our joined hands before she looks back up at me. "What are you doing here, Emilia? Didn't you leave with Carter last night?"

I clear my throat, my cheeks reddening.

"We were just hanging out," Mason says. He moves his chair closer to mine and Lisa grabs her phone angrily.

I lean into Mason and whisper in his ear. "Stop it. I won't play along with this. I won't play a role in hurting Lisa in any way. She's always been nice to me and I'm not going to sit here and let you hurt her."

Mason sighs and turns to look into my eyes, our faces far too close together. "Why did you have to be so sweet, Emilia?"

I glare at him and take out my books. Mason is trouble, for sure. Lisa taps her finger on the table impatiently and stares at me, making me more and more uncomfortable by the second. "So what happened when you left with Carter?" she asks, her eyes moving to Mason's vindictively. "I doubt he just took you back to your dorm."

Mason grits his teeth and stares her down. "You know all about that, don't you? How many times have *you* left parties with Carter Clarke?"

The reminder hurts and I bite down on my lip nervously. I feel caught in between Mason and Lisa, and it's awkward as hell. Lisa looks away, and I try my best to ignore the mental image of her with Carter. I try my best to ignore *both of them* as I attempt to get some studying done, but the atmosphere is tense as hell. It's like every minute takes an hour. This is the last time I'm sitting anywhere near Mason. It's just not worth the stress.

He leans into me again and I'm tempted to swat him away. He chuckles and whispers into my ear. "Look who joined the party?"

He drops his arm back around my chair and grins up at Carter, whose eyes are moving between me and Mason, his expression unreadable.

"Lisa," he says, taking a seat next to her. I'm instantly enraged that he didn't even greet me. Things seemed so perfect this morning, yet now I guess we're back to being distant. I look down at my book angrily. It doesn't look like I'm going to get any studying done here at all, but I don't want to go back to my dorm and face a grumpy Kate either.

Carter seems to struggle to focus as much as I do, and eventually he drops his pen on the table and looks up at me.

"Emilia," he murmurs, tipping his head toward the exit. He gets up and walks toward the bathrooms, and I follow him. Seems like he isn't as unaffected as I thought he was.

CHAPTER 18

arter

Fucking Mason again. Why the fuck is she with Mason? I was hoping Lisa was joking when she texted me — guess not. I walk toward the staff toilet that I know no one ever uses and look around before pulling Emilia in and locking the door behind us.

She gasps and looks at me with wide eyes. "We aren't supposed to be in here," she whisper-shouts, and I chuckle. Why the hell does she need to be so damn cute? I lean in and cage her in with my arms.

"Remind me, Minx. Did we or did we not agree that we'd be exclusive last night?"

Her eyes flash with annoyance and she nods. "We did," she says through gritted teeth.

"So why are you with Mason, holding hands and shit?"

Emilia raises her brows and looks up at me in anger. She puts her palms against my chest and sighs. "Did you see me sleeping with him, Carter? Because last time I checked, all we were doing was hanging out."

I'm hit with uncontrollable possessiveness. Thank fuck we agreed we'd be exclusive, because I don't think I could deal with not knowing whether I'm the only one she's with. I don't want to date her, but I don't want her to date anyone else either. I'm a selfish asshole, but I want her to myself. I step closer to her and push my body against hers. The edges of her lips tip up, as though she's fighting a smile, and I drop my lips to hers.

"Just remember I'm the only one you'll be fucking for the time being. Only me, Emilia." I run my hand over her body and pull her skirt up, my fingers tracing over her thighs. She squirms against me and I smile against her lips before kissing her. She melts against me as our tongues tangle together and I lift her up. Emilia wraps her legs around my hips and buries her hands in my hair while I push her against the door. She moans against my lips when my fingers find their way between her legs. I push her underwear aside to find her already soaking wet. I grin and bite down on her lower lip. "Already wet, Minx? What do you want?"

Emilia whimpers as I trace my fingers around her clit, not touching her where she wants me to. "Please Carter, I want you."

Good enough for me. "I'm going to fuck you against this door, Emilia."

She gulps and nods, her eyes blazing with the same passion I'm feeling. I lift her higher and manage to grab a condom from my wallet. I'm frantic and impatient as I undo my jeans. I grab Emilia's hands and hold them above her head as I align my dick with her. I look straight into her eyes as I push into her, and her lips fall open in delight. She's so fucking beautiful. I grab her by her hips and thrust into her rough and hard. The need to claim her is unreal. I want to be the only thing she can think about.

Emilia moans and yanks on my hair to get me closer, and I lower my lips to hers. "So tight, Emilia. This pussy is mine, you hear me?"

Her cheeks turn scarlet, and she looks at me with wide eyes. I lift her higher so I can push into her at an angle. She bites down on her lip to keep her moans in and I smirk. My Minx is so sensitive. I place my lips against her neck and suck down on her skin, leaving a small kiss mark in return for the dozens she left on my neck and chest last night. I've never wanted to give a girl a kiss mark, but with Emilia a single one isn't enough. I want her in my bed, naked, with kiss marks all over her breasts. She groans when I pull away and I grin at her. She's so needy, so sexy. I thrust into her harder and she moans loudly, getting closer and closer. I wrap my hand over her lips and shake my head. "Quiet, baby. The librarians are fucking psychos."

She pulls me closer and kisses me without abandon, and I almost lose it. "Can't hold it, baby," I murmur. I know she's close and I'm going to be really fucking pissed off with myself if I can't hold on long enough. I grit my teeth and drop my head to her shoulder as I increase the pace. Emilia moans and her legs start to tremble. I almost come right there and then, and as soon as her muscles spasm around my dick, I lose control. I come at the same time as she does, both of us holding onto each other tightly. My entire body feels like it's tingling, and I doubt I've ever come as hard as I did just then. Emilia slumps against me and I hold her up as she rests her head against my shoulder, a satisfied smile on her face. Seems like all I need to do to tie her to me is keep her well satiated.

I pull away and lower her to the floor. She barely manages to stay standing and leans against the door for support. I can't help but grin. She looks so well-fucked.

"Stop smirking," she says, her eyes narrowed. I smile and bite down on my lip as I take care of the condom. "Can't help it, Minx. You just look like you really enjoyed that."

She rolls her eyes, but it's impossible to ignore her sexy glowing expression. I feel oddly proud to be responsible for it. I can't wait to walk her back to Mason and Lisa. I might not be able to call her mine, but just seeing her like this should make it clear to Mason that she *is* very much mine.

Emilia is quiet and nervous as we walk back to the table Lisa and Mason are at. "Chill, Minx," I murmur.

She looks up at me with wide eyes and shakes her head. "I'm terrified people will know what we were just doing," she says, all flustered.

I smile at her indulgently and put my hand on her lower back. She's tense when we're back at the table, and it looks like Mason and Lisa aren't doing much better. They're glaring daggers at each other and I sigh to myself. Emilia takes her seat next to Mason awkwardly and he looks her over with raised brows. His gaze moves from me to her and I smirk. He's not an idiot. He knows what just happened. Emilia sends me a warning look that only works to corroborate my insinuation, and I chuckle to myself. At least it's clear now — Emilia isn't someone Mason can get his hands on. She was always out of his league, but now she's out of reach too, and I intend to keep it that way.

CHAPTER 19

milia

I wake up all of a sudden and sit up in bed, surprised. I blink over and over again, trying my best to get accustomed to the sudden light. Kate must've just come home from a night out. What time is it? It's not unusual for her to wake me up with her drunkenness or noise, but she doesn't usually turn the lights on. I groan and try my best to keep my eyes open.

Kate is sitting on her bed, pressing a wad of toilet paper to her face. I jump out of bed immediately to check on her and she looks at me with wide panicked eyes.

"Nose bleed?" I ask. "How did that happen?"

She shakes her head and dabs her nose, the bleeding luckily subsiding.

"I don't know. It just happened suddenly," she says, trembling. Her eyes are wide and it looks like she might be in shock or something. I rub my hands over her arms and slowly but surely she relaxes.

"Maybe we should go see a doctor. I read that nosebleeds

can be an issue relating to your brain. I don't know. It wouldn't hurt to get it checked, right?"

"No!" she shouts, her eyes flashing with rage. She pushes against my shoulder so hard that I stumble and end up falling onto my butt. She blinks at me and then jumps up in a panic seconds later, her bloody toilet paper falling to the floor.

"Oh my god, Milly. Are you okay? I'm so sorry! I didn't mean it," she says, her voice high pitched and worried. She helps me up and fidgets with my pajamas. "Are you okay?" she asks again.

I nod and grab her shoulders. "I'm fine. Calm down. It's all good."

More than anything, I'm worried about *her*. She didn't get a scholarship, so she's not as concerned with keeping her GPA up. She's just been partying and making new friends that she never even bothered to introduce me to. I'm worried the drinking is getting out of hand. Lately, her behavior seems a little erratic.

I cup her cheek and check her face. She still has a small amount of blood around her nose, but she's not bleeding anymore.

"Seems like you're okay now," I murmur. She nods and drops to her bed.

"I'm sorry for waking you up, Milly. Let's go to bed, okay? We're going to try out that Mexican place this afternoon, right?"

She gets underneath her blanket, and seconds later she's fast asleep. I don't even get a chance to reply to her. I stare at Kate in confusion. Is she that drunk? She seemed fine and alert, yet something is off about her. I'll have to talk to her about all the partying she's doing.

I get back into bed and inhale deeply. Maybe all she needs is to go home for a couple of weeks. Thank god we'll be going next week.

I rush toward the restaurant I agreed to meet Kate at and check my watch. I'm five minutes late. I've texted her multiple times, but it looks like she hasn't even seen my messages yet.

"Hi, I'm a little late, I'm sorry," I tell the waitress at the entrance. "I have a reservation under Emilia?"

She smiles at me, and her eyes crinkle at the edges. My heart warms at the very sight of her. She must be around sixty years old and she's wearing a frilly dress with a checkered apron on top. She's plump in an adorable grandmotherly way, and she barely reaches my chin.

"That's okay, *chiquita*," she says. "You're not so late. *Fashionably* late. My name is Maria, but you can call me Abuelita. Come, I'll show you to your table."

I smile and follow her into the small rustic restaurant. "I think my friend might already be here," I tell her.

She looks up at me and shakes her head. "No. I don't think so."

She leads me to a small table in the corner and lights a candle while I glance around. The place is quiet and indeed, Kate is definitely not here yet.

I grab my phone and ring her, but she isn't answering. Abuelita walks over with a bread basket and some dips and shoots me a concerned look. "You're not being stood up, *niñita*?"

I blush and shake my head. God, that's probably what it looks like, isn't it? Abuelita frowns and walks off again, only to return with a glass of wine.

"Here, grape juice," she says, winking. "You look like you need it, *niñita.*"

I gape at her, but she walks off again. I'm shocked she'd serve me wine without ID'ing me. I have a feeling she's well aware I'm underage.

I take a sip of the wine and smile to myself. It tastes amazing. Abuelita just became my new favorite person. I take another sip as I try to ring Kate again, but she won't pick up. I'm starting to get worried. Surely nothing happened to her?

I can feel my anxiety rise and bite down on my lip. I'm overthinking it. Surely she's fine. I hesitate and then decide to text Carter.

Emilia: *Hey, did you see Kate? She was supposed to meet me for an early dinner, but I can't reach her.*

Devil: *No, but let me check if anyone in my group chats has seen her. Between all of them, someone will know where she is. Give me a couple of minutes, okay?*

I exhale in relief. Of course, Carter will be able to figure out where she is in no time at all. He knows practically everyone, after all.

Devil: *Where are you?*

Emilia: *a small restaurant called La Familia*

Devil: *Okay, don't move. She's fine.*

Emilia: *Is she on her way?*

I fidget with my phone and finish my glass of wine quicker than I should. After fifteen minutes or so, I'm about ready to leave. Just as I raise my hand to request the bill from Abuelita, Carter walks in. Abuelita lights up when she sees him and he hugs her tightly, lifting her off the floor. I look at him in disbelief as he walks up to me. Carter leans in to kiss me on the cheek and then sits down opposite me. I blink in disbelief and he chuckles.

"What are you doing here?" I stammer.

Carter pouts and shoots me a wounded puppy look. "Don't you want me here, Minx?"

I bite down on my lip to hide my smile, but my rapidly reddening cheeks still give away how flustered I feel. Abuelita approaches our table with a stern expression and stares Carter down.

"How can you make such a beautiful girl wait, *Lindo*?"

I raise my hands and shake my head. "Oh no, Abuelita, I wasn't waiting for him. I didn't expect him to come at all. I was waiting for my best friend — Carter's sister."

Carter leans back in his seat and spreads his arms. "Lita, the best things in life are worth waiting for," he says, winking at her. She rolls her eyes and swats him with the menu.

"He didn't make you wait?" she asks me again. I shake my head and smile at her. I adore her. She's so cute and grandmotherly. I already know this place is going to become one of my regular joints.

Abuelita huffs and shoots Carter one more warning look. "Fine. You want the usual?"

Carter glances at me. "Trust me?" he asks. I nod, and Carter smiles at Abuelita. "Yes, please, Lita. The usual for both of us."

She walks away and I lean in. "You haven't told me what you're doing here," I murmur. Carter grins at me. "I was hungry and you happened to be at one of my favorite restaurants all by yourself."

The way he's looking at me makes my heart work overtime. "So where is Kate?"

Carter's expression falls and he clenches his jaw. "One of my buddies texted to say she's with him and a bunch of other people she has no business being with. I'll need to talk to her about this. I can't believe she stood you up to hang out with them."

I exhale in relief. "At least she's okay. I was worried."

Carter looks away and shakes his head. "It'll be good for her to go home next week. From what I can tell, college has been all the wrong kinds of fun for her."

I nod in agreement. "God, I'm so happy you see it too. I thought I was being selfish, or boring, or you know... I don't know. I'm worried about her."

Carter grabs my hand from across the table and intertwines our fingers. "You aren't being selfish, baby. I don't think you've ever been selfish when it comes to Kate. I'll talk to her, don't worry about it."

He squeezes my hand and I nod at him, my heart fluttering. He doesn't usually call me baby outside of bed and I find it sexy as hell. I wonder if he even realizes he did it.

"Enough about her, though. Since we're here now, we might as well enjoy it. Honestly, Lita's food is such a treat. I have to work three times as hard to burn it back off, but it's so worth it."

I smile at him and move to pull my hand back, but Carter holds on tight. I can't help but blush a little. He said we'd only be friends with benefits, but this feels an awful lot like a date.

Abuelita brings over a lot of small dishes that all look ridiculously good. Her eyes drop to our joined hands and she smiles.

"Enjoy," she tells us, before walking off in a rush. Carter grins at me and points at the food as though he cooked it himself and is presenting it to me.

"Amazing, isn't it? I love all the food here, so instead of full dishes, Lita gives me a bit of everything. My favorites are the taquitos and enchiladas, but the empanadas are to die for too."

Carter grabs a spoon and starts filling my plate, and I hold my hands up. "It's okay, I can do it," I tell him, but he shakes his head and continues to serve me food.

He looks at me expectantly and I try not to smile as I grab my fork. I take a bite under his watchful gaze and nod, my lips betraying me and tipping up into a smile.

"It's amazing," I murmur, and Carter's shoulders sink in relief. He starts filling his own plate and for a couple of minutes we both sit in silence, absorbed in the food.

"So when did you discover this place?" I ask. Carter leans back in his seat and grins.

"It was a coincidence, actually. I got lost in my first week here and stumbled upon this place. I was starving and Abuelita fed me the best meal I'd had in weeks. Her food kind of reminds me of home. It's similar to the food you and Mom always used to make, and it kind of made me feel a little less homesick, I guess. I've come back every month since then. How did *you* stumble upon it, though?"

I smile at him. "It was actually featured in a small food blog that I like. Before I came here, I made a list of things I wanted to do, and eating here was on it."

Carter smiles, but it doesn't reach his eyes. He looks away as though he's lost in thought and then turns back to me. "So, what's on your list?"

"This sounds lame, but I want to go see the botanical gardens at Huntington Library. I also want to walk around the Venice Canals and go to all the theme parks. I want to go to all the beaches and I made this list of dozens of restaurants I want to try."

Carter's smile is bittersweet and he nods. "Yeah, those were all things I thought you'd like too," he murmurs. He blinks and his expression becomes unreadable. "We can go do some of that stuff together, if you want. It'd be nice to hang out like the good old days. Me, you, Kate, and maybe even Asher."

For a second I thought he meant he wanted us to go together, just the two of us, and my heart sinks .

"Yeah, that would be amazing."

Carter and I get the bill, and even though I insisted we'd split it, he wouldn't let me. He walks me back to his car and suddenly I'm nervous. I don't want the night to end yet.

"Are you excited to go back home?" Carter asks as he drives me back to my dorm. I nod. "Yeah, I didn't think I would, but I actually missed my dad. I really missed Helen too. I can't wait to be back and have some homemade food."

Carter chuckles. "Yeah, Mom's food is what I missed most too. I miss it less now you're cooking for me every once in a while. It's good to be home, though."

Things are slightly awkward between us, as though neither

one of us knows where the boundary is between being friends and being more. Carter pulls up to my dorm building and we both sit there in silence.

"I'd invite you up, but I think Kate will probably be back by now."

Carter grins and leans into me, his hand brushing over my hair. He pushes my hair behind my ear and looks into my eyes. "Next time," he whispers. I blush and pull away.

He stands by his car and watches me until I've walked through the door, and all the while my heart beats wildly. I wanted to kiss him goodnight so badly, but that isn't what *friends* do.

CHAPTER 20

arter

Emilia, Kate and I are exhausted from the long journey by the time we walk into my house, but that exhaustion is quickly forgotten once my mother jumps up and runs toward us. She wants to hug all of us at once, so we end up in one big group hug.

"My babies are back," she says, her voice trembling. My heart breaks. I need to try harder to call her more and send her some photos every now and then. It can't be easy for her to have a completely empty house all of a sudden, especially since Dad works such long hours. I hug her tighter before stepping back. Mom pulls us into the kitchen where she already has all our favorites waiting. There's carrot cake for me, lemon bars for Kate, and a chocolate cake for Emilia.

"Oh my gosh, you shouldn't have," Emilia says. I can tell she's feeling just as emotional as my mother does and my heart warms. Sometimes it takes being away for a little while to remember just how lucky we all are to have Emilia in our lives. She's the only one that calls Mom every day, and she's the first to thank her for everything she does for us. It makes me feel both grateful and guilty.

I watch Emilia as she busies herself in the kitchen, getting us all plates and cutlery. I'm so accustomed to it, it doesn't even occur to me we should be the one serving *her*. Kate digs into her lemon bar and hums happily.

"Come and sit," I tell Emilia. She looks at me, startled, and then moves to join me at the high chairs by the kitchen counter.

"So, how is college?" Mom asks. She stares at Kate and Emilia, her eyes wide with excitement.

Kate chuckles and leans in. "So much fun, Mom. I've gotten to know so many new people and LA is so cool. It's so different to Woodstock. Honestly, it's amazing."

Emilia nods in agreement. "It's been really good so far. Classes are great. I'm learning a lot and I'm having a lot of fun too."

Mom looks relieved and nods. "How did all your tests and deadlines go?"

Kate shrugs, but Emilia nods seriously. "I think I did well," she says, smiling tightly. I know she's worried about her grades and her scholarship.

I drop my arm to the back of her chair and brush my fingers over her shoulder. "I'm *sure* you did well," I murmur.

Mom smiles at me, her eyes glittering with happiness. It's clear she's happy to see Emilia and me on good terms again, and part of me feels guilty for even remotely risking her happiness.

"Milly told me you're tutoring her," she says and I nod. "Yeah, she'll be fine. She barely needs my help."

Mom glances between the two of us, and her relief is palpable. I know she was probably worried we'd have another tension filled holiday, but that won't be the case this time. Even though Mom never called me on it, she must have known that I was heartbroken after I came home to find Emilia dating

Landon. I've barely come back home since then, using the distance as an excuse. It wasn't a total lie, but it certainly wasn't the main reason. I guess it was a combination of things — every time I came home, I was reminded of what could have been. Every time I was here, I'd miss Emilia that much more. It was just easier to stay away.

"I'm making lasagna for dinner. Please tell me you're staying for dinner, Milly."

Emilia looks at my Mom and shakes her head. "I'm sorry, Helen. I promised my dad I'd cook for him and we'd have a nice little catch-up."

Mom's eyes soften and she nods in understanding, but I can tell she's disappointed. "Maybe tomorrow, Mom," I tell her. "Maybe Emilia can join for dinner tomorrow."

Thankfully, Emilia nods in agreement. She gets up and moves toward the sink with her plate, but my mom takes it from her. "It's okay, honey. You're probably tired, why don't you go get some rest?"

Emilia nods and turns to grab her suitcase. "I'll see you guys tomorrow," she says.

She walks out and Kate moves toward the hallway, probably eager for a shower and some rest. I follow her up the stairs and stop her before she makes it to her room.

"Let's have a chat," I tell her. Kate looks up at me with wide eyes and I tilt my head toward her bedroom. She seems nervous as we walk in, as though she knows she did something wrong. I sit down on her bed and cross my arms.

"You've been avoiding me," I tell her. Kate grabs her desk chair and sits down. Her hands tremble and she clenches them. My little sister has always hated confrontations with me and I've always done my best to prevent them from happening, but this time I'm too worried to stay silent.

"What were you doing with Jake?"

She looks away, as though she can't face me, and shrugs. "Nothing really. We were just hanging out."

I frown at her. Jake is a classic douchebag rich boy. All he ever does is skip classes and smoke weed or whatever else he can get his hands on. The only reason he hasn't been kicked out yet is because of the amount of money his parents donated.

"Jake doesn't just *hang out,* Kate. Don't bullshit me. What was so important that you stood up Emilia? Tell me you weren't doing any type of drugs with that asshole."

Kate bites down on her lip nervously and shakes her head. "Emilia told you about that? I was really just hanging out with him and lost track of time. I promise, I wasn't doing drugs or anything. I spoke to Emilia and she said it was fine and that things happen. I promised to treat her to lunch when we get back to make it up to her."

I run a hand through my hair in frustration. "That's not the point, Kate. I'm worried about you. What the hell are you doing? You're always partying and now you're becoming friends with all the wrong people. What's up with that? I expected so much more from you."

She looks at me with wide eyes and then looks down in despair. "I know, Carter. I did go overboard, I know. I'm sorry. It's just that I don't have a scholarship like you and Milly, so I didn't really feel like I needed to make myself miserable trying as hard as you two do. I just wanted to have some fun. It's been so freeing not being in Woodstock anymore."

I sigh. "I know how you feel, Kate. Trust me, I do. I'm not asking you not to go out at all. I'm just asking you to at least try to maintain a balance of some sort. You can have fun and still excel academically too. You just need to try to find that balance. Promise me you'll try that, okay?"

She nods at me, her head bopping up and down. She seems sincere, and that's good enough for me.

"You know I'm always here if you need help, right? Whether that's tutoring or anything else. I'm always here for you, Kate. I know it gets overwhelming very quickly, moving out and being on your own. But you're never alone, baby sis. I'm always here, okay?"

She nods and the look in her eyes tells me I got through to her. I exhale in relief and rise. I need to try harder to look after her. I need to keep a better eye on her and make sure I'm there for her more than I have been so far.

CHAPTER 21

*E*milia

I'm just about finishing up dinner when my dad walks in. He pauses by the doorway and stares at me for a couple of seconds before he walks toward me. I'm startled when he wraps his arms around me and hugs me tightly.

"You're back, kiddo," he murmurs. I nod against his chest and hug him back. I can't even remember the last time he hugged me. It must've been when I was still a kid.

Dad pulls back and looks at me, his face revealing how emotional he's feeling. "Hey, Dad," I murmur, and he smiles.

His eyes follow me as I serve us dinner. It's almost like he can't believe I'm really here. I haven't actually been gone that long. It's only been a few months.

While I was at college, I felt like he didn't think of me at all and part of me wondered if he might actually be happy that I left, but considering how he's looking at me now, that can't be true.

Dad takes a bite of his food and smiles. "This is delicious, Emilia," he murmurs. I grin at him happily. Before I left home having dinner together was just as rare as it is now, but back then he didn't actually seem to appreciate my cooking, nor did he think of us having dinner together as quality time.

"I may not have said this, Princess... but the house hasn't been the same without you. I've missed you a lot. I'm not very good at saying these things, but that doesn't mean I don't think about you. The house has been so quiet without you, and the weekends are so bleak. I'm very happy to have you back home for a few weeks."

I blink and nod , scared my voice will wobble if I speak now. He missed me? Dad and I aren't very close — we haven't been close in years, but tonight it feels like he's my Dad again.

"I missed you too, Daddy," I murmur. He looks at me, his eyes suspiciously shiny. I never thought of him as an emotional man and usually he isn't, but it seems being so far away from me hasn't been easy on him.

"How is college? Are you enjoying it?"

I nod and repeat the same things I told Helen. I'm surprised when Dad hangs onto my every word. He wants to know about all the different people I've met and every class I'm taking, and I answer all his questions.

"I'm glad you're enjoying yourself, Princess. I'm relieved to know you have the Clarke kids with you. You guys have always had each other's backs and I know you will now too. It's good to know Carter is there to protect you if need be."

I smile. If only Dad knew... in his eyes, it'd probably be *Carter* I need protection from. Though, if it ever came down to it, I know Carter would be there for me no matter what.

I yawn and make my way up the stairs, eager for a shower and my bed. It feels weird to be back in my old bedroom. I've only been away for a few months, but my room already doesn't feel the same anymore. It's weird to think I feel more at home in my dorm room. I rush through a shower and walk back into my bedroom wrapped in a large fluffy towel.

I glance out the window to find Carter walking through his room. He's wearing his old pajama bottoms, but he's not wearing a top. He's got a towel raised to his head and stares at his phone as he dries his hair. He must've just gotten out of the shower too. It's been so long since I've been able to see him through our windows. It's strange, I guess, but I missed this. Messing with each other through our windows is one of those things I didn't realize I loved until it was no longer possible. In the last two years he'd keep his curtains resolutely closed, physically shutting me out. I'm glad we're slowly getting back to where we used to be.

Carter looks up and catches me staring. He grins and looks back down. Seconds later, my phone buzzes on my nightstand. I frown as I walk over to grab it and smile when I realize Carter just texted me.

Devil: *Being a peeping tom again?*

My cheeks turn crimson and I pray he can't tell from all the way over there. I can't believe he knew I was watching him back in high school.

Emilia: *Aw, don't talk about yourself that way. Though, granted, it's weird that you stare at girls in their towels. You creep.*

Devil: *I only ever stare at you, Minx. How does it feel to have your own personal creep?*

Emilia: *I'm kind of flattered.*

Devil: *Now who's the creep?*

I chuckle and glance up to find him standing in front of his window. He's leaning against the windowpane and looking at me.

Devil: *This is nice*

Emilia: *I was just thinking that*

Devil: *The last time I remember seeing you through our windows, you were with Landon. Pretty sure I kept my curtains closed ever since.*

I gasp. He saw me with Landon? Shit. That can't have been

good. I clutch my phone tighter as I decide on how to reply. In the end, I decide to keep it simple.

Emilia: *I'm sorry, Carter.*

Carter walks away from the window and lies down on his bed, and I follow suit. I immediately miss being able to see him and fidget with my phone for a little before making up my mind. I press the video call icon and stare at my screen nervously while I position myself so my good angle is on camera and quickly comb through my hair.

Carter picks up and grins at me. "Miss me already, Minx?" he asks, his voice soft. My heart skips a beat at the sight of him. He's in bed with the sheets pooled around his waist. He's got his phone positioned on his nightstand, giving me an amazing view of his body.

I put my own phone on my nightstand too and try my best to look just a bit more sexy than I usually would.

"Maybe," I murmur.

"You're still wrapped in your towel... not getting dressed?" he asks, his voice husky. I bite down on my lip and nod. I completely forgot about getting dressed. The way he's looking emboldens me and I reposition my phone so he can see my entire body before walking to my wardrobe.

I walk back with panties and the most revealing pajamas I have in hand. In hindsight, they're more cute than anything else, with cute little strawberries on them. Sixteen-year-old me thought they were sexy as hell, though. It's the best I've got here, so they'll do.

I kneel on my bed so Carter can see most of my body and slowly unravel my towel, my eyes on his. He looks so turned on.

"Minx," he whispers. I watch as one of his hands disappears underneath his bed covers and my breath hitches.

My towel drops and Carter groans. I take my time putting my jammies on. Carter is breathing hard as I raise my arms and push my breasts out. My cute little strawberry top covers my chest and Carter groans. "No," he whispers. I bite back a smile and run my hands over my breasts, squeezing just slightly. A moan escapes his lips and his eyes flutter closed for a second. I love seeing him so worked up. I giggle as I pull my panties on and Carter shakes his head.

"You drive me insane, Emilia. I need you. *Now*. I'm so tempted to sneak into your bedroom and fuck you so hard you'll be screaming my name."

If I wasn't scared of our parents catching us, I'd be all up for that. I shake my head and grab my phone as I get comfortable in bed. Carter grabs his own phone too and places it next to him, both of us on our sides, facing our phones. It's almost like he's lying right next to me.

"Soon," I whisper. Carter nods and sighs. I miss him, and I wonder if he feels the same way. He hasn't given me any real indication that he sees me as more than a friend. I know he wants me, but does he have feelings for me? I know I shouldn't even want him to, because we'll end up in the exact same mess we were in two years ago. But hell... I want him to. I want him to feel the same way I do.

CHAPTER 22

arter

I stand underneath the shower and think back to last night. Being on the phone with Emilia like that was surprisingly nice. That girl... the way she teases drives me crazy. I never saw the appeal of phone sex, but with her I'm going to have to give it a try sooner or later. We both fell asleep while still on the phone. When I woke up my phone was dead, and I'm sure hers was too.

I catch a whiff of Emilia's sweet perfume and frown. I left the door to my bathroom open a crack and the fragrance is unmistakable. It takes me right back to our youth. It's her perfume that's always given away her presence. I grin as I dry myself off quickly. I bet she's pulling a prank on me.

I walk out of the shower as quietly as I can and find her kneeling beside my bed, her back to me and three old alarm clocks in her hands. From this angle, I have the perfect view of her ass. She's wearing a warm sweater with a short skirt and thick tights underneath. I wish she wasn't wearing those damn tights so I could catch a glimpse of those amazing legs of hers.

I watch as she sets the alarms to go off at random times before hiding them around my bed. How does she even come up with these random little tricks of hers? Evil little genius.

"So, what's with the alarm clocks?"

Emilia jumps and turns around in shock. "Shit, you scared me," she murmurs. She glances at my bedroom door and I shake my head as I bite down on my lip.

Emilia dashes toward my door, and I catch her before she reaches it. She giggles when I lift her into my arms and playfully pushes against my chest. "You know I hate waking up early during the holidays," I murmur.

Emilia laughs and nods. "Hence the prank, smartass."

"So evil," I whisper. I drop her onto my bed and lean over her. Emilia's eyes drop to my lips and her eyes darken.

"Good thing I caught you," I whisper. "I'd have been pretty damn pissed off if I was woken up by those damn things early in the morning tomorrow."

I drop my lips to her neck and press a soft kiss to her skin. "I'd have to punish you, Minx. Good thing you failed there."

Her breath hitches, and she arches her back, pushing her boobs into me. She turns her head and I pull back a little, my lips hovering over hers.

"Now I wish I succeeded," she whispers. I groan and push my hips against hers, my hard-on settling between her legs.

"Where the hell did you even get those alarm clocks? They look ancient," I murmur against her lips. Emilia buries her hands in my hair and tilts her head, her eyes falling closed. She pulls me closer and I kiss her hungrily. Her hands roam over my back, her nails scraping my skin .

She pushes against me until she's got me on my back and then kneels in between my legs. She leans over me and presses her lips against my body. I thread my hands through her hair when she sucks down on my skin, leaving a mark on my chest, and then another on my abs. She keeps moving lower until her lips reach my towel. She looks up at me, her blue eyes sparkling, and then she places her lips against the towel. She lifts it away with her teeth and presses a soft kiss against my cock. I tighten my grip on her hair. I need her. I'm so fucking turned on, I can barely think straight. Having her lips right there drives me insane.

Emilia grabs my cock and swirls her tongue around the edge, and I almost come right there and then. "I can't, baby. Not after the way you teased me last night. I need you right now."

She ignores me and takes me in deeper, sucking hard. Her mouth is so hot and so tight, it's fucking insane. I pull her away and flip her back over, settling between her legs.

Emilia pouts, but it only makes her look more sexy. "I wanted to try, Carter. I was only just getting started."

My heart skips a beat. "Baby," I whisper, part of me scared to even ask the question. I shake my head and decide not to. "Why the fuck are you wearing these damn things?" I ask as I tug at her tights.

Emilia pulls on my hair and pulls me close. Her teeth graze my ear and my dick jolts. I need to be inside her right now. "Rip them," she whispers, and I groan. This fucking girl.

I do as she ordered and rip her tights right at the crotch. I'm impatient as I push her underwear out of the way. "I want a taste of you," I whisper. "Soon, baby. Sometime soon I'm going to bury my face between those beautiful legs of yours. I'm going to take my time with you, Emilia."

I slip a finger into her to find her dripping wet already. "I want you naked. I want your skin against mine."

Emilia glances at my bedroom door and shakes her head. "We'll need to be quick if we don't want to get caught," she whispers. I groan in annoyance and slip another finger into her, teasing her g-spot the way I know she likes it.

Emilia is breathing hard and looks at me pleadingly. "Please, babe," she whispers, and my heart skips a fucking beat.

She never calls me by any nicknames or endearments, and I freaking love it. "Say that again," I order.

"Please," she repeats.

I shake my head. "Not that."

Emilia grins and pulls on my hair. "Please, *babe*, give it to me already," she whispers. I bite down on my lip and push my dick against her. She squirms in an attempt to get me to push it in and I smile at her. Thankfully, I'm reminded of a condom at the last second and I drop my forehead against hers in annoyance.

"Condom," I whisper. Emilia groans and pulls on my hair a little. I move away to look at her and hold myself up on my forearms. She looks serious and slightly nervous.

"When is the last time you got tested?" she asks.

I frown and blink in confusion. "Um, last month. Coach has us do health checks every month. I'm clean, Minx. I would've told you if I wasn't."

She bites down on her lip and looks away, her expression troubled. She hesitates before she looks at me and I see a brief flash of pain in her eyes. "Did you sleep with anyone since your last test?" she asks, her voice trembling.

I shake my head immediately and then pause, nodding instead. Emilia's expression crumbles and I rush to reassure her. "You, baby. The only one I've slept with is you."

She inhales deeply and pushes against my shoulder in annoyance. I chuckle and press a kiss to her cheek.

"I'm on the pill, Carter. I got on it when we decided to be, um... well...friends with benefits," she says, her voice barely above a whisper.

I blink at her in disbelief. "Are you saying what I think you're saying?"

She nods and pushes her hips against mine. I softened a little during our conversation, but the idea of fucking Emilia without a condom has me harder than ever before.

I push into her and groan in delight. My eyes fall closed as everything but her falls away. "Fuck," I moan. "You're so fucking tight and so fucking wet. Baby, the way you feel around me is unreal."

I pull back out almost all the way and then slam into her again, both of us moaning. I press my lips against hers and kiss her to silence both our moans.

"Fuck, Emilia. I'm not going to last long like this. It's better than I imagined. Damn... this is insane."

She hooks her leg around me and I lift her hips just a little to hit her g-spot as I drive back into her. "How is this, baby?"

"So good," she moans. "Carter, *more*. It feels so different. It's even better."

I nod in agreement and thrust in and out of her harder. "I won't last, baby."

She nods and I kiss her as I thrust into her deep. I come harder than I ever have before and tingles run up and down my spine. I'm barely able to keep myself up and collapse on top of her. Emilia runs her hands over my back and kisses my ear as I try to catch my breath.

"I'm sorry, Minx. I'll make it up to you, I promise."

I hate that she didn't come. I don't want to be selfish with her.

"That's okay, babe," she whispers. "Make it up to me when we have more time and we're not at risk of your family walking in on us."

I chuckle and pull away from her. She sits up and leans back against my headboard as I grab my towel. She sorts out her underwear while I quickly find myself something to wear. It's still quite early, but it won't take long for my mom to come check if I'm up yet. Whenever I'm back for a few weeks, she always tries to spend as much time with me as possible, and while I'd usually love that, I really don't want her walking in right now.

"Looks like you had another one of my firsts today, Minx."

She looks at me with raised brows, and I smile at her. "I've never had sex without a condom before."

She grins and bites down on her lip. "You had two of mine. I've never done that either, but you're also the only one I've ever gone down on."

I grin to myself, my shoulders sagging in relief. I'm a selfish bastard, but I want to be Emilia's one and only.

She gets up and sorts out her hair before walking to my bedroom door. I grab her by her waist and kiss her deeply before letting her go. I just had her, and I already want more.

CHAPTER 23

milia

I've been on cloud nine all day. Being with Carter this morning was amazing. I may need to pull more pranks if it gets him to do me like that. Oddly enough, having sex without a condom felt so much more intimate. I didn't think it'd make much of a difference, but to me it did. It felt better, both physically and emotionally. Can't say I'm a fan of the stickiness between my thighs, though.

"What are you daydreaming about?" Kate asks, pulling me out of my thoughts. "You've literally been smiling to yourself all morning."

I blush and shake my head, which only makes her look at me through narrowed eyes. She hands me the sheet face masks we've been wanting to try, and I unpack mine carefully.

"You've been staring at your phone a lot too. *Emilia Parker,* did you hook up with someone and not tell me?"

I look at her like a deer caught in headlights, unsure what to say. She knows me well enough to know that something is up.

"Sort of," I murmur.

Kate gasps and grabs my shoulders. "Oh, my god. *What*? Tell me everything."

My heart is beating out of my chest. I'm nervous as hell. What am I supposed to say to her? "It's nothing serious. We got together after that party I went to. The one you couldn't come to because you were going to stay in a hotel with Asher."

Come to think of it, Asher came home late that night and she was at our dorm room early in the morning. I guess they didn't end up spending the night together, but she never told me what happened.

Kate looks at me open-mouthed. "Girl, yes. No wonder you came home in the same outfit acting dodgy as hell. I kind of figured that if you'd stayed with one of the girls in our dorm, you would've just showered and borrowed some of their clothes. Oh my god, how was it? And *who* was it?"

I shake my head, already regretting opening my damn mouth at all. "Uh, I don't really want to talk about it. It's not serious."

Kate shakes her head, the gears in her head turning. "I heard from Riley that you and Mason were getting quite close that night. She has a huge crush on him, so she was totally upset about it. She was so mad that he was too focused on you to pay her any attention that she ended up leaving the party early. I even told her it couldn't be anything to worry about, but guess I was wrong. Damn girl, he's hot. Not bad."

I decide to keep quiet and neither confirm nor deny anything, and make a mental note to be more careful at parties. Gossip travels quicker than I expected. I'm relieved that Carter and I ended up leaving later than Riley, or Kate would've heard about Carter carrying me out of the party.

I quietly put my sheet mask on my face and lie down on Kate's bed as still as possible, scared that it'll fall off my face.

Kate lies down next to me and continues to fire question after question.

"So, did you lose your virginity then?"

I squirm a little, feeling uncomfortable, and then hum in agreement. I've been wanting to tell Kate all about these types of things, but I never could. But then again, if she thinks it's Mason...

"Holy shit. What was it like? I heard Mason is really rough in bed and that it's amazing. I can totally see that."

"*Kate*," I admonish.

She chuckles. "*What?* I tell you everything about Asher and me."

I groan and nod. "It was amazing. It was really hot," I tell her honestly. When Carter took me home that night... the way he kissed me and lifted me into his arms, and the way we ended up in bed together. It was ridiculously hot.

"Did it hurt?"

I'm startled by her question, but then I remember thinks that night was the first time I had sex. Thinking back, when I actually lost my virginity, it *wasn't* exactly hot — not even remotely. It was more sweet and comfortable. Carter was so caring and careful with me, but it did hurt a lot.

"Um, a little. Not for very long, though."

Kate groans. "Ugh, I'm so jealous. My first time really sucked. It hurt so much, and it didn't feel that good. Thank God Asher is better in bed now."

"How are things between you two now?" I ask.

Kate sighs. "I'm not sure. I guess we're sort of growing apart. All he ever does is study and work on the company he and Carter are building. We don't really go out, we just sleep together occasionally. I might end things soon. He's just so *boring* these days. He really changed when he stopped playing football."

Oddly enough, my heart goes out to Asher. I know he really enjoyed football, and even more so than Carter, he truly wanted that to be his future. It can't be easy for him to still see Carter training and playing.

"Do you think maybe things have been tough on him recently? Maybe he's struggling to deal with losing one of his dreams."

Kate groans. "I don't know. He hasn't said anything. I'd be there for him if he reached out, but he hasn't. He just sorta alienates himself. It's weird. I feel like he's pushing me away. To be fair, we agreed we aren't anything, so I also don't want to pry. I'm not his girlfriend, ya know? I don't want to be either. We just hook up every once in a while."

"Hmm, yeah," I murmur. I guess she isn't wrong about that. I never really understood their relationship. They run hot and cold all the time. I'm glad Kate seems to be back to normal now, though. For the last few weeks, she seemed a bit off. I can't quite put my finger on it, but she seemed a bit weird. She seems better now that she's home.

"How're you enjoying being home, by the way? Isn't it weird? We've only been gone for a short time, but nothing feels like home anymore."

Kate groans and nods. "I know right! It's so weird. I'm happy to see Mom, though. I think she really missed us. We need to do something fun with her. Maybe a spa day or something?"

I rise and gently peel off my face mask. "Yeah, that sounds like a great idea. Let's book something."

I glance out the window and grimace. It's freezing and snowy. Kate follows my gaze and grins.

"Hey, you know what we haven't done in a while?"

I look at her through narrowed eyes, knowing exactly what she's gonna say.

"Snowball fight!"

She squeals and jumps up, and I can't help but grin. Her excitement is so infectious. She runs down the stairs and I shake my head as I follow her. Being home is clearly good for her, and it's been good for Carter and me too. I haven't felt this close to him in ages. I wish it could last.

CHAPTER 24

arter

"Milly, you and your dad are coming over for Christmas dinner, right?" Mom asks for the hundredth time. Since we've been home, Emilia has been having dinner at home a lot with her dad, and Mom has obviously been missing her. She pretty much monopolizes Emilia's time during the day while her dad is at work, much to both Kate and my annoyance. Mom is always asking Kate and Emilia to help with this and that in a poorly disguised effort to spend more time with them, and unlike Kate, Emilia doesn't have the heart to say no. I'm happy for Mom, but it's freaking irritating. I haven't been able to get her alone all week now.

"Yes, of course," Emilia says, smiling. Mom nods and walks around the kitchen looking stressed as hell.

"Milly, should we make that pecan pie after all?" she asks, her voice high pitched. Kate groans and walks out of the kitchen, and I'm tempted to follow her. Mom is insufferable throughout the entire holiday period.

I sigh and rise from my chair at the counter. "Mom, what

would *you* like?" I ask. I drop my hands to her shoulders and keep her in place, lest she wears down the floors with her endless pacing. I rub her arms and she smiles up at me, relaxing just a little.

"It'd be nice, right?"

Emilia walks up to us and leans against the counter, right next to me. We both face Mom and nod. "Yeah, it'd be nice," Emilia says. Mom has asked for her help with over a dozen dishes so far, and I haven't seen her even remotely protest. Not even once.

"Okay, let's make it. But we'll need pecans. Oh, should we go to the store, Milly?"

I glance at Emilia and try my best to hide my smile. "I'll go," I offer, just a bit too excitedly. Mom looks up at me with such a huge smile that I almost feel bad.

"Okay, I'll text you a list."

I tug on Emilia's sleeve and she nods at me, the edges of her lips tipping up in a small smile. She follows me and Mom freezes.

"Wait, you're taking Milly?"

We both turn back to look at her and Emilia hesitates. I sigh. So close. I almost had her to myself for a couple of minutes.

"Yeah, it's probably for the best," Emilia says. "You know what Carter is like. If we send him by himself, we'll probably just have to go again. Why don't you start making the pie crust while I get the other ingredients? Maybe Kate will want to help with that too. That'd be nice, right?"

Mom smiles and nods, and I exhale in relief. "Oh, that's a great idea, Milly. I'll ask her now."

I grab Emilia's hand and pretty much drag her out the door, pausing only long enough to get wrapped up in preparation for the cold weather. Emilia laughs and follows me to the car.

"So subtle," she murmurs when we're finally in the car. I groan and lean back in my seat.

"I thought I'd never get you alone."

She laughs again, and I grin to myself. "Take a left here," she says.

I frown and do as she asks. "The shopping center is the other way," I murmur.

Emilia shrugs, and I bite back a smile. She continues to give me directions, and it doesn't take me long to realize where she's leading me to. We're headed to the woods that I took her to on her sixteenth birthday. My heart is racing by the time I park the car and Emilia's cheeks are crimson.

"Pull your seat back," she whispers, and I obey. I'm breathing hard, my entire body tense with anticipation. Emilia grins and climbs on top of me, straddling me in my seat. My hands find their way around her waist and I pull her closer.

She drops her forehead to mine and sighs happily. "I love your Mom, but God... I thought I'd never get another second with you."

I chuckle and peck her lips. "I thought the same," I murmur, right before going in for a kiss. Emilia moans against my lips. Her hands roam over my body impatiently and she pushes her hands underneath my sweater. All week I've been wondering if she's been wanting me too, and all my doubts are put to rest. She didn't seem to have any issues staying away, and whenever we did find ourselves together, she was just so *friendly*.

Emilia pulls her lips away only to bury them in my neck. I moan when she kisses my collar bone, sucking just slightly. She pulls at my sweater and I chuckle before taking it off. She inhales sharply when my body comes into view and I bite back a shy smile. She makes me feel so fucking incredible.

I tug on her dress and she lifts herself up so I can pull it free from under her knees. I slip my hands underneath her dress and hold her waist, my thumbs brushing over the underside of her breasts.

"Again with the freaking tights," I mutter, making her giggle.

"Don't rip these," she warns me, much to my dismay.

"I want them off."

Emilia smiles and bites down on her lip before nodding. She rises and tries her best to take them off in the small amount of space we have, nearly elbowing me in the face in the process.

"Just how complicated are these things?" I ask.

Emilia glares at me. "Just be glad I'm not wearing jeans."

In the end she only takes one side off and keeps the other on, but that's good enough for me. She settles back on top of me and undoes the button on my jeans. I grab her hands and raise them to my lips.

"No need to hurry, Minx," I whisper, kissing the back of her hand. She shakes her head and grinds her hips against mine.

"Babe, we don't have time. We're meant to go to the store, remember?" she says, her voice husky. My heart skips a beat and I'm instantly harder. I love it when she calls me babe.

I bury a hand in her hair and push her underwear aside with the other. "If you want it, then you'll need to come for me first," I whisper. She's soaking wet and responsive as hell. It only takes me a few minutes to make her come all over my fingers. Emilia slumps against me and I wrap my arms around her, hugging her tightly. She kisses my throat as she comes down from her high.

"More," she whispers, and I chuckle. Emilia grabs my dick and guides it inside her in one smooth movement.

"Fuck, Minx," I whisper. Emilia grabs my shoulders and rides me deep and hard, her eyes on mine. I thread my hands through her hair and pull her closer, wanting her lips on mine.

She slows the pace, lifting almost all the way up before

sitting down on me again, over and over. I kiss her as though my life depends on it, losing myself in her entirely. I'm panting and she's keeping me at the very edge.

"Please, baby," I whisper. I run my hands over her body and kiss her deeper. "I can't take it much longer."

Emilia nods and rides me harder, taking all of me. She's so freaking tight around me. "I can't, baby," I murmur, seconds before coming deep inside her. Emilia kisses me and then drops her head to my shoulder as I wrap my arms around her. I don't want to let go of her. I wish we could stay like this just a little longer.

"Damn, as soon as we get back Mom and Kate are going to want all of your attention again. Who knows when I'll next get to have you to myself? It's so cold we can't even sneak into the treehouse."

Emilia sighs. "My dad works during the day, babe. I can find excuses to go back to my own house during the day."

I nod and kiss her neck and then her cheek, before finally kissing her lips. I can't get enough of her.

CHAPTER 25

arter

I can't believe how quickly the holidays have gone by. In just a few days, we'll be heading back to LA.

Kate, Emilia and I are lying on the sofa, watching Home Alone like we do every year. I'm pretty sure we have at least five blankets stacked on top of each other. Emilia is sitting in the middle, between Kate and me, and I reach for her hand sneakily. She smiles when I intertwine our fingers. I wish I could raise them to my lips and kiss the back of her hand. I've really missed her. I miss lying in bed with her after sex, talking about anything and everything. I miss holding her in my arms and I miss her lips on mine.

Contrary to what we planned, we haven't managed to get together much. Every time Emilia tried to sneak out to go back to her own house during the day, Kate would either want to go with her, or Mom would find a reason for her to stay. It's not just her body I want, I just want to spend some alone time with her. It's ridiculous that we're so close, yet we're texting and calling to stay in touch.

Kate glances at Emilia and chuckles. "My God, will you get off your phone, girl? Mason won't freaking die if you don't text him back for an hour or so."

I freeze at the same time Emilia does. She locks her phone screen and hides it underneath the blankets nervously, letting go of my hand.

"Mason?" I repeat, my tone harsh.

Emilia stares at the TV while Kate giggles. "Yeah, Mason," she says. "Emilia is seeing him. They've been texting non-stop. It's so sickeningly sweet."

"I'm not seeing him," she snaps, glaring at Kate. Kate bursts out laughing and wiggles her eyebrows.

"Don't lie, I bet you're seeing a lot more of him than anyone else ever does. I guess seeing him is too tame of an expression though." She looks at me and grins. "She's totally banging him."

"Shut up," Emilia says through gritted teeth, and Kate laughs again.

She shakes her head at me amusedly. "She's trying to keep it a secret, but she's always on her phone."

Emilia groans. "I told you... Mason and I — ugh, never mind. Besides, I told you it was low key. Why would you tell Carter?"

Kate looks contrite and bites down on her lip. "I'm sorry," she whispers. "I wasn't thinking. It just seemed like you and Carter are a lot closer again, so I figured he probably knew. I was just teasing you, I'm sorry. I shouldn't have said anything."

Kate looks at me apologetically and sends me a pleading look. I try my best to act like I don't care and shrug at her before turning back to the TV. I stare at it, but I can't focus on what's happening in the movie at all. She's been texting Mason? And what is this shit about her sleeping with him?

Emilia is tense beside me and carefully reaches out underneath the blankets to grab my hand again. Her fingers snake around mine and she entwines our fingers, squeezing tightly. I shake her off and grit my teeth as I cross my arms.

I think back to how she was flirting with Mason at Noah's house party. She wanted to go home with him that night. If I hadn't been there, she probably would have. That was the first time we slept with each other in years. Yet the very next day she was with Mason *again*, the two of them holding hands at the library. Was it him she really wanted that night?

I bite down on my lip in an attempt to keep my emotions in check. I can't believe she's been texting him all this time. She's been all I can think about, but it seems like that feeling isn't mutual. While I've been trying to devise ways to spend more time with her, she's been texting Mason. How the hell did I miss that? I can't even be mad about it. I'm the one that told her I didn't want to be anything but friends with benefits. I definitely don't have a say over who she dates or who she texts. All I can call mine is her body — and that's only because *she* insisted on exclusivity. I thought that's what I wanted and that's what we needed, so why am I so pissed off? This is exactly what I wanted to prevent. This fucking insecurity and all these damn emotions.

Emilia places her hand on my thigh, but I ignore her. She sighs and strokes my leg. I close my eyes and inhale deeply before grabbing her wrist and removing her hand. I get up and walk into the kitchen, needing some space. When did I start to care so much again? I don't want this. I don't want to feel this way.

"You okay, honey?" Mom asks, pulling me out of my thoughts. I blink at her and nod as I take a seat on one of the high chairs. Mom pushes a slice of pie my way and I take a bite. It's chocolate — Emilia's favorite.

"What's on your mind?"

I shake my head. "It's nothing, Mom."

She leans against the counter and smiles at me sweetly. I

don't know what to say to her. I know she wants to help, but I can't tell her about Emilia.

"Is it a girl?" she asks. I look away and Mom chuckles. "That's a yes, then," she murmurs. She makes me a cup of tea and pushes it toward me. We both sip our tea in silence and I push my cake toward the middle so Mom can have a few bites too.

"It's nothing, really," I say eventually. "She — I don't know. She hasn't done anything wrong, but I..."

I sigh and take another sip of my tea. "I don't know, Mom. I guess things are just moving in a somewhat unexpected direction? I was so clear on what I wanted at the start, and I was so convinced I wouldn't be swayed. But now... now I'm finding myself in a position I really didn't want to be in. I promised myself I'd walk away the second it happened, but now I just can't make myself do that."

Mom smiles at me. "Sounds complicated," she murmurs. "But love usually is, and life definitely is. Things rarely go the way you plan for them to, honey. You'll find, though, that some of the best things in life come when you least want or expect them. Just go with it, and see where life takes you."

I bite down on my lip on shake my head. "It isn't love, Mom. It can't be."

Mom chuckles and nods. "Sure," she says, obviously in disbelief. I cannot be in love with Emilia. That's the one thing I didn't want happening. I guess it's just possessiveness. I want her to be mine alone. That doesn't make it love.

Emilia walks into the kitchen, and Mom straightens. Emilia quietly takes a seat next to me and I take another sip of my tea, ignoring her. I'm being irrational. I shouldn't be mad at her at all, but I just feel so fucking betrayed.

Emilia reaches for a slice of cake and grabs my fork to take a bite. Mom smiles at her when she sighs happily and pours her a cup of tea. Emilia takes it and grins up at Mom. "Thank you," she whispers.

She's such an integral part of my family. I absolutely can't fall in love with her. Mom seems so happy to have both of us sitting here. If I fuck shit up again, I'll be breaking her heart again, like I did two years ago.

"Something on your mind?" Mom asks her. She glances at me and frowns. Emilia shakes her head.

I cross my arms and involuntarily grit my teeth. Mom chuckles and glances from me to her. When we both remain quiet, Mom clears her throat and shakes her head. "Let me go check if the laundry is done," she murmurs before walking out, leaving us sitting alone.

Emilia turns toward me and places her hand on my bicep. "You're misunderstanding things," she murmurs. I turn to face her and smile, catching her off guard. I bury my fingers in her hair and gently cup the back of her neck, my thumb stroking over her throat.

"You don't owe me an explanation, Emilia," I murmur. I lean in until my lips are hovering right over her ear. "It's only your body I want. I couldn't care less who you give your heart to. Just remember that your body is mine."

I pull away from her and her eyes flash with anger. "Fine. Whatever. For the record, I wasn't texting Mason. I haven't spoken to him since we got back home. I was re-reading some of the texts *you* sent me last night. Kate knows I'm seeing someone, and she somehow ended up assuming that it's Mason, and I just never corrected her. If you're going to act like a dick to me, then at least do it knowing all the facts."

I stare at her in surprise and then look away. I get so fucking worked up when it comes to her I can't even think clearly. I can't stand the idea of her with Mason. I'm possessive as hell and I want more of her than we agreed on. I'm falling for her all over again, when I was so sure I'd stay in control of my emotions. When the fuck did this even happen? How could I have *let* this happen?

Emilia jumps off her chair when I remain silent and glares at me before storming off. I'm tempted to follow her, but I resist. A bit of distance is exactly what I need. I need to get myself in check.

CHAPTER 26

milia

Kate drags me to a house party that I've been dreading. "Come on, it'll be so much fun. We haven't been out since we came back from home. We're both overdue some fun. Besides, it's *Mason's* party. How could you not go?"

The reason I don't want to go is *because* it's Mason's party. I have no doubt Carter is going to be there too, and I'm not in the mood for more bullshit or misunderstandings. He's been avoiding me recently and when he tutored me last week he was so distant and polite, making a move on him felt wrong. I feel like I'm being pushed back into the friendzone and I hate it.

Kate entwines our fingers and pulls me straight toward the kitchen for a drink. For once, I'm not at all opposed to a shot or two. I clink my glass to Kate's and down it; the tequila burning my throat. Kate squeals and high fives me. "I told you this would be fun!"

I can't help but giggle. "Okay, fine, you were right," I say.

Kate narrows her eyes and groans. "Ugh, look who's here. The fun police."

I follow her gaze and find Carter approaching us. His eyes roam over my body hungrily and I smile to myself. I'm wearing a short black skirt with a cute long-sleeved crop top and thigh-high boots. I was a little chilly on the way here and should've probably taken a jacket with me, but the look on his face is so worth it. He looks pretty damn good himself. He's wearing dark jeans and a tight black t-shirt that showcases his muscles spectacularly. He's so much more relaxed off-season. He's still working hard, but he isn't watching films all day or training while still trying to keep his grades up. At least now he can focus a bit more on his company and his degree.

Carter leans against the counter, his arm brushing against me. "What are you two doing here?" he asks, shaking his head. Kate shrugs and I follow suit. Carter's eyes roam over my body and he grits his teeth. "Aren't you cold in that?"

I huff in disbelief and glare at him. It's nowhere near as cold in LA as it was in Woodstock. I'm tempted to snap at him but decide to ignore his remark instead.

"Ugh, you know nothing about fashion," Kate says, rolling her eyes. She elbows me and tips her head toward the kitchen door before wiggling her brows. I follow her gaze and watch with dread as Mason walks toward us, a wicked grin on his face. I groan internally. This is about to become a shit show.

"Emilia," he murmurs. He glances at Carter and grins even wider before hugging me tightly. He lifts me right off the floor and twirls me around, ignoring my glare.

"Put me down," I whisper-shout and he laughs. Carter clenches his jaw as he looks at the two of us, his eyes flashing with anger.

Kate lights up at the sight of me with Mason and she grins. "It's so good to finally meet you. I've heard so much about you, but oddly enough we've never met," she says, beaming up at Mason. He wraps his arm around my waist and smiles at Kate. I try to step away, but he just pulls me even closer.

I tip my head toward Kate and smile at Mason. "This is my best friend, Kate." Mason smiles at her and grins wickedly as he pours us all another drink.

"You two look so much cuter together than I imagined. I'm so excited!" Kate says. Carter takes another shot and I sigh as I rise to my tiptoes to whisper into Mason's ear.

"It's a misunderstanding. Hard to explain right now. She thinks you and I are... seeing each other."

Mason bursts out laughing and glances at Carter, who is taking yet another shot. He leans in and whispers into my ear. "Do you know how many times Carter has messed me with me? I'm definitely not letting go of this chance for payback."

I roll my eyes and push against his chest, but he wraps his arms around me, making it look like we're hugging. I rise to my tiptoes and whisper into his ear. "Don't push it too far. He's already being weird."

Mason's smile wavers, and he nods, letting go of me. I resume my position next to Carter and take the drink Mason hands me. I sip it and glance over at Carter's phone to find him texting Lisa. I'm instantly uncomfortable. Why is he texting her?

One of Kate's friends walks into the kitchen and walks straight over to her, grabbing her hand. "Wow, so this is where all the eye candy is hiding," she says, her eyes ping pong-ing between Carter and Mason, as though she can't decide who she wants to ogle.

"Riley, right?" Carter says, smiling at her. He moves closer and leans into her. I didn't even remember her name. So why does he?

"I remember seeing you at pretty much every game and every afterparty. Thank you for your support," he says. I feel guilty instantly. I purposely avoided going to his games because I was trying my best to avoid him. By the time we decided to be friends again, the season was already over.

Riley beams and places her hand on his arm. She bats her eyes at him and he leans in even further. I look away, my stomach twisting painfully. Mason grabs my hand and pulls me closer. "Don't fall for that shit," he whispers. "I've played that game many times. He's fucking with you. There's no way he's even remotely interested in her. Fuck her."

He brushes my hair out of my face, and I smile up at him. "I know," I murmur. "But he can play that game all by himself. I'm not playing. This is bullshit. We aren't kids anymore. I'm not gonna stand here and allow myself to be upset over something like this."

Mason nods in understanding, his expression sad and frustrated, as though he knows exactly how I feel. "What would you like to do... drink, dance or go home? I can take you home if you want."

I tilt my head and then grin. "Drink *and* dance," I murmur. Mason laughs and pours me a shot before pulling me along. We make it to the makeshift dance floor, and much to my surprise Kate is dancing with a guy I don't know.

"Who is that?" I ask.

Mason glances over, his expression clouding over. "Jake," he says uneasily. Jake? The same guy she stood me up for? Kate's eyes meet mine and she winks at me before disappearing in the crowd of people. She seems fine, so I probably shouldn't be worried, but I dislike Jake instantly.

"I need another drink," I murmur, and Mason nods in agreement. He leads me back to the kitchen and my heart twists when I see Carter standing with Lisa, their heads bowed together. He's got his arms wrapped around her and she's looking up at him. The way he's looking at her... how could I forget? How could I forget that I'm no longer the only girl in his eyes? I can't do this. I refuse to do this. I turn back to Mason and try my best to smile. "I think I'll just go home," I murmur, my voice breaking.

Mason nods and glances at Carter and Lisa through narrowed eyes. He grins suddenly and grabs my shoulders. "Let me take you home," he says loudly, catching Carter and Lisa's attention. I sigh and shake my head. Why does he insist on messing with Carter when I just told him I don't want to play along with any of these games?

I roll my eyes and move to walk out of the kitchen, but Carter grabs my wrist and pulls me back. I turn to look at him, and then glance at Lisa, my brows raised. Carter grits his teeth and walks up to me. "I'll take her," he tells Mason. I can tell from the look in Mason's eyes that he's about to mess with Carter even further, and I shake my head in warning. He winks at me and then glances at Carter.

"Buddy, I don't think you quite get it," Mason says, and Carter locks his jaw.

"She's going home with *me*," Carter says through gritted teeth.

"Stop it," I tell Mason, shaking my head, and he nods, taking a step away. I exhale in relief and look up at Carter. "Let's go home," I tell him. "We need to talk."

CHAPTER 27

milia

I'm fuming by the time we walk into Carter's apartment, but he seems to be just as mad. I walk straight into his bedroom and he follows me in. My eyes are flashing with anger as I sit down on his bed.

"What the hell is wrong with you?" I snap.

Carter glares at me and crosses his arms. "What do you mean what's wrong with *me*? What did *I* do?"

I grit my teeth and inhale deeply. "You've been avoiding me and now you're flirting with Riley. What the hell is up with that?"

Carter chuckles humorlessly. "*You've* been flirting with Mason for weeks, yet now you're objecting to me doing the same thing? Did you think I didn't notice the way he's always lifting you up and twirling you around like life is some goddamn movie? He's always touching you and the two of you are always whispering to each other."

He walks up to me and buries his hand in my hair. "But you

know what, Emilia? That's fine. Fuck it. Do what you want, and I'll do the same. You promised me your body — and to be fair, that's all I wanted from you. You never promised me your heart and I never asked for it. It's none of my business if you want to date Mason. Hell, fall in love with him for all I care. All I care about is that I'm the only one you're sleeping with."

I look at him in disbelief and bite down on my lip. I look away in an attempt to hide just how deeply those words cut me.

"We've already destroyed our friendship once before by getting feelings involved," he says. "We promised we wouldn't do that again. Hell, when we went home for the holidays I was reminded of what was at stake, and *fuck*. My mother adores you, and your friendship with Kate is finally back to where it was. What the fuck were we thinking getting together at all?"

I look up at him. "You regret it?"

Carter shakes his head. "Yes, and no."

I sigh and walk to Carter's wardrobe. I grab one of his t-shirts and then walk into his bathroom, slamming the door closed behind me.

Carter looks at me pleadingly when I walk back into the bedroom, but I ignore him and get into bed instead. He sighs and gets up to brush his teeth. I'm curled up into a ball by the time he joins me in bed, my back turned to him. Carter moves closer and wraps his arms around me, spooning me.

I turn to face him, and he lowers his lips to mine. He kisses me slowly, gently. "I hate arguing with you," he whispers. "My heart can't take it."

I wrap my arms around his neck and pull him closer until our bodies are flush against each other. I kiss him, and by the time I pull away again, we're both breathless.

He drops his forehead to mine and I sigh. "It this enough for you, Carter?" I ask. "Just sex, and nothing more? Never being able to call me yours, or to even hold my hand in public. Is this what you want?"

Carter hesitates and closes his eyes.

"You saw how much we hurt Mom when we weren't on good terms. You also saw how happy she was a few weeks ago, when we were all back home and hanging out together. Are you willing to risk her happiness? What about Kate?"

My heart breaks just listening to him. He won't risk his family's happiness in an attempt to find our own. I know I hurt him when I called things off years ago, and I hurt him even further by dating Landon. He pretends like he's over that, but maybe he isn't. Maybe he's still scared I might hurt him again, but maybe it's more than that.

"Is it Lisa?" I ask. "Is she the reason you're pushing me away when things have been so perfect for so long?"

Carter frowns and shakes his head. "No, baby. Fuck, of course not. Why the hell do you keep asking about her?"

I look away. "I saw the way you were holding her tonight. The way she came running to you in tears a few months ago, and the way you carried her in your arms and consoled her. I know she's in love with Mason. Are you just sleeping with me to get over her? Am I a rebound?"

Carter looks at me with wide eyes and shakes his head. "No. *No.* God, no. Lisa and I are just friends, Minx. I'm definitely not in love with her or anything. I don't know what you're seeing, but I assure you, there are no feelings there."

I bite down on my lip and look up at him. "Is she just a friend, or is she more?"

Carter looks away. "Does it matter, baby?"

I inhale deeply and shake my head. "No, I guess it doesn't."

I sigh and hide my face in his neck. "Carter, would it really be okay with you if I went on a date with someone else? Would you not care at all? Would you be fine with it if I truly fell in love with someone else?"

Carter bites down on his lip and nods, lying to both himself and me.

"So that's all I am to you, huh? Just someone you sleep with."

Carter pulls away to look into my eyes and shakes his head. "No, Emilia. Of course not. You're one of my best friends, you always have been. You know that."

I laugh humorlessly. "Your best friend," I repeat, a wry smile on my face. I look into his eyes, my broken heart on display.

"I love you," I whisper.

Carter freezes and stares at me with wide eyes. He blinks and pulls away. He pulls a hand through his hair and sits up, leaning back against the headboard.

I've never felt this vulnerable and exposed before. I feel like I just cut my chest open to hand him my heart.

Carter rises and turns to walk away, but I grab his hand and stop him. He turns back to face me, his expression guarded. I inhale deeply and look into his eyes, my heart beating a thousand miles an hour. I've never been this nervous before. "I meant it."

Carter pulls his hand out of mine and shakes his head. "Emilia, no. We agreed this was just sex. Don't do this."

He looks at me pleadingly and I look back at him, my eyes shimmering with unshed tears.

"I've been keeping these words in for so long, Carter. Part of me is tempted to take them back. To keep going the way we are. But I can't. I keep losing more of myself to you, and if you won't give me anything back, I'll end up being a shell of the person I am now. I can't do this."

I wrap my arms around myself and inhale deeply. "I'm sorry, Carter. Let's just end things here."

He shakes his head and grabs my shoulders. "Minx, please, no. Things are good between us, aren't they?"

I close the distance between us and drop my forehead to his chest. "Things are amazing between us, Carter. But I want more. I want all of you. I want to be able to call you my boyfriend and I want to go on dates. I want to spend nights together when we aren't hooking up and just hanging out. I want to hold your hand across campus and wear your jersey during the next season. I want more than just your body... I want your heart. I want to be able to call you *mine*," I whisper, my voice breaking. A tear escapes my eyes and runs down my cheek. I sniff and pull back, wiping my face.

"Let's end things here, before I fall even further. I think I might still be able to get over this. I think with time I can be your friend, the way you want me to be. But I can't do that while we're sleeping with each other. Every time you touch me, my heart races. Every time you kiss me, I fall a little deeper. I can't do this anymore."

Carter cups my cheeks and wipes my tears away with his thumbs. He looks devastated, but he isn't telling me to stay. Instead, he just nods. I try my best to keep it together while my heart falls apart. I inhale deeply and try my best to smile.

"I'm going back to my dorm," I murmur. "I think we can both do with a bit of space."

I get dressed in a rush and turn toward the front door. Carter grabs my hand from behind before I reach it, and I turn back around, a tiny burst of hope lighting within.

"Stay," he whispers. "Please, Emilia. Stay,"

I bite down on my lip and look into his eyes. He looks torn and anguished, and I hate that I put that expression on his face. "Why?" I ask. "Why should I stay?"

Carter looks at me and then glances away, letting go of my hand. I bite down on my lip as hard as I can to keep myself from bursting into tears.

"Forget what I told you today, Carter. I'll get over it, okay? Don't worry about it."

I smile at him as brightly as I can and walk out of the door.

Big fat ugly tears fall down my cheeks as soon as the door closes behind me. What was I thinking when we started off? How could I have thought for even a second that I'd walk out of this unscathed?

CHAPTER 28

milia

"You've been miserable all week. How long are you going to keep this up?" Kate says. "Didn't you say that Mason was just a hook-up, anyway? It was bound to end at some point. You knew that, didn't you?"

I glance up at her and take the tub of ice cream she's handing me. "Yeah, I knew," I whisper. I'm glad I won't have to keep lying to her anymore. Since Carter and I are over now, I won't have to keep coming up with excuses when she asks me where I am or what I'm up to. I won't have to keep roping Mason into this endless web of lies. It's better this way, for everyone.

Kate groans and pulls on my hand. "Come on. I can't take much more of you being this miserable. The best way to get over someone is to get under someone else. Let's go find you a rebound."

I grimace. I can't stomach the idea of sleeping with someone else. I just want Carter. Kate stares at me expectantly and I sigh. "I guess a drink won't hurt, but I don't want a rebound."

She nods and walks to my wardrobe. I'm not at all surprised when she pulls out one of my sexiest dresses. "Go on, go shower. And for God's sake, wash your hair."

I groan and force myself out of bed and into the shower. I can't help but think of Carter. Does he miss me? Has he replaced me yet? If it's just sex he wanted from me, then he's probably already found someone else to give him that. I wonder if what we had was special to him at all.

By the time I walk out of the shower, Kate is dressed, her hair and makeup done perfectly. I glance at the makeup and hair styling tools she's got laid out and sigh. She's totally going to do a full makeover on me. I sit down and let her do whatever the hell she wants while I sip the vodka mixer she hands me. It doesn't take her long at all, and by the time she's done, the bags underneath my eyes are barely visible.

"Come on," she says, grabbing my hand. "One of my friends is throwing a party in the woods. I've been a few times, and it's always wild. I think it's just what you need."

I frown at her. "A party in the woods? Why does this sound like the start of a horror movie?"

Kate rolls her eyes and drags me along. By the time we get there, I'm already eager to leave, but I don't want to let Kate down. She greets countless people that don't look remotely familiar to me and I honestly can't even introduce myself. I just want to go home and watch a chick flick in bed. Preferably with an entire pint of ice cream.

Kate hands me a drink and I take it from her eagerly. Maybe a drink or two might breathe some life back into me, but I doubt it. Kate looks at me with pity and shakes her head.

"Cheer up, okay?" she murmurs, and I nod, unsure how else to reply. If I could've cheered up, I would've done it long ago. I don't really enjoy feeling this way either.

"Jake!" Kate yells, and I narrow my eyes. I don't like this guy. Jake walks up to us and wraps his arms around her. He looks genuinely excited to see her, and I feel bad for hating him on sight, when he's done nothing to deserve that.

"This is Emilia," she says. Jake looks at me and smiles before turning back to Kate.

"Your best friend?" he asks, and she nods. Jake takes another look at me and smiles lecherously. I look away and take back the remorse I felt for judging him too early. He's clearly a pig.

Jake wraps his arm around me and I take a step away, throwing my own arm around Kate instead. She smiles up at me, but her smile is forced, and I feel guilty immediately. I didn't do anything to cause Jake to behave that way, so why does she look annoyed with *me*.

"She's a bit heartbroken. I thought she could do with a bit of fun," Kate says.

Jake's eyes roam over my body, and he grins. "Fun, huh?"

Kate stiffens and I look away awkwardly. She clears her throat and looks at him with raised brows, and he snaps out of it. "What the hell is with him?" I whisper into her ear.

Kate sighs and shakes her head. "He's usually really nice," she whispers, sounding defensive.

Jake grabs two bags out of his pockets and holds them up for us. "If it's fun you need, one of these will sort you out," he says.

I stare at him in disbelief. "Is that what I think it is?" I whisper.

Kate bites down on her lip and looks at me. "You wanna try?" she asks and I shake my head, my eyes wide.

"What the hell is that?"

Jake and Kate both chuckle. "Weed," he says, holding up his left arm. "And coke," he says, holding up his right arm.

"*Cocaine*?" I murmur in disbelief, and Jake bursts out laughing.

He looks from me to Kate and grins. "I love you small-town girls," he says, amused.

I glare at him and pull on Kate's hand. "We're fine, thanks," I snap.

Jake winks at me and presses a kiss to Kate's cheek. "Come find me later," he murmurs.

I watch him walk off and then look at Kate. "Tell me you've never taken him up on his offer. What a complete psycho. Drugs, really?"

Kate smiles at me and brushes my hair out of my face. "Chill, Milly. I'm far more responsible than you seem to think I am, okay?"

I nod at her in relief and take the drink she's handing me. I didn't notice it at first, but left and right people seem to be doing illegal drugs like it's nothing. I'm familiar with weed and though I haven't ever done it, I can kinda get why people might find that interesting. But these people here are *snorting* all kinds of stuff. It's insane. Kate laughs at my expression and I shake my head.

"Seriously, how do you even know these people?"

She throws her arm around my shoulder and takes a sip of her drink. "Some of them are in my arts classes, and then I kind of just got to know more and more people. I don't even know. How does anyone at college know anyone?"

I shrug and nod. Fair enough. I've gotten to know so many people lately, yet I can't always remember how I know them.

"Still though, I'm not really comfortable around this crowd," I admit. I really wanted to try tonight. I wanted to try to have some fun and hang out with Kate, but I'm feeling really out of place here.

"Kate!" someone shouts. I turn around to find a girl that

looks vaguely familiar walking up to us. I've seen her talk to Kate at parties before, but I've never met her.

Kate tenses. "Jen," she says, smiling tightly.

"You good? What are we doing tonight?" Jen says.

Kate looks at me nervously and shakes her head. "In hindsight, this is probably not really your kind of party. How about we just go home and eat more ice cream?"

Jen rolls her eyes and walks away, but I sigh in relief and nod. I want nothing more than to be in bed right now. Besides, the entire vibe of this party is weird.

"Love you, Kate," I murmur. She smiles back at me and brushes her hand through my hair. "Love you too, Milly. Come on. Let's go eat more ice cream until you finally get over that douchebag."

CHAPTER 29

arter

I take another swig of my beer and stare at the TV. I'm startled when Asher snatches the bottle out of my hand.

"Dude, what the fuck?"

He sighs and puts the bottle down. "How long are you going to keep this up?" he asks, gesturing around us. I glance at the mess I've made. The living room is littered with pizza boxes and beer bottles.

"Have you even moved from the sofa all week? Have you been going to classes?"

I look away and inhale deeply. "I went to a few."

Asher sits down at the edge of the coffee table and looks at me sternly. I hate it when he gets all serious on me.

"If you were gonna be like this, why the hell did you let her walk away? You're a fucking moron. This is Emilia we're talking about. The same girl you've been in love with your entire life. The girl you're fucking crazy about loves you back, and you let her walk away? You let her end things? Are you stupid?"

I groan and drop my arm over my eyes. "It's not that simple.

148

Do you have any idea how much my mother loves Emilia? Fuck, can't you see what it'd do to Kate and Emilia's relationship if we started dating? Their friendship only just recovered. I was in part to blame for the way Gabby manipulated her. I can't be responsible for taking another friend from her."

Asher sighs. "Carter, you two aren't kids anymore. Your Mom would be happier than *you'd* be if you two dated. Pretty sure she always planned on having Emilia as her daughter-in-law someday, just not when you were teenagers. And Kate... well, she does have a propensity toward selfishness. I literally have no idea how she might react, but she's not a child. She'll get over it."

He rises and kicks my leg. "Get up, dude. You fucking stink. I don't get what's wrong with you, man. Why the fuck are you acting like you and Emilia breaking up is a given? All these things you're worried about are only an issue if you two ever break up. Even *my* pessimistic ass can't see that ever happening. You two are so fucking obsessed with each other. It's about time you finally date."

I sit up and run a hand through my hair. Part of me wants to believe him. Part of me wants to believe that Emilia and I can be together, but I don't dare to hope. I gave her my heart when we were younger. She wouldn't date me, but she was with someone else just a few months later. I want to believe that she means what she says, and that she truly does love me. But what if I'm wrong again? What if her feelings are as fickle as they were back then? What if we start dating and end up losing it all? I know I'm an asshole. I'd disappoint her in a million different ways, and eventually she'd leave me. Can I risk breaking my mother and my sister's hearts just on the off chance that we might work out? I know I shouldn't, but God, I want to.

"Okay, if you're going to act all heartbroken, we might as well go out," Asher says. He pushes me toward my bedroom and grins. "Noah is throwing another one of his big ass parties. Let's go."

I drag my feet as I get ready. I don't want to go. I just want to lie on the sofa and watch reruns of Friends, but Asher isn't having it.

The party is loud and packed, and I'm so not in the mood for it. I recognize a couple of the girls that are looking at me with interest, but I can't even imagine being with anyone that isn't Emilia. I ignore them and walk straight to the kitchen. I already need another fucking drink. Asher shakes his head and pours me a drink, only to freeze all of a sudden.

I follow his gaze and find Kate in some guy's arms. She's dancing and giggling. I narrow my eyes and try to get a better look. "Is she with fucking Jake?" I say through gritted teeth.

I glance at Asher and clap him on the back. His face is white and he looks as devastated as I've probably been looking all week. "What the hell is happening between you two?" I ask.

Asher shakes his head. "We ended things a few weeks ago. I don't know, man. I guess she just lost interest or something. I wasn't fun enough."

I frown and pour him a drink. "My sister is a fucking asshole," I tell him, meaning every word. I love her to bits, but she's a dick. Only Emilia thinks she's an angel. Asher taps his cup against mine and empties it in one go before refilling it. I bite back a smile. He took me out to cheer me up, but it looks like he's the one that needs some support now.

I glance back at Kate and shake my head. "Be right back," I tell Asher. Kate doesn't notice me until I'm standing right behind her. I tap her on the shoulder and she looks at me wide eyed.

"Carter... I didn't realize you were coming today."

Jake grins up at me and tries to shake my hand, but I ignore him. "Why are you with him?" I ask.

Kate smiles up at me. "We're just dancing, that's all."

I grit my teeth and look at Jake in annoyance before looking back at Kate. She grins at me and shakes her head.

"I promise, it's just dancing. I'm just having a bit of fun. Balance, right?"

I nod and look at her through narrowed eyes. "Fine," I say, shaking my head.

I shoot Jake a warning look and he tenses. He's a thin, puny little guy. Even if he's got something to say, he wouldn't dare.

"If I find out you two do any more than dancing, I'll find you," I tell him, a bright smile on my face. Jake grits his teeth and looks away. Kate pushes against my arm and I shake my head as I walk away. I don't want her hanging out with him at all, but it's not my choice to make. All I can do is warn her and keep an eye on her.

I glance around the room as I walk back to Asher. In the back of my mind, I can't help but think that Emilia must be here if Kate is. I want to see her. I've missed her like fucking crazy. We haven't so much as texted in a full week now. I've gotten so used to having a dose of her every day. Even when we don't see each other, we usually at least call or text.

I tense when Mason walks into the kitchen with a shit-eating grin on his face. He heads straight toward me and I already want to punch him in the face. "Carter, my boy," he says, smiling even wider. I look at him blankly. I just know some utter bullshit is about to come out of his mouth. "Heard Emilia finally ditched your ass. I'm so glad she's finally available now."

I move without thinking and grab the collar of his shirt. "If you so much as go near her, I'll fucking kill you, Mason. Don't you dare mess with her."

Mason chuckles and pulls himself out of my grasp. "Aw, Carter. You seem to be under the impression that you still have a hold over her. The second you let her go is the second you lost the right to keep me away. Hell, if anything, you've paved the way for me, man. After pouring her heart out to you and getting rejected, I'll look like freaking Prince Charming to her."

He laughs and takes a big swig of his drink while I grit my teeth and try my best to remain in control of my temper. I so badly want to wipe the floor with his damn face.

Mason looks at me provocatively and then walks out, as though he knows he just accomplished what he set out to do. I close my eyes and inhale deeply. What the fuck did I do? How could I have let her go?

CHAPTER 30

arter

I'm nervous as hell as I wait for Emilia to get here. It took so much effort to convince her to come over for tutoring. I can't blow this now. I glance down at my outfit and brush my hands over my t-shirt. I purposely wore a tight black t-shirt with my old dark jeans. It's a combo Emilia loves on me.

I'm already by the door when the doorbell finally rings. I and rest my head against the frame for a second in an attempt to not look overly eager. When I open the door, my heart skips a beat or three. She looks so stunning. Emilia is wearing a tight dress that showcases her body perfectly.

I drag my eyes away and step aside to let her in. "Hey," I murmur nervously.

She beams up at me and grins. "Hey," she says. She's subtle, but I see her check me out the way I just checked *her* out. She walks to the coffee table and drops on the sofa. She crosses her legs and takes out her books.

"I... uh... I'll make you a cup of coffee," I murmur.

She frowns and shakes her head. "I'm good, thank you."

I gulp and turn to walk to the kitchen. "I'll make you one, anyway."

I can feel her eyes on me all the way to the kitchen and drop my head against the refrigerator door. I'm being way too awkward. I inhale deeply and make her a cup of coffee. My hands are trembling as I put it down in front of her.

She looks up at me and smiles. "How have you been?" she asks. She seems so unaffected that I'm already second guessing myself. It's been two weeks since she ended things, but she seems to be happier than she was before. She said she loved me, but it looks like she's already over me.

I sit down next to her and inhale deeply. "I missed you, Minx. I've been fucking miserable."

Her smile wavers, and for a second I see hope in her eyes. That's all I need. All I need is a small sign.

Emilia looks down and takes a big gulp of her coffee, as though she's trying to ignore what I said. I glance at her cup and look away. "Did you miss me?" I ask her, unable to resist. Emilia sighs and frowns at me.

"I thought you said we should try our best to remain friends. That us becoming estranged all over again would defeat the point."

I sigh and run a hand through my hair. "I thought you said you loved me?"

She glares at me and then looks away. "I told you to forget about that."

"I can't. It's all I've been able to think about."

Emilia takes another sip of her coffee and puts it back down with force, a small amount of coffee still in it.

"What do you want me to say, Carter?" she snaps. God, I didn't think this would be that hard. Why can't I just get it right?

Emilia grabs her book and puts it back in her bag. "I can't be around you," she tells me, her voice breaking. "What was I even thinking? It's too soon, Carter. It's literally been two weeks. I can't sit here and pretend we're fine. Let's not do this, okay?"

She grabs her bag and throws it over her shoulder. I panic and grab her arm, pulling her back. She looks back at me, her expression anguished.

"Emilia, wait," I whisper. I'm panicked and nervous as hell. Without thinking, I grab her cup and empty it on the floor before thrusting it back into her hands. She glances at the mess on the floor and then at the cup, bewildered.

"Look inside it," I tell her. "I had this whole plan. I even made a Pinterest account to help me think of ways to ask you. I wanted to do something cute, but I fucked it all up."

Emilia blinks at me in confusion and then looks inside the cup. Her hand trembles as she looks back at me. I drop down on one knee and repeat the same words I had etched inside the cup.

"I love you, Emilia. Be my girlfriend?"

She just blinks at me instead of answering, and I panic even further. "I... when you told me how you felt, I panicked, baby. I was reminded of three years ago, when I was head over heels with you and everything just fell apart. I was devastated, but that was nothing compared to me finding you kissing someone else just a few months later. I just... I was scared the same thing would happen. That you love me now, and in three months you might change your mind. When it was just sex, I felt like I was in control. It was easier for me to tell myself I wouldn't get hurt again. Needless to say, that was straight up stupid. I was worried that you'd break my heart, and it wouldn't just be me that'd be hurt by that, you know? I was so worried that my selfishness would end up hurting my family. It was actually Asher... he made me realize my worries aren't warranted, because they all relate to us breaking up. And hell, I don't think we ever will."

Emilia drops to her knees too and pushes her finger against

my lips. "You're rambling, babe," she whispers, her eyes twinkling. "*Yes*. Hell yes."

I drop my forehead to hers and smile. "Yes?" I repeat.

"Yes," she says. Emilia throws her arms around my neck and I pull her flush against me, hugging her as tightly as I can.

"Fuck, those two weeks without you were the worst. Never again, baby. I'm never letting you go again."

Emilia smiles up at me and shakes her head. "I'm never going to give you a chance to."

I smile and thread my hand through her hair. "You're mine now," I murmur against her lips. "My girlfriend."

Emilia bridges the distance between us and kisses me. Her hands roam over my body and I smile against her lips. I pull away and pull her up with me before lifting her into my arms and carrying her to my bedroom.

"I love you," I tell her.

She smiles at me so widely that my heart skips a beat. "I love you too," she whispers. I put her down on my bed and hold myself up on top of her.

"Say it again."

Emilia giggles and runs her hands over my body. "I love you, Carter."

"Again."

"Babe, I love you."

"One more time."

Emilia laughs and pulls me closer, her lips finding mine. I can easily lose myself in her. In fact, I'm planning on doing just that for the rest of the day.

"I adore you," I whisper. "I'm sorry I was such a fool. I'm sorry it took me two whole weeks to fix things. Thank you for being you, and for being mine."

Emilia shakes her head and cups my face. "I'm glad you had some time to think things through. Considering everything we've been through it does make sense."

She bites down on her lip, a hint of insecurity in her eyes. "Maybe we should keep things a secret for now. We can just date without the pressure of Kate and your family. Do you think that'll settle some of your worries? That way if things do go wrong like you feared, they won't know. We'd be able to step back and try our best to be friends without the additional scrutiny from them."

I drop my forehead to hers. "Do you think it's lame that I'm insecure about us?" I don't dare to tell her just how badly her getting with Landon affected me. She was my everything, but I can't have meant that much to her if she started dating someone else so soon after I left. I'm terrified of it happening again. I'm scared she'll break my heart again.

"No, babe," she whispers. "I think it's hot as hell that you're honest about it. I'd rather you tell me these things so we can work it out together, instead of you leaving me guessing. It really hurt to think you only wanted my body. It hurt to think I was falling in love while you just... *weren't*."

I press a kiss to her forehead and then another one to her nose. "Minx, I'm pretty sure I've been in love with you all my life. I don't think I ever truly fell out of love with you."

She kisses me and grazes my lower lip with her teeth. "I *definitely* never fell out of love with you," she says. "The only reason I agreed to the whole friends with benefits thing is because I wanted whatever you would give me."

I turn us over in bed and pull her on top of me. Emilia rests her head on my chest and I play with her hair.

"Are you sure you'd be okay with keeping it low key for a while?"

Emilia turns and presses a kiss to my neck. "Yes, Carter. I just want you to be mine. The rest will come."

CHAPTER 31

arter

I wake up alone and pat the other side of my bed, annoyed to find it empty. I yawn and make my way to the bathroom to freshen up before walking out of my room to find Emilia. She's in the kitchen wearing nothing but one of my t-shirts and it looks hot on her. I walk up to her and wrap my arms around her waist from behind.

"Morning, baby," I whisper. She turns in my arms and wraps her arms around my neck. She smiles up at me and my heart skips a beat.

"Morning," she murmurs. She rises to her tiptoes and presses her lips against mine. I cup the back of her head and deepen our kiss, taking my time with her. She tastes like tooth-paste and coffee. I grab her waist and lift her on top of the kitchen counter. Emilia wraps her legs around me and pulls me closer. I groan and nip at her lips. "We should go back to bed," I murmur. I'm already hard again.

We both jump at the sound of a door closing behind us. Emilia looks up at me with wide eyes when Asher walks into the kitchen. He looks just as awkward as we do, but he recovers far quicker.

"Thank God you two got back together. I don't think I could cope with Carter's miserable ass for one more second," he says, grinning up at Emilia.

I lift her off the counter, and she looks at me in question. I just shrug. "He's my best friend and he lives with me. I couldn't *not* tell him."

Asher shakes his head. "If you two are going to subject me to any type of PDA, then I demand to be fed."

Emilia laughs and walks over to the coffee pot to pour him a cup. "Fair enough," she says . Asher takes the mug from her and ruffles her hair like she's a child. The outrage on her face is cute as fuck.

She glares and pushes him toward the dining table. "Do that again and you can forget about being fed," she warns him. Asher smiles as he takes a seat. I help Emilia finish the breakfast she was making and use any excuse to sneak little touches and kisses in. By the time we have breakfast on the table, she's as frustrated as I am.

"How did you like the coffee cup?" Asher asks Emilia.

I groan and run a hand through my hair. "She didn't even finish the damn coffee. I ended up having to throw her coffee on the floor to show her the message."

Asher bursts out laughing, and Emilia blushes. She places her hand over mine and I raise it to my lips. Asher looks away and smiles. "I can just tell you two are going to be one of those sickeningly sweet couples."

I shrug and grin at my girlfriend. "We're not like that," I say, and Emilia nods in agreement. Asher looks at our entwined hands and shakes his head.

"You guys gonna tell Kate?"

I glance at Emilia, and she shakes her head. "We just kind

of thought we'd enjoy dating first," she murmurs, and Asher grimaces.

"Yeah, she'll find a way to make your relationship about her," he says bitterly. Emilia frowns at him but remains silent. I can't even blame Asher for his resentment toward Kate. She really fucked up with him.

"I don't think we can hide it for very long, though," Emilia murmurs. I nod. At some point we'll need to tell her, but I'm definitely not looking forward to that.

"Hey Minx," I whisper. Emilia leans into me and looks at me with raised brows. "Will you go on a date with me tonight?"

It's been years, but we haven't ever truly dated. We had that first date in the lake at the summer cabin, and then Emilia's sixteenth birthday, but neither was a true date. I want to make up for all the time I missed, and I want to spoil my girl just a little. Saying *I love you* isn't enough, I want to show her I mean it.

Emilia blushes and nods at me. "I'd love to."

I'm antsy the rest of the day. I dropped Emilia back at her dorm after breakfast, and I've been counting down the minutes since. I've never been an insecure person, but today I actually changed my shirt three times. Emilia has seen me in pretty much every outfit I own, and she's seen me grow through all my awkward phases, but I still want to look good for her. It's like being in an official relationship with her makes everything feel brand new.

I'm nervous by the time I leave. Emilia asked me to pick her up around the corner of her dorm, and I hate that we're going out of our way to hide our relationship. I never should've agreed to that, but I also don't want to deal with Kate once she finds out. I kinda want to enjoy some peace and quiet with my Minx, before Kate inevitably blows up.

"Hey," she says as she walks up to me. I lean back against my car as my eyes roam over her. She looks amazing tonight.

She's wearing a loose summer dress that showcases her boobs beautifully. She's so stunning... I can barely believe she's mine.

"Hey," I whisper. I pull her toward me and kiss her, but she pulls away. I frown, but she avoids my gaze and hops into my car.

She's quiet on the way to the restaurant, and I can't help but worry. Does she regret making our relationship official? I don't understand why she isn't as excited as I am.

Thankfully, her eyes light up when I park in front of La Familia. She grins up at me and I step out of the car and run around to open her door. I grab her hand and entwine our fingers as we walk to the entrance. Lita smiles at us when we walk in and glances at our joined hands, her eyes dancing with excitement.

"You two came to your senses, huh?" she says. I nod and lean in to hug Lita, lifting her right off her feet.

"I told this boy he was crazy for not making you his girl-friend," she tells Emilia.

I nod in confirmation and Emilia blushes. "Don't worry, Lita," I tell her. "She's mine now, and I'm not letting her go."

Lita claps me on the back and leads us back to the same table we had last time.

"You look far more relaxed," I say. Emilia looks up at me, startled. She bites down on her lip, her expression falling.

"I was just worried about being seen with you. I don't want Kate to find out. I know we'll have to tell her eventually, but I don't want to do it right now."

I sigh and nod. "I know what you mean, but I also don't want to hide it. We're finally together after so many years, it seems stupid to keep it hidden for even a second longer."

Emilia nods and smiles sadly. "I know, babe. Just a few months, though. Let's just have a few months together before we tell her. I have a feeling things won't be the same anymore once we do."

I nod and look away, unsure what to say. "What are you going to tell her, though? How are you going to justify spending nights with me or hanging out together?"

Emilia looks down and I just know I'm not going to like her answer. "Random hook-ups and tutoring?"

I sigh and close my eyes. "We tell everyone this summer, okay? The academic year is almost over, anyway. We'll tell them when we go home. This summer I want you in my bed, Minx. I want to be able to throw my arm around you on the sofa and go on dates without having to make any excuses."

Emilia smiles at me and nods. Truthfully, I'm just glad we're finally together. Part of me is glad we're on the same page, though. A few months of dating without any pressure from my family is exactly what we need.

CHAPTER 32

milia

Kate looks at me through narrowed eyes and crosses her arms. "Where have you been lately?" she asks. "I've barely seen you in weeks now. I mean, I know I've been going out a lot... but more often than not you don't even come home all night. What's up with that?"

I glance at her nervously. I didn't mean to do it, but I've mostly been avoiding Kate. Things between Carter and I have been even more perfect than I could've dreamed, and I've been scared of anything ruining our happiness.

I shrug and try my best to smile at her. "I followed your advice and decided to have more fun," I say.

She grins at me and shakes her head. "*Finally*. I thought you'd be upset when things didn't work out with Mason, but it looks like you full-on went on the rebound, huh? Good for you, girl. I've missed you though. Feels like we've barely seen each other."

I nod and sit down on my bed. I'd planned to go over to Carter's today, but maybe I should hang out with Kate instead. I can't even remember the last time I hung out with her. When was it? A month ago? She and I have continued to grow apart ever since we started college, and for once I don't want to be the one fighting for our friendship. I've done more than my fair share of that.

Kate smiles at me and glances at her phone. "Carter has been texting me pretty much every day recently, asking about my grades and all kinds of shit. I think Mom asked him to do it or something, because he's being *so* annoying. I just texted him to say I'm coming over so he can tutor me on a few of the subjects I'm failing. That might get him off my back, but it'll be boring as hell. You wanna join? We can catch up as well."

I'm startled and instinctively grab my phone. Carter and I were meant to study together today, and I was planning on staying over after. I was going to make us dinner and try out a new recipe that Helen sent me the other day. I check my phone, and indeed, Carter messaged me.

Devil: *Kate texted asking if she can come over. I said that it's fine, but I forgot to check with you. I know we had plans. Is it okay if she joins?*

Emilia: *Of course, babe. I'm with her now. We'll go to your place together.*

"Yeah, I'll come with you," I tell Kate. "I doubt he's trying to be annoying. I don't think it's your Mom, either. She's been trusting us to be responsible. I think he's probably just worried about you."

Kate rolls her eyes. "Like hell he is. It's Carter."

I grab my bag and throw it over my shoulder while Kate puts on her shoes. "Come to think of it, if you and I have barely hung out, then you and Carter must not have seen each other in ages."

I shake my head and bite my lip. "He's still been tutoring me, so we see each other often enough. I'd probably be failing a bunch of my classes if he didn't help me out."

Kate laughs. "Right, I forgot. You're both huge geeks."

I'm nervous as we make our way to Carter's place. We've managed to avoid both of us being with her at the same time, so this'll be the first time we'll all be in the same place since Carter and I started dating. I'm not sure how to act around Kate anymore. I've gotten so used to touching Carter and being in his lap or in his arms. It'll be strange to have to hide our relationship in her presence.

Carter opens the door just as we walk up. His eyes drop to my lips and he bends down and leans into me, before thinking better of it. He hugs me instead and then moves to hug Kate.

"Sup, bro?" Kate says as she barges in. I follow behind her. There are only two more months left before we go home for the summer. We'll need to tell Kate soon, but I just don't want to.

Carter winks at me as he walks to the sofa, both of us dropping to the floor by the coffee table in our usual spots. Much to both of our surprise, Kate actually does study for a couple of hours, pausing only to ask Carter questions.

"So how have your grades been?" I ask. She hasn't shared much with me, and I've gotten quite used to her being too hungover to even attend her classes. I probably should've checked in with her a bit more often, but I'm wary of treating her like a child.

Kate grimaces and shakes her head. "Let's just say that I might actually need Carter to tutor me every week if I want to save my GPA."

I shake my head and focus on my own work. Only a handful of tests left before we're finally done. I can barely believe how much time has passed, and how quickly it's gone. I'm actually pretty excited to be back home for the summer. I know Carter will be training for the new season, but at least we won't have classes on top of that too. This will probably be our last summer with not too many responsibilities. Next year I'll probably want to find an internship.

"Shall I make dinner tonight?" Carter asks. I grin to myself and try my best to hide my smile as I shake my head. I'm planning on making fake cake pops today. I bought a batch of Brussel sprouts that I'm going to coat in chocolate and serve to Carter for dessert. It's going to be the perfect trick, and I can't wait. I smile as sweetly as I can and Carter narrows his eyes.

"No, I already planned what I wanted to make. You can cook next time, okay? I wanna try a new recipe your Mom sent me. I'm getting just a little homesick, so I thought it might be nice."

Carter nods and Kate claps in excitement. "Oh my gosh, yes! I can't wait," she says. I grin and get up to prep the food.

As expected, Carter follows me into the kitchen. He wraps his hands around my waist and pulls me flush against him. I rise to my tiptoes as his lips find mine, and Carter lifts me on top of the kitchen counter. "I can't deal with you sitting so close and being unable to touch you," he whispers. "I want everyone to know that you're mine. I don't want to hide this any longer."

I smile against his lips and pull away. "This summer," I promise. "I think it's time we tell everyone too. Let's tell your parents and Kate together."

Carter drops his forehead against mine and sighs. "I can't wait," he whispers. "There's no way I can stay away from you all summer."

I nod in agreement, but part of me dreads the thought of telling them nonetheless.

CHAPTER 33

*E*milia

I'm nervous the entire way back to Woodstock. Carter and I haven't really discussed what we'd do or say when we went back, and I'm worried.

Kate storms into the house excitedly while Carter and I follow behind her.

"You're being really quiet. You okay?" Carter whispers. I nod and help him carry our luggage into the house. I know my dad isn't home yet, so there's no point in going back to my own house yet. I might as well say hi to Helen first.

Helen smiles at us as we walk in, her eyes glittering with unshed tears. She walks up to Carter and me and hugs us both, forcing us into a group hug. Carter chuckles and throws his arms around us, lifting us both off the ground.

"Missed you, Mom," he says. She smiles up at him and grabs our hands.

"I'm so glad you're back," she says, her voice trembling. Kate throws herself at us and joins in on our hug, squeezing us all tightly.

"Yeah, missed you, Mom," she says.

Helen leads us all to the kitchen and the three of us smile in delight when we find the counter filled with our favorite foods. She went all out for us.

"Helen," I murmur. "You shouldn't have."

She throws her arm around my shoulder and shakes her head. "All my babies are finally back for the summer. I'm just so happy, Milly. The house hasn't been the same without you three."

I hug her tighter, my heart breaking. I don't like the idea of her being at home all by herself. She's gotten so used to having us around.

"I have a dozen recipes for us to try, Milly." She glances over at Kate and grins. "And I booked a spa day for the two of us, Kate."

Kate squeals happily, making me laugh. She's been in high spirits all week, and I'm happy to see her so excited. I was worried she'd hate coming back, or that she'd be bored. I'm hoping her excitement will make it easier for her to accept the news of Carter and me dating.

I glance at him as he takes out slices of cake for the three of us. Helen made each of us our favorites. Carter grabs my slice of chocolate cake and grins wickedly before taking a bite. I lunge toward him and snatch the fork out of his hand.

"Don't even," I warn him. His arm snakes around my waist and he pulls me flush against him, my breasts crashing against his chest. Carter grabs the fork from my hand and brings another serving to my lips. Just as I'm about to close my lips around the fork, he pulls it away and shoves it in his mouth.

"You... you... you don't even like chocolate!" I shout. I glare at him and grab my fork back, turning my back to him in annoyance. "I can't believe you ate my cake."

I pull my plate toward me and wrap my arm around it protectively. It isn't until Helen bursts out laughing that I remember we aren't alone. She glances at Carter and me and smiles in relief. "I see you two are back to your usual antics. I knew being in the same city again would be good for you two."

Carter looks into my eyes, silently telling me this would be a good time to tell her, but I shake my head. I'm nervous. I don't know for sure how to tell her, but I don't think right now is the right moment.

Carter looks disappointed but nods. Helen chats non-stop as we all eat our cake. It's obvious she's beyond happy to have us back, and I'm terrified of ruining her happiness so soon. I know Kate isn't going to like us dating, and I don't want to create any conflict.

"Come on, let me help you take your luggage home," Carter says. I nod and rise, grabbing one of my bags while Carter gets the rest. He's quiet as we walk into my house, and I know he's annoyed with me.

"This week, okay?" I murmur. Carter sighs and carries my luggage up the stairs. When we reach my bedroom, he drops it all on the floor before sitting down on my bed. I walk up to him and sit down in his lap. I cup his cheek and turn his face toward mine. Carter looks at me dejectedly.

"I love you, Emilia. I love you with my heart and soul. I know things aren't going to go as smoothly as we want them to, but I also won't hide how I feel about you. We've done enough of that. It's time we start living *our* life."

I rest my head on his shoulder and press a gentle kiss to his neck. "I love you too, Carter. Let's tell them at the end of this week, okay? Let's give your Mom a bit of time with us before... *you know*."

Carter nods and tilts my face up. I kiss him and smile as I push him flat on his back. He grins wickedly and looks at me through lowered lashes. "You know what, baby? I've never had you in your bed."

I chuckle and straddle him, not at all surprised to find him hardening already. Carter turns us over so he's on top and kisses me until I'm breathless. His lips move to my neck and he trails a path down to my chest.

"Off," he says, yanking on my clothes. I giggle and grab his t-shirt, pulling it over his head. We're both impatient as we undress each other. I pull him toward me as soon as we're finally naked in my bed.

Carter leans over me and kisses me so tenderly that my heart feels ready to burst. "More," I murmur. "You can't stay away too long. Besides, my dad should be home in an hour or so."

Carter groans and glares at me as his fingers find their way between my legs. He keeps me right at the edge, and no matter how I squirm or plead, he won't give in.

"Please, babe. Come on," I urge. Carter chuckles and reaches for his jeans. He grabs a pouch from his back pocket and holds it up for me to see.

"Payback for the goddamn Brussel sprouts dessert. I'm upping my game, Minx."

He takes out a device that's shaped like an egg and grins as he pushes it between my legs. I bite down on my lip and look at him in curiosity. Even while we've been dating, we never stopped playing pranks on each other, but they've never been this daring. My heart is racing when Carter grabs his phone and uses an app to turn the device on. It starts vibrating deep inside me and I nearly come there and then.

"I dare you to keep it in throughout dinner, baby," he says, grinning wickedly. "Try not to come."

He laughs and I try my best to glare at him, but I'm feeling too damn good. "Ugh, playing dirty, huh?"

I'll need to think of a way to get back at him for this. He's definitely going to keep me right at the edge for hours. "Damned Devil," I mutter under my breath, making him laugh.

Carter leans in and kisses me, pulling away to look into my

eyes. "I love you, Minx. You're the girl of my dreams. You know that, right?"

I nod and thread my hands through his hair. "I love you more, Carter."

He shakes his head and kisses me again. "Impossible," he whispers. I pout when he pulls away and grabs his clothes.

"I've stayed away too long already. Mom will definitely come find me soon. Tonight, though, baby. One way or another, I'm having you."

I fall back on my bed as Carter walks out the door, intent on making myself come at least once. There's no way I can get through dinner otherwise. I'm going to be a needy mess by the time I finally get Carter alone again.

CHAPTER 34

arter

Emilia's face is flushed as we sit down for dinner. I bet she wishes Mom didn't invite her dad over tonight. She squirms in her seat opposite me and I smile to myself. I'm so fucking hard just watching her. She's doing really well hiding her arousal, but my Minx has always been transparent to me. The way she bites down on her lip, her rapidly rising and falling chest, and those rosy cheeks of hers... Her eyes meet mine and she looks at me with such desperation and arousal that I have to bite down hard on my own lip to keep myself in check. This was meant to torture her, so why the hell am I the one that's suffering?

"Honey, you did so well," her dad says.

Emilia smiles up at him while I nod in agreement. "4.4 GPA. That beats mine," I tell him proudly, and he nods.

"You've done well too, son. Your dad told me you're starting your own company?"

I nod awkwardly and clear my throat. "Yes, sir. We've secured all the required funding and are just about finalizing

172

the platform we're building. We'll go through a round of security testing soon. I actually hired some of the best hackers to try and get into our systems. We have a lot of testing left to do, but we should be up and running in a year or so. I'm currently working on building relationships with big corporations. I'm looking to make our platform as user-friendly as possible, so I want it to be possible to do things as simple as grocery shopping with one of our cards. It's the partnership stage that'll make or break the business as I envision it."

I don't dare to tell him we've acquired funding to the tune of *millions*. It still makes me nervous to think of all the responsibility Asher and I have taken on. We cannot fail — it simply isn't an option.

John nods and glances at me with interest. "Sounds very technical. I'm sure you'll do fine. I'm proud of you, kid."

Dad nods and claps me on the back. "You *have* done well, Carter. We're all really proud of you."

I look down and nod in thanks. I've stayed as quiet as I can about my business. Neither Asher nor I are the bragging type. Besides, our business can't even be called a start-up yet.

John turns toward Kate and smiles at her. "How have you been doing at college?" he asks.

Kate looks up at him, startled, and then looks back down. "Um, it's been okay," she says. "I've had a lot of fun."

To my surprise, John bursts out laughing and nods at her. "Good for you, Kate. Emilia and Carter have always been incredibly serious, but you're only young once. I'm glad you're at least enjoying your youth. Make sure you help them have fun a bit too, okay?"

Kate grins up at him and nods. She hasn't actually told me what her current GPA is. It can't be great if she won't tell me. I'm worried Kate is having *too much* fun. Emilia and I have been so wrapped up in each other that neither one of us has paid much attention to her. I'm not even sure what she's been up to, or who she's been hanging out with. I don't want to be an annoying brother, but it wouldn't hurt to keep an eye on her.

Mom walks in with a whole roasted chicken that looks delicious, and before I even have a chance to, Emilia jumps up to help her. The two of them carry in dish after dish, and I stare at the table in surprise. Mom has clearly outdone herself — she's prepared us a whole feast.

I glance up at Emilia and grin to myself as I grab my phone. I open up my app and increase the vibrations . She jumps and looks at me with wide eyes, shaking her head subtly. I grin up at her, tempted to increase it even further, but I want to keep her at the edge, not push her over it. Not at dinner, at least.

My phone buzzes and I glance at it in surprise, only to smile when I realize it's Emilia.

Minx: *Turn it off, I'm dying*

Carter: *But I like seeing you all hot and bothered*

Minx: *Either make me come right now, or turn it off. I'll make you pay for this babe.*

She glares at me and I try my best not to smile. I increase the pace slightly every few minutes, and the way she's looking at me has *me* at the edge.

"Food's great, but you're barely eating, Emilia," I say. She bites down on her lip and slowly raises her fork. She glares at me as best as she can, but her flushed cheeks destroy the image she's trying to convey.

My phone buzzes, and I glance at it.

Minx: *I want you. Now.*

Mom rises to clear the table while Dad shows John a bottle of whiskey that I'm sure they're about to sample. I want to help Mom and do the dishes, but I'm scared my girlfriend might actually kill me if I make her wait any longer. I bet Emilia and I can sneak away for a few minutes.

Carter: *Meet me in my bedroom? I'll sneak out now. Follow me in 2 mins.*

Emilia grins at her phone and I smile as I stealthily leave the room, praying no one will notice.

My heart is racing and I'm rock hard by the time I enter my bedroom. I grab my phone and switch off Emilia's device seconds before she walks through the door. She glares at me and pushes against my chest before pulling my head down toward her. I smile against her lips and kiss her. I lift her onto my desk and Emilia undoes the button on my jeans with practiced ease. She yanks them and my boxers down in one go before grabbing my dick with impatience.

I chuckle and push her underwear aside. The device I pushed into her slips out easily — she's that wet. It drops onto my desk and she pulls me closer.

"I love you Carter, but if you don't fuck me right now, I think I might murder you."

I laugh and push into her slowly, making her wait another few seconds. Emilia's eyes fall closed when I'm all the way inside her and her muscles spasm around my dick, gripping me tightly.

"One thrust was all it took, huh, baby?" I tease. She glares at me and wraps her legs around me as the last few tremors run down her spine. Emilia grins and pushes against my chest. I step away in confusion and she laughs as she fixes her underwear.

"Baby, *no*. Minx, you can't do this to me," I murmur. Emilia shrugs and glances at my erection with satisfaction.

"You left me hanging all night. Payback's a bitch," she says as she hops off my desk. I look at her open-mouthed and in total disbelief. Emilia merely winks at me and walks out the door.

I'm a fool for messing with my girl... I should've remembered who I'm dealing with. My girlfriend is *Emilia Parker*, after all.

CHAPTER 35

arter

Emilia has been eyeing me from her window all morning now. I'm sure she thinks she's being subtle, but I know her too well. I always wondered how she times her pranks so well. Turns out she just waits until she sees me walk into the shower. Can't believe it took me this long to figure that out. How much mayhem could I have prevented if I'd known that a few years ago? I grin to myself and shake my head. Like I actually would've stopped her.

I walk into the bathroom and leave the door half open as I step into the shower. Sure enough, just a couple of minutes later, Emilia sneaks into my room. I watch her from the corner of my eye and try my best to act like I haven't noticed her. She pauses by the doorway, where I'm sure she thinks I won't notice her, and ogles me shamelessly. I'm tempted to ask her to join me, but I also kinda want to figure out what she's up to. She hesitates, as though she struggles to drag her eyes away from me, and eventually moves away.

I keep the shower running as I step out and dry myself off as quickly as I can before sneaking out of the room. Emilia is making my bed as I walk into my bedroom, so she definitely fucked with it somehow.

I walk up to her as quietly as I can, the sound of the shower masking my footsteps. When I'm within reach, I grab her from behind and pull her flush against me, her back against my chest. She jumps and looks at me with wide eyes.

"Oh shit," she whispers.

I smile at her and drop my lips to her neck. "Tell me what you did, Minx. I guess leaving me hanging last night wasn't bad enough?"

She grins evilly and I know whatever she did is going to be good. "Please, tell me it isn't the cockroaches again. No matter how many times you pull that one, I won't ever get used to it. You'll give me a heart attack, baby. Do you want to give your boyfriend a heart attack? No, right?"

She leans into me and giggles. "It's not the cockroaches, Carter," she murmurs. I exhale in relief and run my hands over her body, pausing at her breasts.

"Are you ready to forgive me for the vibrating thing last night?" I ask cautiously. I wouldn't put it past her to get me all worked up again this morning, only to make me suffer for the rest of the day. Emilia turns in my arms and nods. She rises to her tiptoes and presses her lips against mine. I kiss her deeply and slowly, wanting all of her.

"Missed you, baby," I whisper.

Emilia smiles against my lips. "You saw me last night," she murmurs.

I sigh and drop my lips back against hers. "It's not enough. I want you with me all the time."

"Me too," she whispers. Emilia deepens our kiss before pulling back, both of us panting. "Let's do it again when we're on a date... *the egg thing*. Just not with family around."

I look at her with wide eyes and grin. I *knew* she loved it. "I can just imagine you sitting in a movie theatre, popcorn in your lap and your thighs quivering. Hmm, I wonder how many times I can make you come during one movie?"

Emilia smiles and looks at me admonishingly, but I know she'd enjoy the hell out of that. I can't wait to give it a try.

I lift her into my arms and move to put her down on my bed, but she clings to me with all her might and shakes her head. "No, don't," she says, her voice high pitched. I look at her through narrowed eyes and then move my gaze to my bed.

"Minx, what did you do?"

She grimaces and looks up at me apologetically. "Itching powder... it's only a super mild one, but it'll still be annoying. I definitely don't want that up my butt."

I shake my head and place her down on my desk instead. "It's my own fault for dating a petty evil little genius."

Emilia pushes against my chest and glares at me. "Who are you calling petty," she says.

I burst out laughing and peck her lips. "I called you evil too, but it's the petty bit you take offense to?"

I lean in and kiss her. I'll never get enough of this girl. She moans against my lips and moves her hands over my body restlessly. "I'm not petty," she says, yanking off my towel.

I nod and tug at her dress. She raises her arms for me and I pull it off. "Yeah, you're not petty, baby," I say, placating her.

Emilia grins as her underwear comes off and pulls me closer. "You'll say anything when I'm naked."

I chuckle and shrug. I can't deny it, because she's right. I can't even remotely think straight when I'm touching her. My fingers find their way between Emilia's legs and her eyes fall closed. I get her right to the edge and then push into her. She moans into my ear as I enter her and tightens her legs around my hips. I lift her into my arms and thrust into her at an angle, slowly, , making sure I'm hitting all the right spots inside her. It's taken some time to figure out her body, but with time it's become much easier to make my girl come on my dick. Just a few carefully controlled thrusts, and she shatters around me. I put her back on my desk and accidentally knock over the glass of water I left on there last night. It shatters on the floor, but I barely notice it. "I'm so close, baby," I tell her. Emilia nods and rakes her nails over my scalp as she moves her body in sync with mine.

"Fuck yes, Emilia... fuck. I love you so fucking much," I whisper, right before coming hard. My entire body tingles and I'm pretty sure I'm seeing stars the entire time it takes to catch my breath. I drop my head to her shoulder and kiss her neck.

I've only just managed to calm my raging heart when my door swings open and a concerned Kate walks in. She freezes when she spots Emilia and me and gapes at us. We're both still naked, and I'm still deep inside Emilia.

"What the hell are you doing!" she yells.

I snap out of it and glare at her. "Get the fuck out, Kate. What the fuck?" I return.

Her eyes roam over my room, pausing on the clothes on the desk and the shattered glass and the water on the floor. I jump into action and grab my towel to cover myself and help Emilia into her dress.

Just as Kate turns around to leave, Mom comes rushing in. She takes one look at our disheveled states and Emilia's position on my desk and turns back around. "Kids," she says. "You've got some explaining to do."

Yeah, we fucking do. I wish I'd just told them the very second we got back. Hell, I should've just sucked it up and told them months ago. I'm sure Emilia and I will both pay for that now.

CHAPTER 36

milia

My heart is pounding as we walk down the stairs. This isn't how I wanted them to find out. I can't believe we got caught having sex. Carter grabs my hand when we reach the hallway and I turn toward him. It's not until he strokes my shoulders that I realize I'm trembling.

"It's okay, baby. They were going to find out one way or another. I admit this isn't ideal, but it is what it is. We'll deal with it, okay?"

I gulp and nod at him nervously. Carter looks so confident and unwavering, and I wish I could just borrow a bit of his grit. He leans in and brushes his nose against mine before grabbing my hand with a smile on his face.

"Come on," he says. We walk into the living room with our hands entwined. I clutch Carter's hand with all my might in an attempt to keep from panicking.

I can barely look at Kate and Helen. I'm proud of Carter and of our relationship, but right now, right in this moment... I'm ashamed as hell.

"Right, so…" Carter says. He tugs on my hand and I look up at him. He grins before looking at his mother and sister. "Emilia and I are dating."

I glance at Helen and I'm surprised to find that she doesn't really look mad like I thought she'd be. She looks a little surprised and scandalized, but the edges of her lips turn up into a reluctant smile.

Kate, on the other hand, looks furious. "*Dating?*" she repeats. Carter lets go of my hand and wraps his arm around my shoulder instead. "Yep," he says. Kate looks at me and I involuntarily shrink into Carter. She's looking at me like I'm the vilest thing she's ever seen.

"Emilia, tell me this is a joke," she says, her voice harsh and unyielding. "Tell me you guys are pranking us or something."

Carter's grip on my shoulder tightens and I inhale deeply before shaking my head. "It's not a joke, Kate. We're dating."

She leans back on the sofa and stares at me with so much malevolence that I can't help but shudder.

"How long?"

Carter sighs and starts to draw circles on my shoulder with his thumb — his attempt to calm me down a little. Usually that would've set me at ease, but right now it just makes me feel even more on edge. It makes me feel like we're provoking Kate unnecessarily.

"It's been a few months," Carter says, and Kate bursts out laughing. There's no humor in that laugh, though… only malice.

"Jesus, Emilia. You were fucking Carter and Mason at the same time?"

Carter and Helen both freeze, and it's my turn to soothe Carter. I look up at him and smile reassuringly before shaking my head.

"No," I tell Kate. "Mason and I have never been together. I said I was seeing someone, and you just assumed it was Mason.

I couldn't correct you and tell you it was Carter, so I kind of just let it go, and it all ended up spiraling out of control."

Kate looks at me with raised brows. "Couldn't correct me, or wouldn't? You've been lying to my face for months now. I've never asked anything of you, Emilia. The only thing I ever asked was that you stay away from Carter. What kind of friend are you? How could you betray me like that? How could you look me in the eye and lie to me for months?"

I'm filled with shame and heartbreak. I knew I'd be letting her down when I followed my heart, and I did it anyway. I knew she'd react like this, and I decided Carter was worth it. I still believe that with my heart and soul, yet every single word that comes out of her mouth makes me feel like I'm being cut a thousand times over.

Kate looks at Carter and grins at him. "If she's been lying to me, then she's probably been lying to you too. Loyalty clearly doesn't mean shit to her if she can go behind my back like that. How long until she does it to you? Can you really be sure that she hasn't been screwing Mason?"

Helen straightens and pins Kate down with an angry stare. "That's quite enough, Kate," she says, her voice soft. "I know you're angry, but don't say anything in the heat of the moment that you'll regret."

Helen looks at us and tips her head toward the door. "You two... just go upstairs for now. We'll talk later."

I hesitate, wanting to speak to Kate, wanting to explain myself, but Carter tugs on my arm and walks me out of the living room.

"Give her time," he says, sighing. He grabs my hand and pulls me up the stairs. Carter leads me into his room and lifts me into his arms as soon as the door closes behind us. He sits down in his desk chair and places me on his lap. It's not until I feel his thumb glide over my cheek that I realize I'm crying.

I look up at him as the first of my sobs escapes my lips. "She hates me," I whisper, my voice breaking. Carter inhales deeply and pulls me closer. I rest my head on his shoulder while his arms wrap around me.

"She doesn't hate you," he whispers. "She's just shocked and angry. We've been keeping this from her for so long now. Give her some time to calm down first, and then we'll try to talk to her, okay?"

I sniff loudly and Carter presses a kiss on top of my head. He rubs my back while I try my best to stop crying. "I'm sorry... I don't mean to cry. This must be so hard on you too," I murmur.

Carter smiles and presses another kiss to my hair. He leans back in his chair and repositions me so we're both comfortable. "No, I pretty much expected exactly that. I'm not hurt, baby. Just annoyed my little sister is being an asshole. She'll get over it, Minx."

"No, she won't. We should've told her months ago."

Carter sighs and presses a kiss to my temple. "And ruin the first few months of our relationship? Why would we want to add more strain when our relationship was still so new? Don't second guess yourself now, Minx. We did the right thing for us."

The door opens behind us quietly, and I jump off Carter's lap in surprise. Helen walks in, a concerned look on her face. I wipe my tears away and try to pull myself together, but I know she sees straight through me. Helen sighs and walks up to us. She cups my cheeks and wipes away the last few stray tears on my cheeks, a sad look in her eyes. She steps back and looks at the two of us, her lips slowly transforming into a smile. "So you two finally got together, huh? I always knew you'd find your way back to each other."

I look up in surprise and she chuckles. She pushes a few strands of my hair behind my ear gently and shakes her head. "You two have my blessing," she says. My eyes fall closed and I exhale in relief. I was terrified she'd be disappointed in us. I don't know what I would've done if she was.

"Kate will need some time, Emilia," she says, her voice gentle. I bite down on my lip and nod.

"What can I do? How do I make this better?"

Helen shakes her head. "You can't. You know what she's like, honey. She'll get over it eventually, but in the meantime she's going to feel betrayed and she'll lash out at the both of you. Just keep in mind that she's hurt, and that she didn't mean any of the things she just said. Have some patience, okay? Everything will fall into place."

Helen wraps her arms around me and I hug her back tightly, barely able to keep a new bout of tears at bay. I sniff and squeeze my eyes close, trying my best to stay in control of my emotions. Helen squeezes tightly and then pulls back. "Things will be okay, honey. Don't you worry."

I hope she's right.

CHAPTER 37

*E*milia

I glance at the mirror and grimace at my reflection. I've been crying all day and my eyes are puffy and red. The makeup I was wearing has turned into a horrible mess. I guess the way I look accurately reflects how I'm feeling. I sigh and try my best to clean up my face.

The sound of the front door closing snaps me out of my thoughts. Dad's home. Shit. I'll need to tell him about Carter too. I wasn't this nervous when I told him about Landon, and to be honest, he didn't seem to mind me dating so much. It'll probably be okay, but I'm nervous nonetheless.

My heart is beating loudly as I walk to the living room. Dad looks up when I walk in and freezes.

"What happened?" he asks, his tone concerned. "Did you cry? Who made you cry?"

I bite down on my lip and tip my head toward the sofa. "Dad, have a seat," I murmur, my voice barely above a whisper. "There's something I need to tell you."

His eyes widen, and he sits down on the sofa anxiously.

"You're worrying me, Emilia. What happened? Why have you been crying?"

I shake my head and smile at him. "It's nothing serious, I promise."

"Are you pregnant?"

I freeze and stare at my dad with wide eyes. "What the hell, dad? No. *No*. Oh my god. No."

I run a hand through my hair and shake my head. "Nothing like that, gosh. I... I'm dating someone."

Dad looks at me through narrowed eyes. "You're dating a boy? He made you cry?"

I bury my face in my hands and shake my head. "This is coming out all wrong."

I groan and stare up at the ceiling before looking at my dad. "No, Dad. It's Kate that made me cry. We had an argument... because I'm dating Carter."

Dad stares at me speechlessly. "Carter Clarke?"

I nod. It's not like we know another Carter.

"You're dating Carter?"

I nod again.

"No," Dad says.

I frown at him, tensing. "What?" I ask, confused by his intense response. Dad pauses as though he isn't even sure why he doesn't like the idea of Carter and me dating.

"You two... haven't you been friends for years? You two grew up together. Why would you date Carter? Besides, you only just started college. You shouldn't be dating anyone. You should be focusing on school."

I inhale deeply, feeling truly worn out. Kate's words are still grating on me, and Dad's response on top of it has me feeling like crying all over again.

"I don't get it, Dad. You didn't say much when I dated Landon. Yet when it's Carter you suddenly don't approve?"

Dad runs a hand through his hair and sighs. "It's not that.

It's just that Carter and you... I always thought you were as close as *siblings*. I've been trusting him to take care of you in LA, and now you're suddenly dating?"

Dad shakes his head and sighs again. "It was bound to happen, I guess. But you're only eighteen, honey. I don't know. I'm just surprised."

I nod, unsure how to reply to that. I inhale deeply and glance out the window, my eyes landing on the treehouse.

"Well, we're dating. I thought you should know."

Dad nods and tugs on his tie. I shake my head and smile at him. "I'm going for a walk, okay? I need some fresh air."

Dad nods eagerly, as though he can't wait to get out of this conversation, and the edges of my lips tip up in a reluctant smile. I'm trying my best not to take his response personally. I guess it's odd for him that I'm dating Carter, when he's seen us grow up together. When we were younger, we were notorious for our feud, so I shouldn't be surprised that most people can't imagine us ending up together. I guess my Dad is just one of those. He'll come around, though. There's no one Carter can't win over.

I'm absentminded as I walk through the yard. I wasn't even planning on going to the treehouse, but that's where I end up nonetheless. In the place where it all started. This is where I met Carter and where we eventually both lost our virginity. It's where he asked me to be his, all those years ago.

I place my palm against the handrail by the stairs and let my hand trail over it as I walk up . I go inside, expecting the treehouse to be empty, but instead I find Carter sitting on the floor. He looks up at me with a knowing smile and pats the pillow beside him.

"What are you doing here?" I ask.

Carter grins and pulls me over, positioning me in his lap. He wraps his arms around me and kisses my temple. "I had a feeling you'd end up here tonight, and I could do with some solitude myself."

He lies down and I reposition myself so that I'm a bit more comfortable, draping my leg over his and resting my head on his chest. We both lie there in silence for a few minutes, both of us lost in our own thoughts.

"I told my dad that I'm dating you. He was... surprised."

Carter tenses and buries a hand in my hair. "You should've told me. I can't believe I didn't think of it. I should've been with you when you told him."

I shake my head and press a kiss to his neck. "It's okay."

Carter runs his hand over my back soothingly and I snuggle in closer. He turns so we're both on our side and cups my cheek. He looks into my eyes, looking more vulnerable than I've ever seen him look before.

"I love you, Emilia. Promise me we'll get through this together. No matter what Kate or anyone else throws at us, promise me we're in this together."

I smile and press a quick kiss to his lips. "I love you too, Carter. I promise. I promise we're in this together. I'm fully aware that things won't be easy for a while, but when have things ever been easy for us? I'm not willing to give up. I let you go once, and I won't do it again. I love you too much. You're my better half, Carter. It sounds lame as hell, but I don't think I'll ever feel complete again without you."

Carter exhales in relief and kisses me so sweetly that my heart skips a beat. "Thank God," he whispers. I look into his eyes and smile. So long as we've got each other, we'll be just fine.

CHAPTER 38

arter

Emilia is on edge as I carry her luggage to my car. I know she's having second thoughts yet again, and I'm hoping she won't change her mind at the last second. I've had to convince her to come to the summer cabin about a thousand times now. She hasn't missed a trip in years, so why should she start now?

Kate glares at Emilia's luggage in dismay and walks to Dad's car, slamming the door. Emilia and Kate have barely spoken in two weeks now. No matter what Emilia tried, all that's been coming out of Kate's mouth has been pure venom. I haven't been spared either, but I don't care as much as Emilia does.

She stares at Dad's car with such a sad expression that I'm wondering if it might've been better if she and I both just stayed here. Dad and John walk up to us, and I stare at John with raised brows. Why the hell is he carrying luggage?

He grins at me and throws his bag at me. "Thought I'd finally join for once," he says. "Your Dad has been inviting me for years. Besides, heard you're taking two cars this year, anyway."

I blink at him in disbelief. He hasn't explicitly said that he doesn't like me, and until I started dating Emilia I never once felt like he didn't. Yet these days he's always popping up everywhere, unwanted. So long as he's home, there's not a chance of me seeing Emilia. I was hoping we could spend some nights together over the summer, but she doesn't want to come over thanks to Kate, and John has banned me from his house when he's not present. Since I'm planning on spending the rest of my life with Emilia, I don't really want to cross my future father-in-law by disobeying his rules. I haven't had much alone time with my Minx at all. I was really looking forward to finally sharing a room with her, but I have a feeling that won't happen now.

John walks over to the passenger side of the car and I freeze. I'd been planning on holding Emilia's hand while driving and singing dumb songs with her at the top of our lungs. Guess that's not happening either.

Emilia sees my crestfallen expression and bursts out laughing. She rises to her tiptoes and presses a quick, sly kiss to my lips. I grab her and pull her back, kissing her properly. She pulls back with a mischievous smile. "I miss you," I whisper. "You're right here, yet it feels like we've barely spent any time together."

She nods and grabs my hand. "I know, babe. Hopefully, we'll be able to spend some time together at the cabin."

I glance back at my car and grimace. "Not with your dad there, we won't."

Emilia chuckles and presses another kiss to my cheek. "We'll find a way," she whispers.

I'm tense as I get into the car. I want Emilia sitting next to me, not in the back. She winks at me from the mirror and I inhale deeply. I've played football games with thousands of spectators, yet now I'm suddenly nervous sitting here next to John — the same guy I've known almost all my life.

He fiddles with the music for the first couple of minutes,

touching every single button he can get his hands on. I have a feeling he's doing it to wind me up, but I honestly couldn't care less about the music.

"So, Carter," he says eventually. I tighten my grip on the steering wheel and glance at him. "What are you planning on doing after college? You going pro?"

I shake my head. "No, I don't think so. I obviously have high hopes, but realistically I know my chances aren't that high."

"So what are you going to do?"

I glance at him nervously. "I told you about the company Asher and I are building, right? I'll probably be doing that full-time. We're looking to end up in Silicon Valley."

John frowns. "I thought that was just a hobby of yours. You're actually planning on doing that full-time? What a waste of a degree. How many of those companies even succeed? Are you really willing to take on all that risk? What kind of stability will you have? How much debt will you end up with?"

I hear the questions he isn't asking. What kind of stability will I be able to give Emilia? It's a question I've been asking myself more and more often. I don't see my future as just mine anymore. Every vision of the future I have includes her.

"Asher and I are limiting the amount of personal debt we're taking on. We bought an apartment together that we've put up as collateral. I know the odds of us succeeding aren't as high as I'd like them to be, but we have something amazing. If we pull this off, the return will be unimaginable."

I glance at Emilia through the mirror, and she nods at me proudly. She's always believed in me, and I'm working as hard as I can to make sure I don't let her or myself down.

"How about just getting a job? A steady income. The market is tough as it is, why risk it when you've got a perfectly respectable degree?"

I nod. "I know. I do understand your concerns, but our business plan is solid. If I didn't follow through on this, I'd regret it for the rest of my life."

John stares at me and nods before looking away. I've never been the type to strive for someone's approval, but I want his. I want to make Emilia feel the way she makes me feel whenever I see her with my Mom.

John is quiet for the remainder of the journey, but I can tell he's gearing up to question me more. He probably just can't think of anything right now, but it'll come. Part of me can't help but wonder if freaking Landon got the same treatment.

I inhale deeply as I park the car. I feel like I'm going from the frying pan into the fire. John in the car and Kate at the cabin. I'm sure Emilia is feeling just as emotionally worn out as me. I wink at her as I lift our luggage out of the trunk and she smiles up at me sweetly.

"So," John says as we walk into the cabin, and my hackles are immediately raised. "I understand there are three bedrooms? One for you, one for Kate, and one for your parents?"

I nod warily. John tips his head to the two large sofas in the living room. "How about you give your bedroom to Emilia, and you and I can sleep on these sofas? Even a big guy like you will fit on one of these."

I close my eyes in defeat while Emilia jumps up. "Oh, no, Dad. You take Carter's room. He and I can sleep on the sofas. No problem."

John looks at us through narrowed eyes and shakes his head. "No way, kiddo," he says, before looking at me. "You and I will be sleeping on the sofas, *far away* from Emilia."

I look down in amusement. Message received, loud and clear. I nod at John and Emilia groans as though she wants to argue with him, but I place my hand on the small of her back and shake my head ever so slightly.

"Go on, you go upstairs. I'll be fine here."

Emilia looks into my eyes and I nod at her as reassuringly as I can. She glares at her dad and crosses her arms.

"Dad, you know we're not kids anymore, right?"

John shrugs. "You'll always be a kid in my eyes. Besides, you aren't even old enough to drink yet. How about we have this discussion again when you're actually old enough to enter a bar, kiddo?"

Emilia huffs and turns around, stomping up the stairs in annoyance. I smile to myself, wishing I had her guts. I'd have loved to try and convince John to let me share a room with her, but I'm too scared to be disrespectful.

I guess I'll have to try and sneak into my bedroom at some point...

CHAPTER 39

arter

Emilia is quiet as we hike through the woods, like we do every year. She keeps glancing at Kate with so much heartbreak in her eyes that I can feel my own heart breaking. I was hoping Kate would get over us dating sooner than later, but she hasn't. If anything, she's making it seem like ignoring Emilia is easy. I grab Emilia's hand and she looks up at me with sad eyes. I wish I could make things better, but I don't know how. I've tried talking to Kate, but there's no getting through to her.

Emilia entwines our fingers and holds onto me tightly. I raise our joint hands to my lips and kiss the back of her hand as we walk. This entire trip has been tense so far. Kate won't speak to Emilia, Mom is caught between the two of them, and John keeps throwing questions at me that I don't know how to answer. The only one that seems to be enjoying this trip is Dad.

I exhale when we reach the canoes by the water. I can't wait for this day to be over already.

"Kate," Emilia says, surprising us all. "Wanna go together?"

Kate glances at the canoe and then at Emilia before raising

her brows. "Like I'd get on a boat with a backstabber like you. What? Are you itching to throw me off or something?"

I sigh and shake my head at Kate. "What the hell is wrong with you, man? Me dating Emilia has nothing to do with you. Mind your own goddamn business and stop being so fucking selfish."

Hurt flashes through Kate's eyes and she turns to glare at Emilia. "I see you've turned my own brother against me. Good job, Emilia."

Emilia inhales deeply and looks up at the sky. Even I don't know how much more of this bullshit she can take. I don't want her to have to deal with this at all. Mom looks torn, as though she doesn't know what to do or say.

I grab Emilia's hand and pull her closer. "We're leaving," I tell my mother. She looks startled, but she doesn't stop us. Not even John tries to intervene this time. I pull Emilia along and start down the path we just came from. Usually we'd canoe around the lake and then back to the cabin, but even I don't want to be anywhere near Kate right now.

"She's a fucking nut job."

Emilia sighs and shakes her head. "She's just hurt."

I pause and turn to face her. "Minx, are you insane? Why the hell are you still standing up for her? She's not a fucking child. So what if we hid our relationship from her? It's none of her goddamn business."

Emilia shakes her head. "It's not that simple, Carter. She made me promise to never fall for you back when we were in high school. It's the only thing she ever asked of me, and I broke my word. She told me she and I would be done if I ever dated you, and I decided to do it, anyway. I'm not saying she isn't to blame at all, but I'm just as much to blame. I guess I didn't think she'd end a ten-year friendship, but I knew it was a risk. I thought being with you was worth that risk, and I'm paying for it now. It's shitty, but I'm not mad at her for the way she's acting. I broke her trust, Carter. I lied to her and misled her. I'm dating her *brother*; the one guy she didn't want me to pursue. I'd probably be mad too."

I run a hand through my hair, unsure how to feel. I understand what she's saying, but I still think Kate is being unreasonable. "I just want us to be happy, Emilia. I want us to be happy together, and I want those around us to be happy too. That can't be so much to ask."

I walk to the small makeshift pier by the lake and inhale deeply. Emilia wraps her arms around my waist and rises to her tiptoes. She kisses me and I deepen our kiss, needing more of her. I can't even remember the last time I got to have her completely to myself. Emilia pulls back and looks at me through narrowed eyes.

"Hey, do you remember when you crashed my first date?"

I glance at her and look away, annoyed at the mere thought of her with someone else.

"Fucking Tony," I mutter.

Emilia laughs, the sound making my heart skip a beat. "You're so petty," she says, pressing a kiss to my lips.

"You're mine. Even then, you were mine," I whisper, my hands closing around her waist possessively.

Emilia looks into my eyes and nods. "Yeah, I was. I've always been yours, Carter. And I always will be. I still remember, you know. Back then I was falling for you so hard... it terrified me. I wasn't sure if you felt the same and you were about to leave for college too."

I lean in and press another kiss to her lips while my hands slip underneath her t-shirt. "I was falling for you too, baby. Hell, by then I was already deeply in love with you. Why do you think I tried to give you a better first date?"

Emilia giggles and glances at the water beside us before looking at me with raised brows, a challenge in her eyes. "It was a phenomenal first date. It was so good, I think we should do it again."

I laugh and pull her t-shirt over her head, letting it drop to the ground. It'll take the others some time to get back. They're usually on the water for hours, and we're on private property, which means I get to have Emilia to myself for a few hours in complete privacy. She tugs on my t-shirt and I take it off, the rest of our clothes soon following.

"Come on," she says, pulling on my hand. Her eyes drop to my crotch and she giggles. I shrug. "Can't help it, Minx. Whenever you're naked, I automatically get hard."

She shakes her head and lowers herself into the water carefully. She sighs in delight as the water hits her body. She watches me as I enter the water, her eyes roaming over my body. She holds her hands out and I swim up to her. She doesn't hesitate to throw her arms around me and I lift her up just a little. She wraps her legs around me and I sigh in delight.

"You drove me crazy that night, you know. I wanted you so badly and the way you moved against me, fuck. I really wanted to slip inside you."

Emilia laughs and kisses my chin, and then my cheek, before finally kissing my lips. "I wanted it too, you know. I watched you all the time... through the window."

I laugh and trap her lower lip between my teeth. "I know," I whisper against her lips. "I put those shows on especially for you. Walking around half naked, jacking off with the curtains wide open. I was teasing you."

She grins and shakes her head. "I know that now, but back then? It was so hot, Carter. Damn."

I walk us to the posts underneath the pier and press her back against it. "I've wanted to fuck you here ever since that day. It's been almost four years, Minx."

Emilia chuckles and threads her hands through my hair. "I guess it's your lucky day, babe," she whispers, and I get even harder. Emilia kisses me and rubs her body against mine so that I almost slip into her every single time she moves.

"Baby, you'll drive me insane," I whisper. Emilia smiles smugly and I kiss her. Two can play this game. I tighten my grip on her ass and push against her the way I know she likes, and before long it's her that's panting.

"I love you," she whispers. "I want you, Carter."

Just hearing her say that has me close. I always knew sex with Emilia would be incredible, but I underestimated how good it'd be. Just having this connection with her is insane. I look into her eyes as I slip into her and her mouth falls open, a small moan escaping her lips. "You're so fucking tight around me, Emilia."

She tilts her hips and tightens her legs around me, taking me in even deeper. "I love this," she murmurs. I lower my lips to hers and thrust into her slowly, taking my time with her. Emilia's hands roam all over my body, her nails raking over my back desperately. "More," she whispers. I love it when she's this turned on and demanding. I suck down on her lower lip and fuck her harder, silencing all her moans with a kiss. We're both frantic, wanting more of each other, more of how amazing this feels after a couple of really shitty weeks. It doesn't take us long to lose control and the second I feel her muscles tighten around me, I come right along with her.

"I love you," I whisper, dazed. Emilia smiles and rests her head on my shoulder, both of us panting.

She leans back against the wooden post; her legs still wrapped around me and the two of us still intimately connected. "This is what I wanted that night," she murmurs.

I kiss her gently and shake my head. "I'm glad we didn't," I whisper. "We were both virgins, baby. It would've been impossible, and it would've hurt. It's much better this way."

Emilia nods and looks up at me like I'm the only thing she can see. She makes me feel so fucking loved.

"Would you still have done it if you'd known the fallout would be this bad? Would you still choose to be with me?" I ask.

Emilia smiles with so much love in her eyes she doesn't even need to give me an answer. "Yes," she says. "A thousand times over, Carter. You're worth every risk. This is worth everything."

I drop my forehead against hers. Just a few hours together makes me forget about all the shit we've been through in the last couple of weeks.

"I'm going to marry you someday," I whisper.

Emilia smiles and tilts her head to kiss me. "I know," she whispers against my lips.

I look into her eyes and I just know she is it for me. "Move in with me."

Emilia freezes and stares at me with wide eyes. "What?"

"I'm serious, Emilia. I don't want to be without you. I'm going to get so busy with the new season. I'll have to leave soon for summer training, and I can't imagine coming home after a long day and not seeing you. I want to spend every free second with you. I want to wake up with you and go to bed with you. I want you to be the first thing I see when I wake up and I want to kiss you goodnight every single night. Besides, you're meant to be rooming with Kate, do you really want that?"

Emilia looks at me, completely shell-shocked, and I can't help but chuckle. "Just think about it, baby," I whisper before pressing a lingering kiss to her forehead. There's nothing I want more than living with Emilia, but ultimately the choice will be hers.

CHAPTER 40

milia

All I've been able to think about for the last week is Carter's question. I can't believe he actually wants me to move in with him. Even crazier is that I can't think of many reasons to say no. I want nothing more than to spend more time with him, especially once he starts to get busier with football. I'm terrified of pushing Kate even further away, though. I doubt she'll accept us moving in together, and I don't want to make things worse. Even if things between me and her never get better, I don't want to be responsible for ruining Carter's relationship with his sister.

I pause in front of Kate's bedroom door. She's been in her room since we got back from the cabin, and I admittedly went out of my way to avoid her when I should've tried harder to make things up to her. I hesitate before knocking. I'm not surprised when she doesn't reply and open her door, my hands trembling.

"Kate?" I murmur. She's sitting on her bed with her laptop on her lap and glares up at me.

"Get out."

She slams her laptop closed and crosses her arms. My heart is beating loudly and I'm oddly scared. I don't know what to do or say. This helplessness is killing me.

"I'm sorry," I tell her for the millionth time. Kate rolls her eyes and looks away as though she can't even stand to look at me. "I never meant to hurt you, Kate. I definitely never meant to break my promise. None of this was intentional. Carter and I... it just happened."

Kate looks at me and frowns. "Are you seriously standing there and telling me the two of you getting into a relationship *just happened*, like it wasn't a conscious choice you made?"

She huffs and I bite down on my lip, unsure what to say. She's right, I did choose to be with Carter, and I did it knowing it would hurt her.

"Did lying to me just happen too? Was it fun for the two of you to sneak around, leaving me clueless? You've been going behind my back for months now, Emilia. *Months*. You're supposed to be my best friend, but you've been lying to my face this whole time."

I shake my head. "I never meant to, Kate. Of course I didn't mean to do any of that. Carter and I just wanted to be sure our relationship would last before telling you about it."

Kate laughs and rolls her eyes. "What, so it was all for my sake? You lied to me and broke your promise for *my* sake?"

She looks away, disgusted. I don't even know how to defend myself, because she isn't wrong. I did do all of those things, but at the time I genuinely thought I was doing the right thing.

"Why, Emilia? Why did it have to be Carter? I've always welcomed you with open arms. When the kids at school used to make fun of you for not having a mother, I defended you. Every Mother's Day I made sure you'd join me to buy a gift for my mom, so you wouldn't miss yours so much. When your dad was too busy to teach you how to drive, I convinced my own dad to teach you instead. I've always shared everything with you. I've invited you on every trip and we've celebrated every holiday together. Even when I was sick, I'd always make sure Carter would take you to school or pick you up. And this is how you repay me? I asked one thing of you, Emilia. Just this one thing. All I asked was that you don't go after my brother."

I look down at my feet, my heart breaking. "Kate, I tried. I swear I did. I never meant to fall in love with Carter. I fought the feelings I had for longer than you can imagine. Falling for him wasn't a conscious choice. I tried to get over him for months, *years* even. I've been so scared to let you down or to hurt you, but not being with Carter was tearing me apart. We're both so much happier together. I know you're worried us dating might change things or that we might break up and ruin everything, but we won't. I promise you, nothing like that will happen."

Kate shakes her head and inhales deeply before looking up at me. "I want nothing to do with you, Emilia. I don't trust you. You're nothing but a leech — hanging onto me and sucking all the happiness out of my life. You won't stop until all I've got is yours. You've already won over my parents, and now Carter. You play the innocent role so well that you had me fooled for years. But I see you for what you are now. You're nothing but a sad girl wishing for someone else's life. I'm done with you. I've already put in a request with USC to change roommates. I never want to see you again."

I inhale sharply, my heart clenching. I swallow hard and will myself to say something, to do something... but I can't. I can't speak another word without bursting into tears. I take a step back before turning away, a tear running down my cheek.

"Fine. I understand," I murmur. I inhale deeply and walk out of Kate's room. I'm surprised to find Carter standing in the hallway, a worried expression on his face. Did he see me walk into Kate's room?

He opens his arms and I walk up to him. He closes his arms around me and hugs me. "It'll be okay," he murmurs. "Give it time, baby. Everything is going to be okay."

I shake my head and clutch him tighter. This time it won't be okay. This time things won't work out. But if being with Carter is costing me my friendship with Kate, then I might as well not hold back. Nothing I do or say will make her forgive me.

"I'll move in with you. If you meant it, then I'll move in with you. Kate already put a request in to change roommates, so we don't have to if you don't want to."

Carter pulls away and looks at me excitedly. "Of course I meant it," he says, his eyes twinkling with affection. He leans in and presses a chaste kiss on my lips. "I'd love nothing more, Minx. I'm so ready for us to do this right. I want it all with you."

I nod happily and rise to my tiptoes to kiss his cheek. "My scholarship pays for room and board costs, so I can even pay rent."

Carter threads his hands through my hair and shakes his head. "Let's save that money for our future and for emergencies. I've got rent covered."

I nod at Carter, my heart soaring. Our future together... I love the sound of that. "Are you sure Asher will be okay with it?"

Carter smiles at me endearingly and nods. "I wouldn't have asked you if he didn't agree. He owns the apartment as much as I do, and he's fine with it. He may have suggested he'd like some home-cooked meals, though..."

I chuckle and hug him tightly. "I'll go back with you. When you leave for summer training, I'll go back with you. I don't want to be here without you."

Carter nods and presses a kiss on top of my head. "I'd love that, Minx."

CHAPTER 41

arter

I'm giddy with excitement as Emilia and I walk into my apartment. *Our* apartment, now. Usually I'm tired and cranky from the trip, but today I'm buzzing. Emilia seems nervous as I put her luggage down.

"We'll have the place to ourselves for a few weeks. Asher went home to see his parents and he won't come back until the new term starts."

I grab her hand and pull her closer. She smiles at me, but the smile doesn't reach her eyes. When is the last time I saw her smile? I sigh and wrap my arms around her, hugging her tightly. She's lost weight and she's got bags underneath her eyes that she never used to have. I'm worried about her. Worried that I did this to her. To us. That I won't be able to make it better. I hope I'll be enough for her. That I can make up for what she's lost because of me. I just want Emilia to be happy.

I grab her hand and pull her along. "So this is *our* bedroom now," I murmur, unable to hide my smile. Emilia looks up at me and grins. A real grin, this time. She looks around in wonder and slowly but surely, the light in her eyes returns.

"Ours, huh?" she says.

I laugh happily, unable to contain my excitement. My heart is overflowing with happiness, and I want to make her feel the same. "Is there anything you want to change?"

Emilia looks around and shakes her head. "Not really. Can we add some of my candles and maybe we could use my bedsheets? It'd add a little bit of color."

I move to stand behind her and wrap my arms around her. "Do whatever you want, baby. This room is as much yours as it is mine from now on." She turns to look at me with just a hint of insecurity in her eyes. "I want you to feel at home here, Minx. I'm serious when I say it's your place too."

She bites down on her lip and looks at me with wide eyes. "And you're sure Asher is okay with it?"

I nod. "You'll be sharing a room with me, so it's not like he's losing out on any space. Besides, you were already here often, anyway. Not that much has changed. He seems pretty excited at the idea of having some of your food, though. He may have mentioned it half a dozen times. I still eat most of my meals with our nutritionist and my team, but since Asher stopped playing he's been on his own food-wise, and he can cook about as well as I can. All he eats these days is canteen food and cup noodles. You don't have to if you don't want to, but I think he'd really appreciate it if sometimes you'd cook for him too? I don't know, it's up to you."

Emilia smiles and nods happily. "I have to cook for myself anyway, so it's not even like I'd be going out of my way at all."

I nod and press a kiss to her cheek. "Thank you, baby. He's had a pretty rough time recently. Things haven't been great for him since he got injured and had to stop playing. The shit with Kate hasn't helped either, though he refuses to tell me what exactly happened. I think she cheated on him or something. I really don't know."

Emilia stiffens in my arms and stares at me with wide, panicked eyes. "You knew?" she whispers. I grin and kiss her forehead. "Minx, Asher and I live together. Besides, remember when I sneaked into my bedroom that night you and Kate stayed over? Kate was obviously in Asher's room."

She blinks and then blushes, as though she can't believe she missed that. She groans and drops her head to my chest. "I'm so stupid... how could I not have realized that? I mean, I was pretty sure you knew, but I wasn't a hundred percent certain."

I laugh and shake my head as I start to unpack. "I guess I did distract you *thoroughly* that night, huh?"

She blushes and pushes against my arm before wheeling her suitcase into the bedroom. It's a little silly, I guess, but I'm pretty happy to see her things next to mine.

"Here," I murmur, pointing at my wardrobe. "You can have half. I think we have space for another wardrobe if this one isn't big enough."

Emilia shakes her head and bites down on her lip, her cheeks rosy. I think us moving in together is finally sinking in, because her eyes sparkle with the same excitement I'm feeling. We unpack together, and slowly but surely, my bedroom starts to look more like *ours*. I never cared much for this kind of stuff, but Emilia's cute little candles and decorations definitely make the room look nicer. By the time we're all done, we're both exhausted. My stomach grumbles loudly and Emilia chuckles. She grabs my hand and pulls me toward the kitchen.

"Your mom gave us food for at least a week or so."

I gasp happily and make a run for the fridge, making Emilia laugh. "Shit, Minx. How could I have forgotten? Mom's food, yes!"

She giggles and hops onto the counter while I warm up the food. I push her legs apart and stand between them. She smiles at me and closes her legs around my hips, pulling me in closer. She wraps her arms around my neck and pulls me in for a kiss. I kiss her gently, taking my time with her. I kiss her until we're both breathless and rest my forehead against hers.

"I love this. I love you. It feels like it's been forever since we've been alone together. Since we've had a moment of true peace."

Emilia sighs and buries her face in my neck. "I know. I'm sorry," she whispers.

I pull back to look at her, my brows furrowed. "It's not your fault, Minx. None of this is your fault. This is a shit situation to be in, but life isn't perfect. We're in this together, remember?"

She nods, but she stares into the distance as though she's tortured by a memory I don't know about. I bet Kate said some shit to her that's still hurting. Emilia tries her best to smile at me and hops off the counter. She walks away and starts to set the table. I sigh and open one of my cupboards, only to pause and stare at it in amusement. All of my jars still have googly eyes on them. I chuckle to myself and turn to look at Emilia, a huge smile on my face. I love her to bits, and I know she loves me just as much. Things won't be easy for a while, but there's nothing she and I can't get through. I know her heart is broken, but I'll mend it.

CHAPTER 42

$\mathcal{E}$milia

Carter grabs my hand and pulls me closer with a huge smile on his face. I grin up at him and rise to my tiptoes to kiss him. Shouts and hoots erupt around us and I pull away shyly, reminded that we're standing in the kitchen at someone's house party.

Carter has been so over the top with our relationship — he's always introducing me as his girlfriend to every single person we come across, and he's always touching me one way or another. If he isn't holding my hand, then he's got his arm wrapped around my waist. He's doing it even more since the new term started, and I secretly love it. I've waited years to call him mine publicly, and I'm glad he's as excited about it as I am.

The last couple of weeks have been amazing. It's just been us and a mostly empty campus. I've taken the time to explore LA properly while Carter was at football training, and we've had dinner together every single night, though he always brought home his own food on strict orders from his coach. It's almost felt like a much-needed holiday. Some days it's hard to believe that this is our life now. I thought for sure that we'd struggle to adjust to living together, but that hasn't been the case at all. It's been amazing seeing each other at night after a long day, especially now that classes have started again. If anything, both of us are a little disappointed Asher is back now, and the apartment isn't just ours anymore.

"Can't believe it took you two this long to admit that you're dating officially. We all totally knew."

I turn around to find Mason walking toward us with Lisa in tow, huge grins on both of their faces. Mason walks up to me and pulls me away from Carter. "Man, can't believe I lost my chance," he says jokingly. Carter looks at him through narrowed eyes and Lisa slaps his arm.

I chuckle and move back toward Carter. He pulls me flush against him, my back against his chest and his arms wrapped around me. "You never stood a chance," Carter says, and I nod in agreement.

Lisa shakes her head and smiles at me. "I can't believe he's that cheesy and clingy," she tells me. I blush and look away. I'm relieved to find that she genuinely looks happy to see us together. Part of me still had some doubts that I struggled to put to rest.

"You should see them at home. They're so irritatingly cute together," Asher says. "More often than not they just forget I'm there, and they do this weird thing where they communicate without talking, or something, it's just half sentences. I can't figure out how they understand each other at all. So weird. It's a good thing Emilia is so nice to me, or I'd have so many more complaints. Feels like I have this weird mixture of a mother and sister now."

Mason laughs and claps Asher on the back sympathetically. Asher glances at us and shakes his head, but I know he's really happy for us.

Carter tenses behind me and I turn to look at him, only to

come eye to eye with Kate. We haven't run into each other since classes started and neither Carter nor I have tried to get in touch with her for a while. We both thought it'd be best if we gave her some time, but it's been weeks now. She glances at us, huffs, and then turns to leave. I straighten and move to follow her, but Carter grabs my hand and shakes his head.

"Let me just talk to her," I say. "It's been a couple of weeks, maybe she's calmed down a little." I can tell from Carter's expression that he doesn't believe she has at all.

"Baby, I don't want you to get hurt any further," he murmurs, his voice soft. I rise to my tiptoes and press a kiss to his cheek before rushing after Kate.

"Kate!"

She stops and turns to look at me as I try to squeeze through the crowd. She looks away as though she doesn't even know me and continues walking.

"Kate," I shout, grabbing her hand as soon as I'm within reach. She shakes me off with force and looks at her hand in disgust, as though I'm some vile insect.

"Please, can we talk?"

She sighs and looks at me emotionlessly. Her eyes are red and I can't help but wonder if maybe she's as heartbroken as I am.

"What the hell do you want? I told you I want nothing to do with you, which part of that did you not get?"

I inhale deeply and look down at my feet before facing her again. "Kate, please. I'm sorry. I'm so sorry for hurting you. Please, won't you give me a chance to make it up to you? You've always been like a sister to me. I love you, Kate. You're my *family*."

She rolls her eyes and crosses her arms over her chest. "You should've thought of that before you seduced my brother."

I sigh and run a hand through my hair. "I don't get it. You were seeing Asher for such a long time. He's Carter's best friend, just like I'm yours. Surely you understand how it feels? I never set out to hurt you or break my promise. I was in love with Carter long before you ever even asked me to stay away from him, and I tried my best nonetheless. It was killing me inside, Kate. I've loved Carter for *years*. I don't expect you to like it, and I don't even expect you to forgive me so soon, but please... can't you try to be happy for me? Please, won't you give me a chance to earn your forgiveness? Please, Kate, don't shut me out."

Her eyes flash with anger, and she looks at me with raised brows. "Just because I dated Asher doesn't mean it's okay for you to date Carter. Just because I made a mistake doesn't mean you should be making the same one. You definitely shouldn't be throwing things I told you in confidence in my face."

I inhale deeply and shake my head. I can't figure out whether she's misunderstanding on purpose or if I'm just not making myself clear. "That's not what I'm trying to do at all. I'm just trying to make you understand. Surely you understand how it feels? Wasn't it the same with Asher — knowing better, but being unable to resist? This was never about you, Kate. I'm not trying to hurt you and I'm not trying to take anything from you. I truly love him."

She grits her teeth and looks away. "That's bullshit, Emilia. You could've had anyone you wanted, but you *chose* to go after Carter. Don't give me all this tortured bullshit. You knew full what you were doing and you did it, anyway. I've said it before and I'll say it again. If you date Carter, then we're done. Our friendship is over. Make your choice."

I stare at her in disbelief. "It's been over ten years, Kate. You'd throw away our friendship because I fell in love with Carter?"

She shrugs and turns to leave. I inhale deeply and make up my mind. "Fine," I say, stopping her in her tracks. "If that's truly what you want, then that's how things will be. I won't ever give up on my relationship with Carter. I've chosen you over him before, and I have been doing that for years. I chose you over him even after you ditched me for Gabby, and I regretted it for years. I won't do it again. I love you, Kate... but this time I'm choosing my own happiness."

She laughs humorously and shakes her head. "Of course you do. You've always been a selfish bitch. I didn't even realize you've been going behind my back for years, you're just that good. I bet you thought you could have it all. That you could betray me and we'd all still be a happy family. Things won't work out for you, Emilia. You don't deserve happiness. Carter can do a lot better than you, and it won't take him long to realize it. When he finally leaves you, where will you be? I'll be counting down the days, Emilia. I'll be waiting until you're finally out of our lives forever. I bet I won't have to wait very long at all. After all, not even your own family loves you. How could Carter?"

She laughs and walks off while I try my best to keep from falling apart. Part of me knows she's right. I *did* betray her, I *did* lie to her, and Carter *can* do better.

CHAPTER 43

milia

"Come on," Asher says, pulling Mason and me along. I giggle and sway a little as we make our way into the stadium. We've been tailgating before the game, and I'm already buzzing pleasantly. Mason wraps his arm around my shoulders and maneuvers us through the crowd. Carter managed to get us seats on the lower level and I couldn't be more excited.

"You look cute," Mason says, pointing at my clothes. I'm wearing Carter's jersey with jean shorts, and I'm giddy as hell. "The paint is a nice touch too," he says.

I glance down at my outfit and grin. "It's the first game of the season. Scratch that, it's the first college football game I've ever attended, and *my boyfriend* is playing. Of course I went all out! Don't worry, I brought face paint for you too."

Asher and Mason both groan and look at each other. "Of course she did," Mason says to Asher. I forced them both into Carter's jersey too. By the time I'm done with them the three of us will look all matching and supportive as hell.

Mason is antsy when we sit down and almost jumps out of

his seat when the cheering squad walks onto the field. His eyes are on Lisa and I don't think anything could've distracted him. His eyes are glued to her the entire time and I can't help but smile to myself. He's obviously in love with her... she's the only one who doesn't realize it. "You know she wants you too, right?"

Mason tears his attention away from her for a single second and shakes his head. "No, she doesn't. It's my brother she wants. It's him she sees when she looks at me."

I punch his arm and shake my head. "You're a fool. *You're* all she sees. You just don't want to acknowledge it."

He smiles sadly and takes a big swig of his beer. He leans back in his seat and stares at Lisa, and my heart breaks right along with his. I don't understand why they won't reach for the happiness they both want.

"He won't listen," Asher murmurs into my ear. "I'm not sure what the story is there, but I'm pretty sure it's quite complicated."

I nod and sigh. From what he's told me, it does sound like there's a lot standing between them. It's so heartbreaking to see how much they clearly love each other, yet they stay away.

"Talk about complicated," Asher murmurs. He tips his head toward the row in front of us and I look over to find Kate sitting next to Jake. He's got his arm wrapped around her and his head close to hers.

They must feel our gazes on them, because they both look up. I'm not at all surprised to find that Jake's eyes are bloodshot. He's probably high on something. "I don't understand what she sees in him," I murmur.

Asher laughs humorously. "He's *fun*, unlike me."

I rest my head on his shoulder and sigh. "Her loss."

The three of us watch the game and ignore Kate and Jake as best as we can. It isn't hard to do in the excitement of the game. The energy is amazing, and I can't believe I missed out on this last year. Carter is even more magnificent on the field than he was in high school. There's definitely a huge difference between the way he played then and the way he plays now. The endless training he does has clearly made a huge difference. I can totally see him going pro.

"Come on," Asher says as soon as the game ends in a win for us. He pulls me along and maneuvers us through the crowd before I even have a chance to ask him where we're going. Before I know it, we're standing on the field and Carter is running up to us. He throws his helmet on the floor and lifts me into his arms. "Emilia," he whispers, breathing hard. I grin and press a kiss to his lips, despite the sweaty mess.

"You were amazing," I say. Carter grins and twirls me around happily. He sets me down and claps Asher on the back before looking behind him. Asher and I turn to find Kate walking onto the field, her hand in Jake's. Asher grits his teeth and Carter tries his best to keep his expression neutral, but it's obvious to me that he isn't happy to see her with Jake.

"You were amazing, bro," she says, smiling. He grins and hugs her, ignoring Jake altogether. My heart clenches painfully. I'm glad Carter and Kate are doing okay now. She was just as mad at him as she was at me, but she ended up forgiving him. I just wish she'd give me a chance too. I miss her like crazy, even though I'm doing my best to act like I don't.

"Thanks, baby sis," he says. "We're gonna have some drinks after. You wanna come?"

Kate hesitates and then nods, much to my surprise. Carter is clearly surprised that she said yes too, but he hides it much better than I did. I feel almost invisible as we make our way to the house party we agreed to meet at. Kate is laughing with Jake and Carter, while I just feel oddly left out. Carter is visibly torn between us, and I hate that. I hate everything about this. I miss Kate. I miss the way we used to be. Part of me thought that things would still be perfect between us all. That Kate would actually become even more of a sister instead of a friend once

Carter and I got together, and that she'd be happy for us. I didn't realize how many hopes I had until everything fell apart. I didn't realize I'd been counting on her eventually forgiving me. What if she doesn't? How will that affect Carter and me?

"You okay, baby?" Carter murmurs as he wraps his arm around me.

I look up at him and try my best to smile. "Yes, of course," I whisper. Kate glances at us and finishes her drink, her eyes flashing with annoyance. I watch as she sneaks off to the bathrooms with Jake, only to return minutes later, giddy and smiling. I should be glad to see her so happy, but something just doesn't feel right. I always feel like the happiness she portrays around Jake isn't genuine — like she's just tipsy and buzzing. Her smile drops when her eyes meet mine, and she clenches her jaw before looking away.

Carter pulls me closer and presses his lips against my temple. "Let's go home, Minx. It's been such a long day for me. All I want is to lie down on the sofa with you and hold you in my arms."

I turn in his arms and smile up at him. "I'd love nothing more," I whisper right before pressing my lips against his.

CHAPTER 44

arter

I've been running around all day, trying to get everything in place for the surprise I'm planning for Emilia. It's taken some time to get her to smile properly again. It almost feels like our happiness is cast in shadows. I can tell Emilia is still sad, even though she tries so hard to hide it from me.

I turn the fairy lights on and look around the living room, pleased. I wasn't really sure what to do, but I thought she might enjoy a little throwback of sorts. A reminder of happier times, of when we started to fall in love with each other, all those years ago.

I've transformed the living room to be as close to what I made our spot in the woods look like on her sixteenth birthday. There are pillows all over the floor, and I managed to fish out the old little cardboard projector I used that day. Instead of using a white sheet like we did that night, we'll be using an empty white wall instead. I check my watch and glance around the room. I'm worried she won't like it, or that she might think it's not original enough. Other than the fairy lights and the pillows, I've got countless balloons filling up the ceiling. I got us a nice bottle of champagne too, and I got desserts from her favorite bakery. I hope it's enough. I hope she'll be happy.

I'm tense as Emilia unlocks the door. She walks in and freezes. She stares at me open-mouthed and I grin. "Surprise, baby," I murmur.

She smiles from ear to ear and runs up to me, jumping into my arms. "Oh my gosh, Carter. This is amazing. Is this all for me?"

I twirl her around in my arms before setting her down on the floor, my arms wrapped around her. I lean in and kiss her, taking my time. I drop my forehead against hers and sigh.

"We've both been so busy recently, we haven't even had time to go on a date. I just wanted to do something nice for you."

She grins up at me happily, and my heart skips a beat. When is the last time I saw her looking this happy? I should've done this ages ago. I bury my hand in her hair and pull her close.

Emilia smiles and wraps her arms around my neck, her lips finding mine again. "I'll never get enough of you," I whisper. She giggles and pulls me down onto the pillows.

"It's just like my sixteenth birthday. Do you remember that?"

I nod and hold my arms open for her. I expected her to snuggle into me, but she pushes against my chest and straddles me. I blink in surprise and wrap my hands around her waist.

"I wanted you to be mine then... did you know? I was so in love with you then, Carter. I was just as in love with you then as I am now," she says.

I look up at my beautiful girlfriend and count my lucky stars. After everything we went through, we found our way back to each other.

"I guess the time wasn't right for us then," I murmur. Emilia nods and leans over me, her lips finding mine. I sigh happily as she kisses me.

"There's one thing I wanted that night that we didn't do," she whispers. I raise my brow, and Emilia grins wickedly.

"We didn't have sex that night. We should definitely recreate and improve that memory."

I laugh and turn us over so I'm on top of her. "Baby, we've got all night. Asher offered to spend the night with Mason so we could have the apartment to ourselves."

I lower my lips to hers and kiss her deeply, savoring her. Even when I've got her this close, it isn't enough. Emilia's grip around me tightens, as though she's feeling the same need that I am — that intense desire to be closer.

"I love you," I whisper. "I love you so much, Emilia. You're without a doubt the best thing that's ever happened to me."

She blushes and looks at me with such adoration, I know she feels the same way. "I love you too, Carter. You're my favorite person. You're my other half."

My heart skips a beat and I kiss her to hide the blush that's tinting my cheeks pink. The way she makes me feel... it's unreal.

Emilia looks up at me with her bright blue eyes and grins before tugging on my t-shirt. I laugh and take it off.

"I planned this entire cute ass date for you, but all you want is my body, huh? What happened to wining and dining your date?"

Emilia giggles and tugs at my jeans impatiently until she's got them off. She pushes against my chest and turns us over. I put my arms behind my head as she straddles me. I watch her with fascination as she slowly lifts her dress up and takes it off, teasing the hell out of me.

"I fucking adore you," I whisper.

Emilia grins and takes off her bra. I reach for her, my hands roaming over her body. "So fucking magnificent."

She shakes her head and giggles. "You're so extra."

I turn us over again and tug her underwear off, taking my time kissing every inch of her body. I pause on her inner thigh and look up at her. "I need a taste of you, baby," I murmur.

She looks at me in surprise, and I smile. I kiss her right between her legs and drag my tongue over her wetness. She moans loudly and I'm instantly even harder. Her skin is so smooth and slick and I love having another one of her firsts. I want her coming on my tongue, and it doesn't take me long to get her there. I've fantasized about going down on her, but this is way hotter than I expected. I'm throbbing by the time she comes.

"Need you, baby," I whisper.

Emilia nods. "Please, Carter. I want it," she says, panting. I grin and align myself before pushing in slowly. Emilia's eyes fall closed and the way she moans drives me insane. I fuck her slowly and steadily, wanting to enjoy every second of this with her. It's been so long since I've felt this close to her. Since we've completely lost ourselves in each other. I want this happiness to last.

"I love you," she whispers. She pulls me closer and grazes my neck with her teeth. Her lips are so close to my ear and every single one of her pants and moans gets me closer.

"I can't hold on," I murmur. Emilia nods and sucks down on my neck, marking me. I increase the pace and hold on to her tightly, thrusting into her hard. She moans louder, and I lose it. "Fuck yes, Emilia," I groan.

I collapse on top of her and kiss her neck over and over again. I take her into my arms and turn us over so she's lying on my chest. I press a kiss to Emilia's hair and she sighs happily. I want all our days to be like this.

I sigh and pull her up with me, grabbing the champagne. She smiles at me and grabs my t-shirt from the floor. She pulls my tee over her head and throws my boxers at me. The two of us snuggle up on the pillows on the floor, each of us a glass in hand.

"Here's to us," I say. "To the love we share and the life we're building. I love you, Emilia. I promise you I'll work hard to make you happy every single day for the rest of our lives."

Emilia clinks her glass against mine and looks into my eyes. "Me too, Carter. I count myself lucky every single day. I love you so much, babe. I promise I'll try to make each day happier than the last."

I wrap my arm around her shoulder and kiss her temple. My heart is overflowing with happiness. I can easily see myself spending the rest of my life with her, just like this.

I grin as she selects The Notebook on Netflix. She laughs and presses a kiss to my cheek.

"You know I don't even like this movie, right?" she says.

I laugh and shake my head. "Fuck, really? I hate it too."

Emilia shrugs and presses play. "Screw it," she says. "It's a tradition now."

I grin up at the screen and hold on to my girlfriend even tighter. I want to spend the rest of my life creating more traditions with her. I'm already looking forward to it.

CHAPTER 45

arter

Emilia keeps twisting and turning in bed, unable to sleep — and keeping me up too. I groan and pull her against me, spooning her. "Can't sleep again?"

She inhales deeply and nods. We've been happier than ever before, but Emilia isn't the same. Ever since Kate ended their friendship, Emilia has lost her spark. She doesn't eat well and doesn't sleep, and I recently noticed she keeps wanting to frequent places that Kate might be at. It's clear she's hoping seeing each other often will make Kate give in, eventually. It's not a bad theory, but I don't like seeing her so defeated every time Kate ignores her or sends her a dirty look. I don't want to see her hurting, and I hate there's nothing I can do to make things better.

Emilia's phone vibrates as it lights up the room. I nuzzle her neck when she reaches for it. "I don't know this number," she mumbles before picking up. I can't hear what's being said, but Emilia tenses in my arms, a small shudder running down her body.

"What's wrong?"

She's shaking by the time she ends the call and gets out of bed, her eyes wide. "We need to go," she says, her voice trembling. She fumbles around in the dark until she finds the light switch and I throw my arms over my eyes with a loud groan when the room is suddenly bathed in light.

"Babe, what the hell?"

Emilia rushes to get her clothes on and throws jeans and a t-shirt my way. "It was the hospital," she says. "I... they told me to come as soon as possible. I don't know what's going on. They just told me Kate was admitted and I need to come right now. I guess she never changed me as her ICE contact."

I frown at her, confused, and try my best to get dressed as quickly as possible. "Ice?"

Emilia glances at me, annoyed, and nods. "*In case of emergency*, Carter. Come on, we gotta go."

I swallow hard and follow Emilia out the door, my heart racing. Kate was admitted to the hospital? What the hell could've happened?

"Did the doctors say anything at all?"

Emilia is trembling and shakes her head. I try my best to remain calm as we drive to the hospital. Emilia is already freaking out — I can't panic, too. I'm trying not to worry until we know exactly what's going on.

By the time we walk into the hospital, Emilia has tears running down her face, her shoulders shaking. "I'm Emilia Parker," she tells the nurse at the front desk. "I got a call to come in. I'm Catherine Clarke's ICE contact."

The nurse looks up and smiles at Emilia before checking her computer. "Miss Clarke is on the eighth floor. Are you related?"

Emilia falls silent, so I nod in her stead. "I'm her brother," I tell the nurse. She nods at the two of us and directs us to go upstairs. My heart is racing as we get closer to her room. When we walk in, Kate is fast asleep in a hospital bed, an oxygen mask covering half her face.

I'm shaking as badly as Emilia by the time the doctor approaches us. "What happened to her?" I ask with more force than required.

He looks up at me, recognition flashing through his eyes. "Carter Clarke?" he says, surprised, before shaking his head and looking down at his clipboard. "I apologize. I attended one of your recent games with my son," he says, smiling tightly.

I nod and try my best to smile back, but I'm seconds from yanking the clipboard out of his hands.

"My sister?" I repeat. The doctor glances at Kate and inhales deeply, as though he's bracing himself. "Your sister overdosed, Mr. Clarke. We found an opioid in her system. Benzoyl-methylecgonine, to be precise."

I frown at the doctor, and he clears his throat, his expression tense. "It's cocaine, Mr. Clarke."

I shake my head in disbelief. "There's no way. Kate would never do that. My sister isn't like that."

The doctor glances at Kate and then back down at his paperwork. "She was very lucky she was admitted in time. She was mid-seizure when she was brought in. Based on the amount we found in her bloodstream, she has more than likely been using for quite some time. Her road to recovery won't be easy. She'll need all the support she can get."

"Who brought her in?"

Kate's doctor shakes his head. "The nurses might be able to tell you. For now, I suggest you focus on your sister. She'll be waking up soon, and I think it might help if you're there when she does."

I nod and sit down in the seat next to Kate's bed, Emilia by my side. She hasn't spoken a word since we got here. All she does is stare at Kate in disbelief and worry.

I grab her hand and lift it to my lips. "She'll be okay, Minx. The doctor said they got her here in time."

Emilia doesn't take her eyes off Kate as she nods, and I pull her closer. "You should call your parents," she says.

I inhale deeply and nod. "I know, but what am I supposed to say? How do I explain this? I mean... I never even suspected she might be using. Maybe weed or something, but coke? Did you ever suspect anything?"

Emilia shakes her head. "In the last few months we lived together, she'd been behaving a bit strange. She was coming back late and staying up all night and day with ease. Sometimes she was a bit short-tempered, but I didn't think too much about it. Come to think of it, a few times she lied about where she'd been, and she did stand me up at La Familia to spend time with Jake instead. At the time it all didn't seem to be connected, but now that I'm thinking about everything, maybe I should've been more concerned. I actually went to a party with her where Jake offered us drugs, and I freaked out. But she said she'd never taken him up on his offer, so I left it at that."

I'm filled with the same guilt that's reflected in Emilia's eyes. We both should've paid more attention to her. I should've done something about her spending time with Jake.

"Maybe... maybe if I'd still been living with her, this wouldn't have happened. If we hadn't gotten together then she wouldn't have started spending all her time with Jake, because she'd be with me instead. With us."

I rise to my feet and pull her into me, enveloping her in a tight hug. "No, Emilia. Would-haves and could-haves won't make a difference. She'll be okay, all right?" I say, even though part of me is also wondering if Emilia and me dating pushed Kate over the edge.

Kate stirs, and I pull away from Emilia to grab her hand. "Hey," I murmur. Kate blinks and pulls away her oxygen mask.

"What happened? Why am I here? My whole body hurts," she says, her voice raspy.

I tighten my grip on her hand and try my best to contain my anger as I push the oxygen mask back over her nose. "You overdosed, Kate. What the hell? Since when have you been using drugs? What the fuck?" I say, unintentionally snapping at her. I really wanted to be patient, but I can't.

Kate's eyes widen and she glances around the room, her eyes settling on Emilia. She narrows her eyes and pulls her oxygen mask down again. "What is *she* doing here?"

Emilia stiffens and smiles at me tightly. "I'll go get the doctor. I'll make the calls too. It's easier that way."

I nod at her in gratitude and turn my focus back to Kate as Emilia walks out the door. "Don't even try to deflect. What the fuck, Kate? Coke, really?"

She looks at me guiltily and then looks away. "I was just having some fun. And since when do you care, anyway? You haven't paid any attention to what I do for months. Why start now?"

I inhale deeply and try my best to stay calm. The doctor walks in and I sigh as I walk out the door, giving him a chance to examine her properly in private. Even now she's in the hospital, she won't acknowledge the impact of what happened to her. How the hell am I supposed to get through to her?

CHAPTER 46

arter

Kate has been on edge since she was discharged from the hospital. I've been refusing to let her out of my sight, and she's been trying everything she can to get away from me. She was okay the first two days, but she's starting to get cagey and frantic, and I have no doubt it's so she can get her hands on more drugs. It's been hard for me to acknowledge, but the doctor is right. The amount of drugs found in her system combined with her current behavior makes it obvious. My sister has been getting addicted to cocaine right underneath my nose, and both Emilia and I were none the wiser. I let this happen on my watch, but I'll be damned if I let it continue.

"Damn it, Carter. Are you never going to let me attend classes? You're being psychotic. I'm going to call the police if you don't let me leave," Kate threatens. She's sweating and her pupils are dilated, and I can't help but worry. She so anxious she seems like she might have a panic attack any second. The doctors warned me she'd be like this and that she needs to come in for outpatient detoxing, but she's been refusing, insisting that there's nothing wrong with her.

I grab my phone and hand it to her. "Call them. I'll call in an anonymous tip too. I'll just tell the police they might want to raid your dorm room because I suspect you're in possession of illegal drugs. What's it gonna be?"

Kate's grip tightens around my phone, and she glares at me. My heart sinks. I was bluffing, but it seems like she truly has a stash hidden away in her dorm room.

My phone buzzes, and Kate looks at it, her eyes narrowing. "Cute photo," she says, holding it up. My background photo is a selfie I took of Emilia and me days after we made our relationship official. Kate glares at it and reads my notifications, her expression falling. I grab my phone from her and glance at it.

"Mom and Dad are on their way," I tell Kate. Her eyes widen and she gulps, her anxiety increasing.

"What the hell? Why would you tell them?"

I inhale deeply and press down on the bridge of my nose. "Kate, you overdosed. You need *help*. Of course I called Mom and Dad."

She glances at me through narrowed eyes and crosses her arms. "Did *you* call them, or was it Emilia?"

I hesitate, and Kate grins. "Of course it was Emilia. That fucking bitch. I bet she's real happy this happened to me. Now she'll get to show Mom how much better she is once again."

I stare at my sister with wide eyes. "What the hell is your problem with Emilia? She rushed to the hospital the second she got the call and she's done everything for you since then. She cooks for you, she scheduled all your doctor's appointments, you're wearing *her* clothes right now and she's picking up Mom and Dad from the airport because I can't leave you alone. Why the hell are you so ungrateful?"

The front door opens, and Emilia walks in, followed by Mom and Dad. My parents are both a mess and Mom's eyes are red from the tears she undoubtedly shed. I can't help but be angry with Kate for causing so much heartache. For causing so much damage to herself, and then still having the gall to blame someone else.

Mom bursts into tears and wraps her arms around Kate tightly. Kate's expression wavers slightly and I breathe a sigh of relief. She looks a little bit guilty, and that's all I need. All I need from her is some acknowledgment that she did something wrong. I need her to take responsibility for her actions.

I glance up at Emilia to find her staring at her feet. She hasn't been herself lately. It's like she blames herself for what happened to Kate, when logically, neither one of us is to blame. I know all too well how she feels, though.

"Milly," Mom yells. "How could this have happened?"

Emilia walks up to my mother, unable to face her, and shakes her head. "I don't know," she whispers.

"You two were supposed to look after each other, weren't you? Why didn't you tell me something was up with Kate? I would've come and check up on her if I'd known."

I inhale deeply and walk up to Emilia, dropping my hand on her shoulder in solidarity. "Emilia and I didn't know, Mom. Of course we would've intervened if we'd known, but we didn't."

Mom glances at the two of us in accusation, and my hackles are raised. It's Kate she should be blaming, so why is her anger directed at us?

"You two didn't even tell me you started living together. Weren't you supposed to be roommates with Kate?" Mom asks Emilia.

Emilia tenses and bites down on her lip nervously before nodding. "I... Carter and I just thought we'd already shocked you enough. We thought it would be best if we kept this to ourselves."

Kate laughs. "More lies. What a surprise. I didn't even

realize you hadn't told Mom you two were living together. Don't you two talk every day?"

Emilia looks away in guilt. I know she's been purposely vague about us living together, hoping that things would calm down before we dropped another bomb on them. It seems like the two of us can't seem to get anything right. Every decision we make for ourselves keeps biting us in the ass.

"Maybe this wouldn't have happened if you two were still living together. If you two were still keeping an eye on each other," Mom says.

Emilia inhales deeply and nods. I tighten my grip on her and look my mother in the eye. "Emilia isn't responsible for Kate's behavior, and it's ridiculous that you make it seem like she should be. I know you're shocked, Mom. But you can't go around looking to place the blame elsewhere. We need to focus on how to help Kate get better."

Emilia grabs my hands and squeezes tightly. First Kate and now Mom... I can't imagine how she's feeling. Dad looks at us. He hasn't spoken a single word yet, but eventually he turns toward Kate and shakes his head.

"I'm disappointed in you."

Kate reels back in shock and stares at Dad with pain flashing through her eyes. Her eyes fill with tears and she looks down at her feet.

Dad turns to Mom and grits his teeth. "I'm disappointed in you too," he says. "Carter is right. We need to be focusing on how to help Kate get better — not on blaming someone else for Kate's actions. You expect too much from Emilia. She is *not* Kate's keeper. She has every right to live her own life. Do I wish she'd been there so she might have been able to keep Kate on the right path? Yes, of course. Do I expect it from her? Never."

Mom glances at Emilia in apology, but Emilia merely smiles tightly. I know she's blaming herself, but we'll need to look toward the future now. We need to focus on Kate's recovery.

CHAPTER 47

 arter

I'm exhausted by the time I park my car in front of my apartment. I'm emotionally drained and physically worn out. Coach benched me because I couldn't focus well enough and I can't even get myself to care. I've always loved being on the field, but not even that is helping me clear my mind. I'm worried about Kate, about Mom, and about Emilia. It's like every day I watch my family fall apart a little more, and there's nothing I can do about it.

The other day, I overheard Kate blaming Emilia for her own actions yet again. I just stood there and let it happen. I couldn't go in and defend my girlfriend, because it would just make Kate hate her even more. I hate being torn between the two of them, especially since it's Emilia's side I want to be on. It's Kate that's sick, but I feel sorrier for Emilia. No matter how hard she tries, Kate keeps lashing out at her, and I can't protect her without hurting Kate. With every day that Kate refuses to acknowledge her wrongs, my mother and Emilia's spirits dampen even more.

I pause in front of my front door and rest my head against it. Ever since Emilia and I started living together, I've raced back home every single day. Ever since then, it's been our little safe haven. It pains me that I struggle to step foot through the door now. Every day I keep coming up with more excuses to stay away for just an hour longer. I wish I were as brave and as patient as Emilia and Mom are. I inhale deeply and steel myself as I unlock the door.

Mom looks up from the sofa when I walk in and tries her best to smile at me, but she fails miserably. She looks as worn out as I feel with the bags underneath her red eyes. She stands up to greet me, and I hug her. Mom clutches my t-shirt and rests her head against my chest. She doesn't need to say a word for me to know how hard things have been for her. It's been two weeks since Kate OD'ed, and she seems to get more and more vicious by the day. It's not just Emilia she lashes out at— it's all of us now. I rub Mom's back and she inhales deeply, as though she's trying her best to remain composed.

"Hi Mom," I murmur. "Brought you your favorite dessert." I dropped by one of Emilia's favorite bakeries on the way home and got her a chocolate dessert that I'm hoping will lift her spirits just a little. While I was at it, I picked up a lemon tart for Kate and tiramisu for Mom.

Mom lets go of me and takes the bag. "I'll put this in the fridge," she tells me. I nod and watch her disappear into the kitchen before I make my way to my bedroom, where Emilia is undoubtedly hiding. Asher gave up his room for Kate and is currently staying with one of his friends, while Emilia and I gave up our room for my parents. It's only during the day we get to use the room. We've been sleeping on the sofa, tasked with preventing Kate from sneaking out at night. We've even had to install extra locks on the inside of our front door.

I'm grateful Emilia offered our bedroom to my parents, but

I'm worried she no longer feels at home here. Especially considering everything she's had to go through with Kate.

Emilia is sitting on our bed with her laptop in front of her when I walk in. She stares at it dazedly and doesn't snap out of it until the sound of the door closing behind me echoes through the room. She looks up at me and tries to smile the way Mom did.

"Hey baby," I murmur. Emilia closes her laptop and rises to her knees as I walk up to her and wrap my arms around her. "I missed you."

She hugs me tightly and presses her lips to my neck. "I missed you too, Carter."

I bury my hand in her hair and tip her head up. She sighs when my lips come crashing down on hers and she kisses me back with the same desperation I'm feeling. I pour everything I can't say into our kiss. *I'm sorry my sister keeps verbally abusing you. I'm sorry my mother isn't treating you the same anymore. I'm sorry I can't stand up for you more. I'm sorry I can't protect you better.*

It isn't enough. "I love you," I whisper, my voice breaking.

Emilia rests her head against my chest and nods. "I know, babe. I love you too," she murmurs, but I shake my head and thread my hands through her hair.

"No, you *don't* know. Emilia, you're my whole world. You're my rock. I couldn't do any of this without you, and I just wish I could make things easier for you. You're everything to me. Words will never be able to describe how grateful I am for everything you do for me and my family."

Emilia's smile drops, and she looks up at me with tears in her eyes. "You don't blame me?"

I cup her face and shake my head. "Hell no. None of this is your fault, Emilia. Don't ever think that. You've done everything you could. Kate is just looking for someone to blame and you've become her scapegoat. And Mom... I think Mom is just looking for answers. She's convinced *she* must've gone wrong some-where with Kate, and I think Kate's words are getting to her. She's starting to think that treating you the same as Kate has caused this, but that's bullshit. If you hadn't been there, the same thing would've happened. Kate would've just chosen *me* to blame instead."

She doesn't look convinced and turns away from me. I wish I could just get into bed with her and spoon her. I want to hold her until every single one of our worries melts away. We haven't had a moment of privacy since we took Kate home from the hospital.

I hug Emilia from behind and rest my chin on top of her head. "We're at least a little to blame, Carter," she whispers. "We weren't there for her. We didn't notice that she needed us. We might have actually pushed her away a little in our efforts to hide our relationship."

I turn her around to face me, my heart shattering when I see her face covered in tears. I wipe them away as best as I can and press a kiss to her forehead. "Baby, even if we did do all of that, we still aren't to blame. *You* aren't to blame. You can't let her get to you like that. Kate isn't a child. You aren't even remotely responsible for her. I feel guilty as hell too, and I agree we could've done *better*. But that doesn't mean either you or I are *responsible*. You hear me, Minx?"

She nods and wraps her arms around me. I hold her tightly as soft sobs tear through her. I close my eyes and hold my girl until her body stops shaking, all the while wishing I could do more.

milia

I open Asher's bedroom door quietly. Kate is in bed when I walk in, her back to me. I approach her and sit down at the edge of the bed; the mattress dipping under my weight. Kate turns to face me, her eyes flashing with annoyance when she realizes it's me and not Helen.

"What are *you* doing here?"

I sigh and hand her a glass of fresh juice. When she won't take it from me, I place it down on the nightstand instead. "I just wanted to check how you're doing."

Kate rolls her eyes. "I bet you're disappointed to see that I'm doing just fine."

I shake my head and look away. "Why would you think that, Kate? I've always loved you. I've always seen you as a sister. I only want what's best for you."

Kate looks at me in disbelief. "That's bullshit. If you wanted what's best for me, you wouldn't have betrayed me the way you did. I bet you're just feeling guilty now. Guilty that this happened because you and Carter abandoned me."

I look at her with wide eyes, unable to believe what I'm hearing. "*We* abandoned *you*? Kate, we did everything we could to earn your forgiveness, yet all you did was push us away. In the end, we chose to honor your wishes. You told me you never wanted to see me again, and I did my best to make that happen. What more could I have done?"

Kate smiles wryly. "If you actually cared as much as you did, you wouldn't have given up on me so easily. You would've noticed when I needed help. When I was being sucked into a black hole I couldn't crawl out of by myself, the two of you weren't there. Hell, I had nosebleeds from coke overuse and you never even realized — all because you were too busy fucking *my brother*. You haven't been there from the start. You never once questioned me about Jake, not even when I stood you up for him. I was falling deeper into my addiction, and you didn't notice I needed help, because all you could see was Carter."

I close my eyes and inhale deeply, trying to settle my aching heart. "I'm sorry," I whisper. "You're right. I didn't notice that you needed help, and it *is* partly because I was so caught up in Carter. But I'm here now, Kate. I'm here and I'll do whatever I can to make sure you get better."

Kate rolls her eyes. "How can you, when you're the reason I turned to coke and Jake, anyway?"

I stare at her in confusion, and she shakes her head sadly.

"Emilia, the daughter my mother always wanted. The girl of my brother's dreams. The one my dad always praised and defended, even though his praises were scarce. You were the one that got a scholarship to his alma mater when I couldn't do it. Hell, even Carter only got a partial academic scholarship, but you just had to go and get a full-ride. I thought things might be different when we got to college, but even here you were the one people noticed at parties. You were the one my brother spent all his time with. I was falling behind in my classes much more than you ever were, but it's your grades Carter was more concerned about. Even Asher sang your praises. I couldn't even complain about you without everyone jumping to your defense — that's how brainwashed you've got everyone.

"It's only Jake that understood how I felt. The coke made me feel better. God, the euphoria I felt... just a couple of hours of not being reminded how much of a fuck-up I am compared to you. A couple of hours of not feeling like I come second to you. Just that feeling of being as amazing as everyone seems to think *you* are... I craved it. I needed it even more after you betrayed me and turned my brother and mother away from me — both of them convinced you should get away with the unforgivable."

She laughs humorlessly, the sound chilling. "I hate you, Emilia. I really fucking hate you. You're the worst thing that ever happened to me. That day in the treehouse, when you'd just moved in... I wish I'd just turned you away when you intruded on our tea party. I wish I'd never invited you into our lives. My life would be so much better if we never became friends. I was trying to be kind and I was trying to give you an inch, but you took a mile. I was trying to be nice to you, but before I knew it, you infiltrated my family. Suddenly you were everywhere, like a slow-acting poison. My life would be a thousand times better without you."

My heart breaks, and a single tear drops down my cheek, but I catch it quickly. "I never knew you felt this way. When that whole thing with Gabby happened, I offered to take a step back. I told you that if you felt like I was overstepping, I'd stop coming over as much as I did. If you'd told me how you were feeling, I would've done whatever I could to make things better, Kate. I didn't know. I had no idea you thought of me like that all this time."

Kate shakes her head. "What, tell you so you could complain to my mother and brother and make me the villain?

So the both of them would blame me for you suddenly walking out of our lives? Like I'd ever do something that stupid. All I need to do is be patient. Sooner or later they'll see you for what you are. Sooner or later they'll look at our family and they'll realize *you're* the one that wrecked our happiness."

I bite down on my lip as hard as I can to keep my emotions in check, but I can't stop trembling. I've always loved Kate and I've always thought of her as my best friend, so how did I fail to notice that she slowly started to hate me?

"You want me out of your life?" Kate nods and I inhale deeply. "Do you think that will solve anything? You won't suddenly start getting better grades once I'm gone. You won't miraculously get clean. Those things all take hard work, Kate."

She grits her teeth and looks away. "I know. But at least it'd be a step in the right direction."

I rise to my feet and look at Kate, but I don't recognize her at all. When did she change? When did she stop seeing me as a friend? Where did things go so wrong?

CHAPTER 49

$\mathcal{E}$milia

I'm trying my best to get in some last-minute studying at the dining table, but I doubt I'll be able to get much done with the amount of noise Helen is making in the kitchen. William was unable to get more time off work and I guess he's also worried about the medical bills he'll now have to pay for, so he's gone back to Woodstock. Without him here, Helen seems to unravel even more.

She's been acting weird with me lately, and I can't blame her. She tries so hard to act like nothing is wrong, but I know she blames herself for what's happening with Kate. She's been avoiding me and every time we speak her replies are short. She's alienating me slowly but surely, and even though it kills me, I'm not even mad about it. I understand where she's coming from, and I hope with time things will get better.

I rise to my feet and walk into the kitchen. Helen seems to be reorganizing our cupboards and I can't help but frown. Carter and I spent ages putting things in the right place in a way that made sense to us both.

"Hey," I murmur.

She looks up, her expression guarded. "Emilia," she says, and my stomach twists painfully. She only ever used to call me by my name when I was in trouble, but nowadays it's all she'll call me. I wonder if I'll ever hear her call me Milly again.

"What are you doing?" I ask. She smiles and stares at the mess she made. "I just needed something to do. Besides, I can't find anything in these cupboards. My boy clearly has no idea how to organize his kitchen."

I bite down on my lip and nod tersely. Her messing up my organizational system is the least of my worries. "Let me help you," I offer.

Helen shakes her head and puts down a jar with googly eyes on it. "No need, Emilia," she says, sighing. She leans back against the kitchen counter and looks away. "I've actually been meaning to talk to you," she says, looking grim.

I nod and turn the kettle on to make some tea. She's been pacing around me in circles for days now, and she's been looking at me like she has something to say. I knew it was only a matter of time.

"I hope you don't take this the wrong way, but I don't think your presence is helping Kate's recovery. I've heard the arguments the two of you have had, and I think you being here is keeping Kate from wanting to get better."

I stare at Helen in disbelief, my heart breaking. She blames me. She didn't say it outright, but she does.

Helen inhales deeply and looks down at her feet. "Kate is right. The way I've been treating you... it isn't right. I've often put you before my own daughter and I never should have done that. It should've been Kate I taught how to bake and it should've been her going on every errand with me. You're a lovely child, Emilia... but you aren't *mine*. I was trying so hard to make you feel at home with us I didn't realize I was hurting my daughter. In part, the way I was treating you led her to do what she did."

I blink in confusion and move through the kitchen on auto-pilot, just wanting something to do. I make two cups of tea, unable to keep myself from trembling.

"When you and Carter started dating, I should've thought of what it would do to Kate. I shouldn't have given you two my blessing blindly. I should've checked up on her to see how she was taking the news. I should have been understanding of her feelings about you two. I won't make that mistake again."

I take a sip of my tea and scald my tongue, but it doesn't hurt anywhere near as much as my bleeding heart. "What are you trying to say, Helen?" I ask, willing myself to stay strong.

She shakes her head and sighs. "You and Carter aren't children anymore, Emilia. I can't forbid you two dating. All I can ask for now is that you consider taking a break. Give Carter a chance to be there for his family, instead of being caught between you and Kate. His attention should be on Kate, but it's you he checks up on when he comes home. Please, Emilia, give Kate a chance to get better. Just seeing you puts her on edge. I just want her to focus on getting better. I just want my daughter to be happy again. I want to see her smile, Emilia, and she won't do that as long as you're around."

I can barely comprehend what she's saying. She wants Carter and me to take a *break*? From our *relationship*?

"If nothing else, please consider moving out temporarily. I don't think seeing you every day is good for Kate. I know Carter would never dare say this to you, but I'm certain he agrees. It's obvious you're holding Kate's recovery back."

A lone tear drops down my cheek, and I wipe it away furiously. Helen's expression wavers for a second, but then she shakes her head.

"Where would I even go, Helen? This is my *home* now."

Helen nods in understanding and grabs her bag. She takes out a credit card and holds it out to me. "Just find some other apartment. I understand a lot of students do house-sharing. I'm sure it won't take you too long to find something. I'll pay for it until you can get back on your feet. I'm sorry, Emilia. I don't want to have to ask you this, but I need to put my family first. Besides, this apartment is Carter's. It's *his* home, not yours."

Her words hit me right where they hurt most. I glance at the credit card she's handing me and shake my head.

"Please give me some time to think about it."

Helen takes the card back and nods tersely. "I hope you'll make the right decision, Emilia. We're all to blame here, and we all need to work to set things right."

I nod and flee to our bedroom. At least during the day, I get it to myself. I glance at Kate, who's leaning against the wall in the hallway. She grins at me wickedly. "I told you it wouldn't take long. Mom is starting to see you for who you are, huh? Didn't even take as long as I expected. I'm glad even *she* doesn't want you here. Finally, she's putting me first. I doubt you'll be able to make the *right choice*, though. I can't wait for Mom to realize how fucking selfish you are."

I ignore her as best as I can and rush into my bedroom. I lie down on the bed and burst into tears, trying as hard as I can to remain quiet. What did I do for Kate to hate me as much as she does? Is loving Carter truly such a crime?

I don't know how long I've been crying when strong arms wrap around me. Carter envelops me in his arms and I turn around to bury my face in his neck. He caresses my hair gently until my sobs die down. I barely manage to tell him about my conversation with Helen without bursting into tears again. Carter kisses my forehead and shakes his head.

"You're not going anywhere, baby. If it comes down to it we'll move out together, okay? Don't take her words to heart. I want you here. I need you here. I'll talk to her, all right?"

I close my eyes and nod, but my resolve is wavering. I'm starting to think Helen and Kate are right. But even if they aren't, I don't see a way forward. Things will never be what they used to be again.

CHAPTER 50

$\mathcal{E}$milia

I stare at the email on my laptop. One week. It's been one week since Helen asked me to leave, and every single day I'm still here she stares at me in disappointment. My mere presence is breaking everyone's hearts.

I close my laptop and rise from my seat at the dining table just as Kate and Helen return from the hospital. Kate looks annoyed to see me, but at least she looks like she's doing okay. Helen has been accompanying her to the hospital multiple times a week, and it looks like Kate's treatment plan is working. It's not easy on her, though. I can tell she's truly fighting, and I'm proud of her for it.

"Why are you still here?" she asks, crossing her arms. "I thought Mom asked you to leave Carter's house. You really make a habit out of intruding where you're not wanted, don't you?"

Her words still pierce my heart, but I guess I've gotten used to it, because the pain is more numbing than it is searing these days. I just nod at her and glance at Helen. She looks as though she doesn't quite know how to face me and walks toward Asher's bedroom instead.

"She did," I tell Kate. "And you're right."

Kate frowns, and I sigh. "You're right, Kate. You've always shared everything with me — every family trip and every holiday, Mother's Day included. You've always made sure your family included me as much as you could, and I started to get used to it. I started to feel like I belong. Like I belong with your family."

I laugh as a tear drops down my cheek. "You're right. I'm just a sad girl that wished for someone else's life. For your life, specifically. You had it all. Loving parents, a brother to be proud of, and that teased you but was still always there for you. You had everything I never had, and I coveted it. I wanted just a bit of what you had. So every time you included me in things and invited me over, I took all I could get. I coveted what was yours, and I coveted *you*. You were the sister I never had."

I smile to myself as I remember the broken girl I used to be. The lonely nights, the empty dinner table, the condemnation that comes with living in a town as small as ours, and the warmth the Clarke's showed me.

"At first, I just wanted to make sure you'd stay friends with me, so I took on all the chores you didn't want to do. I'd do the dishes and I'd help your mother with the groceries. I did as much as I could to make sure you wouldn't get rid of me, so I wouldn't outgrow my usefulness. Over time, that turned into more, though. I started to enjoy spending time with Helen, and both she and Carter started to treat me the same way they treated you. I loved it, Kate. I loved your house and your family. It was in such stark contrast with my own empty and cold house. I craved the love that was so abundant in your family, and I started to think I could have just a little of it if I just tried hard enough. I started to work hard at everything I did so your Mom would praise me, so that she'd want to keep me in your life. The way she treated me made me miss my own mother a bit less. It made me see what it was like to have a *Mom*, and I wanted more of that. Every decision I've made so far has been because I so badly wanted to belong. To belong with you and your family, and I never even realized that there's no place for me."

Kate smiles in satisfaction, as though she's happy I'm finally seeing reason.

"I hated cheerleading, but I did it because you asked me to, Kate. Did you know I was already in love with Carter by then? I fought my feelings as best as I could because I was terrified of hurting you. I broke both his and my own heart because I loved you more than I loved him."

Kate huffs in disbelief. "Yeah, you did a great job fighting your feelings," she says. I smile at her sadly and look down at my feet.

"I always wanted to study overseas, you know? But instead I applied to USC, because that's where Carter and you were going. I worked my ass off to get here, and all the while you'd been wishing I wouldn't be here with you. I wish I'd known."

I fall silent and try my best to keep my tears at bay. I don't want to cry again. I'm done with everything.

"Boohoo, poor Emilia," Kate says. "Poor Emilia, who has no real family and felt the need to leech off mine. What am I supposed to do with this speech of yours? Am I supposed to feel sorry for you? Newsflash, Emilia. The one that's hurting is *me*. The one that's sick is *me*. Nothing about this situation is about you, but I'm not at all surprised you found a way to *make* it about you."

I close my eyes and inhale deeply. "You're right," I whisper. "You're right about everything, Kate. I've been beyond selfish, and I apologize for leeching off your family. I apologize for intruding and overstepping. You win, okay?"

She looks at me with raised brows, and I shake my head sadly. "I'm leaving, Kate. You won't ever have to see me again. Your mother is right too. You won't get better as long as I'm here. You'll keep blaming me and you'll keep victimizing yourself. I'm done, Kate. I'm done being your scapegoat. Maybe you're right, and maybe I *am* to blame. Maybe I did do this to you. It doesn't matter anymore. I'll leave. I'll give you what you need. It's the least I can do in return for everything you and your family have given me over the years. I don't want to be the one that wrecks your happiness. I don't want to be the reason your family falls apart."

I laugh even though my heart is breaking. I can barely even see through the tears that are blurring my vision.

"Besides, you're right. Carter *can* do a lot better than me. He's destined for greatness, and I'm just a small-town girl from a broken family that he's grown attached to because I've always *been there.* You said it won't take him long to realize it, and he'd eventually leave me. I can see now that he and I could never work out. He might think he loves me, but we'll never recover from everything we've been through. I'll always be the girl that destroyed his family's happiness. I'll always be the girl his sister can't stand, the one his mother can't look at without being guilt wrecked. We don't stand a chance."

I bite down on my lip harshly as tear after tear escapes my eyes and Kate looks at me with wide eyes. "You're actually leaving?" she asks, a hint of concern in her voice. I nod and take a step away from her.

"I'm transferring to a university overseas. I'll have to start all over again, but they're letting me start next month. Like I said, you won't ever have to see me again. You and your family will be free of me. You'll be able to focus on your health and your own happiness from now on. I won't stand in your way ever again. I won't ever reach for something that isn't mine. You win."

Kate and I both jump when a loud thump sounds through the room. I turn around to find Carter standing behind me, his gym bag on the floor.

"What did you just say?" he murmurs, his eyes wide and his voice barely above a whisper.

CHAPTER 51

arter

"Don't do this to me, Minx. Please, I'm begging you."

I drop to my knees, barely able to keep my tears at bay. I don't think I've ever cried in Emilia's presence, but my heart feels fucking destroyed.

"Tell me you aren't leaving."

Emilia looks away and pulls her suitcase from underneath our bed. I rise to my feet and watch in disbelief as she starts to pack. I've been trying to convince her for days not to do this. I've begged my parents and Kate to help me change her mind, but I'm fighting a losing battle.

"No," I shout helplessly, startling her. Without thinking, I grab every item she's packed and throw it all on the floor. I grab Emilia's wrist and pull her toward me, turning us both around until I've got her pressed against the wall.

"Tell me this is some sort of joke. Some sort of scheme. A plan to force Kate to get better."

Emilia gulps as tears escape her eyes. "It's not," she whispers. I lower my lips to hers and kiss her roughly, hoping that shutting her up might change the inevitable. She kisses me back, and I lift her into my arms. She closes her legs around me, and I pull back to look into her eyes.

"Don't leave me.".

Emilia tightens her grip around me. "I have to, Carter. I can't stay where I'm not wanted. I can't stay when I'm causing so much pain."

I shake my head as a tear drops down my cheek. "No," I whisper. "We'll get through this. Kate will get better. Things will return to what they used to be."

Emilia smiles sadly and cups my face. "They won't, babe. Kate is never going to forgive me, and she's never going to want me around. As long as I'm here, she'll use me as an excuse not to get better. I'm tired of taking the blame for everything, Carter. I love her, but I can't do this anymore. Once I'm gone, she'll be out of excuses. She'll be forced to face her problems."

I know what she's saying is true. I know, deep down, that things will never be the same again between Emilia and my family. I know she isn't to blame at all, but somehow everyone is holding her at least partly responsible because they're unable to face their own failures.

"But what about me? What about us? You said you'd marry me someday, Emilia. Fuck it all. If you want, we can just move out of here for the time being. Hell, I can ask Mom and Dad to take Kate home. She's barely attending classes, anyway."

Emilia threads her hands through my hair and looks into my eyes. "You know the hospitals at home aren't as good. They aren't equipped to deal with Kate's problem, and the rumors would be endless. Besides, this isn't a temporary issue, Carter. You know that as well as I do."

I drop my forehead against hers and inhale deeply. "It's got nothing to do with us, Emilia. We're perfect together. I know you love me as much as I love you, so don't do this."

"Carter," she whispers. "I can't stay. As long as you and I are together, Kate will use me as an excuse. She'll use our relationship as ammunition. She's wanted me out of her life for longer than either you or I could even imagine. Your mother asked me to leave too, remember? She'll always see me as the reason Kate resorted to drugs. She'll always think of me as the reason she let it happen — the reason she neglected Kate. And Kate herself... she's made it quite clear how she feels about us, about me. Your dad might not have said much, but his silence speaks volumes. If he didn't agree he would've defended me against Kate's repeated attacks."

I can't deny what she's saying, because I know it's true. "I can't lose you, Emilia. You mean the world to me. You're everything to me."

Emilia breathes in shakily and presses her lips against mine. "I love you too, Carter. But sometimes love isn't enough. Your family needs you now, and they need me to go."

I bite down on her lower lip and kiss her. "I'll go with you," I say.

Emilia shakes her head, her eyes filled with tears. "You know you can't. Your entire future is here. You might still get drafted into the NFL, and your company is here. Besides, your family will just think I'm taking you away when they need you most."

"Then we'll do long-distance."

Emilia pulls on my t-shirt and yanks it off. The way she looks at me tears me apart. She's staring at me as though she's trying to memorize every part of me. I don't want to be nothing more than a memory to her. I want to be the person she *makes* memories with.

"We can't do that, Carter. We can't be together. There's no future for us. I love you with my heart and soul, but I'm not coming back. I'll always be a reminder of one of the toughest things your family has had to go through, and they'll always at least partially see me as the cause of it. Kate is always going to hate me. I can't be with you knowing how much sorrow it would bring them, no matter how much I love you. I can't do that to you, because I know how much it would tear you apart. I can't ask you for a future where you're always torn between me and your family. Where every family occasion is filled with bitterness and tension. You deserve more than that."

I carry Emilia to our bed and lay her down . I don't even care that this bedroom is supposed to be my mom's now. My family is taking everything from me. The least they can give me is a couple of hours with my Minx. I kiss her gently, both our hearts breaking. We're both quiet as we undress each other, both of us aware that there's nothing left to say. There's nothing either of us can do to make things better. Emilia is right, the future we might have is filled with bitterness. And even if I want to follow her to London, I can't. Not when my family is falling apart. She's making the choice I don't have the heart to make. She's looking out for my family when that should be my job.

"I love you," I whisper. Emilia pulls me closer and wraps her legs around me. I push into her, part of me irrationally thinking that I might be able to remind her how good things are between us. What she'll be missing out on if she gets on that plane tomorrow.

I take my time making love to my girlfriend, part of me knowing that it's the last time I'll have her like this.

"I love you, Carter," she whispers, and I kiss her.

"I love you more, Emilia," I reply, meaning every word. I love her so much I could never have made the choice she's making for us, even though I know it's what my family needs me to do. I love her more than anything and everything in the world, but sometimes love just isn't enough.

CHAPTER 52

$\mathcal{E}$milia

Carter is quiet as he drives me to the airport. He looks as heart-broken as I feel, but we both know what we're doing is for the best. We never should've gotten together. We both knew we'd cause heartache if we did, but we underestimated just how much. If we hadn't crossed that line, then he and I would still be in each other's lives, and I wouldn't be losing him. Maybe Kate wouldn't have done what she did, and maybe she and I would've been okay. I know our friendship wasn't in a good state, but maybe some distance and some boundaries would've helped.

"Emilia, are you sure about this?" he asks. I nod, unable to voice the words.

"If you get on that plane today, you and I are over. We'll be done. I won't chase after you, and I won't wait for you to come back. I'll move on with my life. Is that what you want?"

Carter looks desperate as he says it, and he knows full well that he's hitting me right where it hurts the most. I know he's desperate for me to change my mind. The mere idea of him moving on with someone else kills me. The future I envisioned with him will belong to some other girl someday. Eventually he'll become someone else's boyfriend, and someday he'll probably become someone else's husband. He'll probably have a wife that'll have everything I've ever wanted. She'll have Helen as a doting mother-in-law and Kate as her sister. She'll become part of a household that'll always make her feel included and loved. But most of all, she'll have Carter... body, heart and soul.

"I'm trying to do the right thing, Carter. This isn't what I want," I whisper. "What I want is *you*. But more importantly, I want you to be happy. I know you think you and I could be happy together despite everything that's happened, but we couldn't be. You might not admit it to yourself, but part of the reason you loved me was because of how well I fit into your family. Some of our best memories include your parents and your sister."

I don't know how to explain to him how I'm feeling. I hate that he's now blaming me, too. For leaving him. For not fighting for us.

"Do you really think we'd be okay if Kate never got better, because I was always there to take the blame every time she relapsed? Do you think you could still love me if, day by day, you lose a little bit more of your sister? Do you think I could live with myself? What about your parents? Would they ever accept us being together knowing how much suffering we've caused?"

Carter is quiet as he parks the car. He won't even look at me as he takes my luggage out of the trunk.

"Say something," I whisper. Carter looks at me, his eyes filled with the same sorrow I'm feeling.

He puts my suitcase down and threads his hands through my hair. "Part of me is hoping you'll change your mind, and another part of me knows that we're doomed even if you do. I hate feeling this helpless... this heartbroken. Emilia, despite everything, you're still the girl I want to marry someday. I think you'll always be that to me. I can't help but blame my sister, and even my mother, for taking you away from me. For ruining the best thing I've ever had. And I don't want to do that. I want to be there for them and I want to help Kate get better, but how do I do that knowing she's the reason you left me?"

I hug him and inhale deeply, trying my best to keep my emotions in check. "It's not just her, Carter. They're not the only reason I'm leaving. The whole thing with Kate made me realize I haven't been living the life I envisioned for myself. I always wanted to study abroad and travel across Europe. I want to see the Eiffel Tower and the canals in Amsterdam. There's so much I've always wanted to do, yet I sidelined my dreams to follow Kate's dreams instead. She was right when she said I was trying to live her life, and I'm done doing that. I want to know what it's like to stand on my own two feet. I need to learn to be my own person, and not just the dependent girl I've become. This distance... it'll give me a chance to pursue my own dreams, and it'll give Kate what she needs the most right now. It'll be a clean break for the two of us, too. We won't be able to stay away if I'm nearby, and we both know we should."

Carter sighs and kisses me with the same desperation I'm feeling. I don't want to go. I don't want to leave him. But I know it's what's best for both of us. If I stay, we'll only end up resenting each other. Kate is right... if I stay, eventually he'll start to blame both me and himself for the ruin of his family. We'd never recover from that. I'd rather leave while we still have so many good memories together. I'd rather leave while Helen still treats me civilly. The Clarke's have done so much for me over the years, this is the least I can do to repay them. They were the family I never had, and thanks to them I had a childhood I can look back on fondly. But they aren't my family, and the right thing to do now is to take a step back.

"Someday," Carter says. "Someday we'll find our way back to each other, and when we do, I won't let anyone stand in our way again. I know this is the right choice now, but I can't imagine a future without you. I never believed in fate, but if it exists, I know it'll lead me straight back to you."

I smile up at him and nod. "Maybe someday, if the time is right."

I pull away from Carter when my dad pulls up at the airport. He looks devastated as he approaches me and wraps his arms around me. "Are you sure you want to go?" he asks me, and I nod.

"I am, Daddy."

He hugs me tightly and then lets me go, placing his hands on my shoulder. "I love you, Emilia. I'll support you with whatever choice you want to make. I'll be here, okay? If you don't like it there, and you want to come home, just call me, okay?"

I smile at and rise to my tiptoes to kiss his cheek. "Yes, Dad, I will."

I glance at Carter one more time, trying my best to memorize him just as he is right now, and then I turn and walk away, leaving the two men I love most staring after me.

I hope I'm making the right choice for everyone, because it sure doesn't *feel* right. I guess rather than making the *right* choice, I'm making the *only* choice that's available to me. To us.

I hope time might mend my broken heart and set right the wrongs Carter and I unknowingly caused. I hope Kate gets better and I hope Helen will one day retrieve the smile I've always loved. I hope Carter will eventually be happy, and I hope a little part of him will always love me.

Hope. It's all I've got left.

———

End of Book II

AFTERWORD

Thank you from the bottom of my heart for following Emilia and Carter's journey along.

Emilia and Carter's story isn't over yet. Theirs is a trilogy that has so far followed them through high school and college. The last book, The Ruins Of Us, will follow them through adulthood.

The Ruins Of Us is available now, so you can read the final book in Emilia and Carter's trilogy right away.

I truly hope you enjoyed Illicit Promises and would absolutely love it if you left a review. Reviews mean the world to authors, myself included!

They'll meet again as adults, and their happily ever after will be all the sweeter because of everything they've gone through.

I'm always happy to hear from readers, so if you'd like to get in touch with me, you can email me at author@

catharinamaura.com. I'm also pretty active on social media, and you can find all details on my website: www.catharina-maura.com

CPSIA information can be obtained
at www.ICGtesting.com
Printed in the USA
BVHW031712050123
655654BV00001B/59